NEW GEPT

新制全民英檢
初級 寫作測驗
必考題型

國際語言中心委員會/著

英檢出題方向來自**日常生活**

情境融入＋題型演練＝學習效果最佳！

● 掌握解題關鍵

本書第一部分為每一個主題量身訂做「解題焦點」及「重點文法快速查」，歸納考題的重點核心，幫助考生快速掌握解題關鍵。

Step 1

● 勤做題庫演練

在熟讀解題關鍵之後，最重要的就是勤做練習題。透過本書海量的嚴選題目做密集訓練，提高解題的速度及正確率。

Step 2

Step 3

● 全面融會貫通

完成了本書第一部分的文法密集訓練，對各主題的文法觀念已然駕輕就熟，就可以在第二部分「段落寫作」中活用所學。

Step 4

● 本書第二部分將英檢常見的情境融入考題，並歸納整理了7大類，且提供常用的字彙列表，幫助考生輕鬆征服段落寫作。

Step 5

● 寫作

PASS!!

「寫作能力」密集訓練

到底能幫我增強那些能力呢？

快速解題

本書針對每個文法主題量身訂做的「解題焦點」，以一目了然的條列方式，歸納該主題的文法要點，藉著題型的分類加速考生學習記憶，並實際以例句 明解題重點，強化考生的解題技巧，快速掌握解題關鍵。

Focus 解題焦點：
主動語態改成被動語態的題型有三種情況：
一、填入動作者／二、填入接受動作者／三、省略動作者。

一、填入動作者
S + V + O → O + BeV + 過去分詞 + by S
例 A typhoon caused the damage.
☞ The damage was caused by a typhoon.

二、填入接受動作者
S + V + O → O + BeV + 過去分詞 + by S
例 A typhoon caused the damage.
☞ The damage was caused by a typhoon.

三、省略動作者

文法重點一把罩

特別規劃的「文法重點快速查」專欄，針對各個主題，整理解題所需的各類文法、句型、字彙、片語、動詞變化，以表格的方式清楚呈現，不論是查考或是背誦都相當方便省時，為考生的實力大大加分。

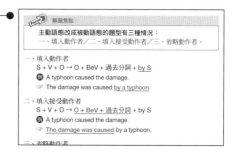

重點文法 快速查!!

問句／答句的合併，句型可分為三類

類型	問句句型	答句句型	合併句型
主詞類	Who + V + O?	S + 助 V	S + V + O
副詞類	Where + 助 V + S + V + O?	地方副詞	S + V + O + 地方副詞
	What time + 助 V + S + V + O?	時間副詞	S + V + O + 時間副詞
Yes/No 問句類	助 V + S + V + O + 地方副詞？ 助 V + S + V + O + 時間副詞？	Yes,S + 助 V. No, S + 助 V not.	S + 助 V + (not) + V + O + 地方副詞 S + 助 V (+ not) + V + O + 時間副詞
	助 V + S + V + (that) + 子句。	Yes, S + 助 V. No, S + 助 V not.	S + 助 V (+ not) + V + (that)+子句。
		Yes, S + have/has.	

自然反射訓練

「實戰演練」針對每個主題的出題方向，嚴選超精華且海量的題目，並提供考生完整而有效率的題庫演練。透過「解題焦點」的活用，有效訓練快速解題的自然反射力，讓你一看到題目就想到答案！

實戰 演練 考題你的合倂能力！

Q1. Who made the mistake?
Bill did.
↳ Bill ＿＿＿＿＿＿

Q2. Who runs the fastest?
Rick does.
↳ Rick ＿＿＿＿＿＿

文意融會貫通

本書「示範解答」醒目標示答案重點，加強視覺記憶，並逐句附加中文翻譯，方便考生參照查考，不用查字典就可以百分之百瞭解文意。另外針對關鍵必考的題型補充相關的必考重點或文法要點，真正讓你培養實力。

Q8. flag / the / in / the / is / wind / flapping
↳ The flag is flapping in the wind.
（旗幟在風中飛舞。）

Q9. the / moon / the / west / rise / in / does
↳ Does the moon rise in the west?
（月亮在西方升起嗎？）
☞ 句尾已提示問號（？），所以要用助動詞 does 開頭來引導問句，主詞是 the moon，後接原形動詞 rise，最後再放地方副詞 in the west 即可。

Q10. flashed / a / just / shooting / by / star
↳ A shooting star just flashed by.
（有一顆流星剛閃過。）

目錄 contents

目錄 contents

PART 2. 段落寫作 |英|檢|最|常|考|主|題|

PART 3. 實戰完整模擬試題

Part **1**

單句寫作

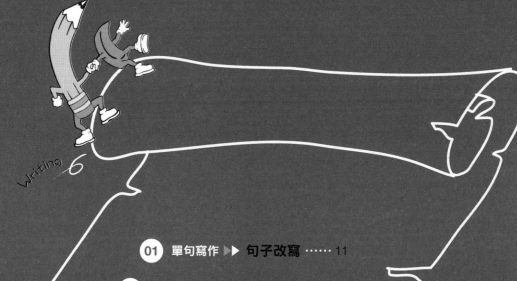

100% 得分要領

- ☑ 勤做題庫演練
- ☑ 釐清文法概念
- ☑ 仔細訂正錯誤
- ☑ 掌握解題線索

Writing 6

單句寫作分三種題型：句子改寫、句子合併、句子重組。基本上，這三種題型所需要的能力大同小異，包括：完整的文法概念、句型的活用、正確的英文語順、對句意的充分瞭解。

想要在單句寫作各個題型中拿到分數，唯一的方法就是**勤做練習題**。在演練各種題目的過程中，考生能夠增加自己解題的經驗，熟悉各種考題的解題線索，提高做答的速度以及正確率。做完練習題以後，重頭戲才要上場，一定要耐心的找出自己錯誤的原因，**仔細訂正錯誤**，而且要不厭其煩地熟讀**相關的解題概念**，在正式應考之前，要重複加強自己曾經做錯的題目，不斷提醒自己不在考場上犯相同的錯誤，應考時要仔細閱讀題目，盡其所能找出所有的**解題線索**，而且在交卷之前，要再次針對自己容易犯錯的地方，確定自己沒有犯一樣的錯誤。

另外，要盡量避免一般考生常犯的錯誤，包括：現在式第三人稱單數的動詞忘了加 -s 或 -es、加入助動詞卻沒有把一般動詞還原為原形、可數名詞沒有加冠詞也沒有改複數形、疑問句沒有加問號、最高級沒有加 the……等。這些地方雖然是最基本的，卻又是最常被忽略的部分，考生答題的時候一定要細心，才能把握住最基本的得分。

TIPS 單句寫作搶分一族

- **Step 1.** 多做練習題，培養解題技巧。
- **Step 2.** 藉由做練習題找出自己錯誤和需要加強的地方。
- **Step 3.** 仔細訂正錯誤，並且熟記相關的文法概念。
- **Step 4.** 務必溫習弱點題型，避免在考場上犯相同的錯誤。
- **Step 5.** 應考時要眼觀四面仔細閱讀題目，絕對不放過任何解題的蛛絲馬跡。
- **Step 6.** 交卷前也不輕言鬆懈，再次針對自己容易犯錯的地方重複檢查。

句子改寫

❶ 句子改寫的題目中，會有一個完整的英文句子和一個不完整的英文句子，考生須依照題目的提示在空格中填入答案，將句子改寫成題目所指定的型式。

❷ 本書針對句型改寫的命題趨向，將考題歸納為 15 種文法主題，百分之百嚴選內容，提供考生有系統的學習。

本書嚴選 句子改寫的 15 種文法主題

常考主題 1. 主動／被動切換（速翻 P12.）

常考主題 2. 直述句／疑問句切換：be 動詞、助動詞型（速翻 P18.）

常考主題 3. 直述句／疑問句切換：一般動詞型（速翻 P25.）

常考主題 4. 直述句／感嘆句切換（速翻 P32.）

常考主題 5. 主詞的切換（速翻 P37.）

常考主題 6. 原級／比較級／最高級切換（速翻 P44.）

常考主題 7. 時態的切換（速翻 P50.）

常考主題 8. 問句／名詞子句切換：疑問詞型（速翻 60.）

常考主題 9. 問句／名詞子句切換：Yes／No 句型（速翻 P62.）

常考主題 10. 直接引述句／間接引述句切換：直述型（速翻 P72.）

常考主題 11. 直接引述句／間接引述句切換：疑問句型（速翻 P77.）

常考主題 12. 直接引述句／間接引述句切換：Yes／No 句型（速翻 P83.）

常考主題 13. 改寫為虛主詞（it）的句型（速翻 P89.）

常考主題 14. 對話／單句切換：不定詞型（速翻 P95.）

常考主題 15. 對話／單句切換：動詞-ing 型（速翻 P103.）

主題 1 | 主動／被動切換

Focus 解題焦點：

主動語態改成被動語態的題型有三種情況：
一、填入動作者／二、填入接受動作者／三、省略動作者。

一、填入動作者

S + V + O → O + be 動詞 + 過去分詞 + <u>by S</u>

例 A typhoon caused the damage.

☞ The damage was caused <u>by a typhoon</u>.

二、填入接受動作者

S + V + O → <u>O</u> + be 動詞 + 過去分詞 + by S

例 A typhoon caused the damage.

☞ <u>The damage was caused</u> by a typhoon.

三、省略動作者

「by + S」在不清楚是什麼人的情況下，或者不特定的人時可以被省略。

例 Someone stole her purse.

☞ Her purse <u>was stolen (by someone)</u>.

重點文法 快速查!!

被動語態的 be 動詞 需隨著時態而改變	
現在簡單式	is／are + 過去分詞
過去簡單式	was／were + 過去分詞
未來簡單式	will be + 過去分詞
現在完成式	has/have been + 過去分詞
現在進行式	is/are being + 過去分詞

GRAMMAR

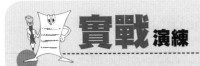
Q1. Careless drivers cause many car accidents.

↳ Many car accidents are caused _____.

Q2. The strong wind damaged thousands of houses.

↳ Thousands of houses were damaged _____.

Q3. The maid cleans the rooms every day.

↳ _____ by the maid every day.

Q4. My father built the house ten years ago.

↳ _____ by my father ten years ago.

Q5. The mechanic will fix our car.

↳ _____ by the mechanic.

Q6. The police have caught the robber.

↳ _____ by the police.

Q7. The shop clerk is helping the old lady.

↳ _____ by the shop clerk.

Q8. Someone stole my bicycle at midnight.

↳ My bicycle _____ at midnight.

Q9. They will cancel the concert if it rains.

↳ If it rains, the concert _____.

Q10. Look! They are knocking down the old building.

⤷ Look! The old building is _____.

Q11. Has anyone sent the letter to Wendy?

⤷ _____ to Wendy?

Q12. Someone paid him a million to do the job.

⤷ _____ to do the job.

Q13. They gave her only two hours to finish the work.

⤷ _____ to finish the work.

Q14. They didn't offer me the job.

⤷ The job _____ to me.

Q15. I will not tell another person the password.

⤷ The password _____ to another person.

示範 解答 ⟶ 中英文對照大解析

Q1. Careless drivers cause many car accidents.
（粗心大意的駕駛人造成很多交通事故。）

⤷ Many car accidents are caused <u>by careless drivers</u>.
（很多交通事故是粗心大意的駕駛人所造成的。）

☞ 介系詞 by 後面接原本主動態的主詞。若原本的主詞是代名詞，則改為被動語態時，by 後面必須用「受格」。例如：He praised me yesterday.（他昨天誇獎我。）→ I was praised by him yesterday.（我昨天被他誇獎了。）

Q2. The strong wind damaged thousands of houses.

（強風破壞了數千棟房舍。）

↳ Thousands of houses were damaged <u>by the strong wind</u>.

（數千棟房舍被強風破壞。）

☞ 注意原句的動詞時態為過去式（damaged），改為被動語態之後仍為過去式（were damaged）。

Q3. The maid cleans the rooms every day.

（女傭每天清理房間。）

↳ <u>The rooms are cleaned</u> by the maid every day.

（房間每天是由女傭清理。）

Q4. My father built the house ten years ago.

（我父親十年前建造了這間房子。）

↳ <u>The house was built</u> by my father ten years ago.

（這間房子是十年前我父親建造完成的。）

Q5. The mechanic will fix our car.

（修車師會修好我們的車。）

↳ <u>Our car will be fixed</u> by the mechanic.

（我們的車會被修車師修好。）

Q6. The police have caught the robber.

（警方已經逮捕搶匪。）

↳ <u>The robber has been caught</u> by the police.

（搶匪已經被警方逮捕。）

Q7. The shop clerk is helping the old lady.

（店員正在協助這名老婦人。）

↳ <u>The old lady is being helped</u> by the shop clerk.

（這名老婦人正接受店員的協助。）

☞ 現在進行式 is helping 的被動式是 is being helped。

Q8. Someone stole my bicycle at midnight.

（有人在半夜偷走了我的腳踏車。）

↳ My bicycle <u>was stolen (by someone)</u> at midnight.

（我的腳踏車在半夜被人偷走了。）

☞ 如果原句的主詞為不特定對象，例如 someone、anyone、they、people…
等，改為被動式之後，可以省略「by + 主詞」。

- -

Q9. They will cancel the concert if it rains.

（如果下雨，他們將取消演唱會。）

↳ If it rains, the concert <u>will be cancelled</u>.

（如果下雨，演唱會將被取消。）

- -

Q10. Look! They are knocking down the old building.

（你看！他們正在拆除那棟老建築。）

↳ Look! The old building <u>is being knocked down</u>.

（你看！那棟老建築正在拆除中。）

- -

Q11. Has anyone sent the letter to Wendy?

（已經有人把信寄給溫蒂了嗎？）

↳ <u>Has the letter been sent</u> to Wendy?

（信已經寄出去給溫蒂了嗎？）

- -

Q12. Someone paid him a million to do the job.

（有人付了他一百萬做這工作。）

↳ <u>He was paid a million</u> to do the job.

（他收了一百萬做這工作。）

☞ 如果原句的動詞為授予動詞，例如 give、send、pay、offer、tell… 等，因
為有兩個受詞（直接受詞與間接受詞），所以改為被動式時，可以有兩
種改法。這裡是以「間接受詞（him）當主詞」的改法。

- -

Q13. They gave her only two hours to finish the work.

（他們只給她兩小時去完成工作。）

↳ <u>She was given only two hours</u> to finish the work.

（她只有兩小時可以完成工作。）

Q14. They didn't offer me the job.

（他們沒有錄用我。）

↳ The job <u>wasn't offered</u> to me.

（我沒有受到錄用。）

☞ 這裡是以原句的「直接受詞（the job）當主詞」的改法，因此必須在原句的間接受詞（me）前面加上介系詞 to。

Q15. I will not tell another person the password.

（我不會告訴別人這組密碼。）

↳ The password <u>will not be told</u> to another person.

（這組密碼不會透漏給別人。）

直述句／疑問句切換：
be 動詞、助動詞型

解題焦點：

本單元主要測驗將直述句改成疑問句後，動詞與主詞字序調換的認知。在本單元，直述句改成疑問句可分成兩種情況：
一、Be 動詞型／二、助動詞型。

一、Be 動詞型
S + be 動詞… → 疑問詞 + <u>be 動詞 + S</u>…？

例 You are in Taipei.

☞ Where <u>are you</u>?

二、助動詞型
S + 助動詞 + V… → 疑問詞 + <u>助動詞 + S + V</u>？

例 She will go to Paris in June.

☞ When <u>will she go</u> to Paris?

重點文法 快速查!!

be 動詞動詞變化一覽表

動詞種類	時態	單數		複數	
be 動詞	現在式	第一人稱	am	第一人稱	are
		第二人稱	are	第二人稱	
		第三人稱	is	第三人稱	
	過去式	第一人稱	was	第一人稱	were
		第二人稱	were	第二人稱	
		第三人稱	was	第三人稱	

GRAMMAR

重點文法 快速查!!

疑問詞會隨著動詞之後的字詞而改變

動詞之後的字詞	對應的疑問詞	例句
地點	Where	Mary is in her room. → Where is Mary?
稱呼／關係	Who	Candy is my friend. Who is Candy?
時間	When	She was born in December. → When was she born?
	What time	It is ten o'clock now. → What time is it now?
原因	Why	The cats are crying because they are hungry. → Why are the cats crying?
動作	What	Vivian is dancing. → What is Vivian doing?
方法	How	Belle will go to school by bus. → How will Belle go to school?
狀況 （形容詞）	How	Jack is sick. → How is Jack?
狀況 （副詞）	How well	How well can Ariel speak English? Ariel can speak English very well.
數量	How much （不可數）	I have spent five hundred dollars on the dress. → How much have you spent on the dress?
	How many （可數）	There are four members in our family. → How many members are there in your family?
多久時間	How long	I have lived in Taiwan for twenty years. → How long have you lived in Taiwan?

Q1. Betty is in her room.

↳ Where _____ ?

Q2. Leo is very sick.

↳ How _____ ?

Q3. Louis and John are my friends.

↳ Who _____ ?

Q4. Jenny's birthday is in December.

↳ When _____ ?

Q5. The dogs are barking fiercely because they see strangers.

↳ Why _____ ?

Q6. Ben is studying.

↳ What _____ ?

Q7. The kids are taking a nap in the bedroom.

↳ What _____ ?

Q8. They are going to the library this afternoon.

↳ Where _____ ?

Q9. Celina will go to Australia this summer.

↳ What _____ ?

Q10. His flight will arrive in Taipei on January 15.

↳ When _____?

Q11. They will go to Kaohsiung by train.

↳ How _____?

Q12. Terry can speak English very well.

↳ How well _____?

Q13. Danny has spent NT$10,000 on fixing up his motorcycle.

↳ How much _____?

Q14. He has eaten 4 pieces of fried chicken.

↳ How many _____?

Q15. They have lived here for twenty years.

↳ How long _____?

示範 解答
中英文對照大解析

Q1. Betty is in her room.
（蓓蒂在她房裡。）

↳ **Where is Betty**?
（蓓蒂在哪裡？）

Q2. Leo is very sick.
（里歐病的很重。）

⤷ How <u>is Leo</u>?
（里歐好嗎？）

Q3. Louis and John are my friends.
（路易士和約翰是我的朋友。）

⤷ Who <u>are Louis and John</u>?
（路易士和約翰是什麼人？）

Q4. Jenny's birthday is in December.
（珍妮的生日是在十二月。）

⤷ When <u>is Jenny's birthday</u>?
（珍妮的生日是在什麼時候？）

Q5. The dogs are barking fiercely because they see strangers.
（那些狗叫得這麼兇是因為牠們看到了陌生人。）

⤷ Why <u>are the dogs barking fiercely</u>?
（為什麼那些狗叫得這麼兇？）

Q6. Ben is studying.
（班正在讀書。）

⤷ What <u>is Ben doing</u>?
（班正在做什麼？）

Q7. The kids are taking a nap in the bedroom.
（孩子們在臥房裡午睡。）

⤷ What <u>are the kids doing in the bedroom</u>?
（孩子們在臥房裡做什麼？）

Q8. They are going to the library this afternoon.
（他們今天下午要到圖書館去。）

⮡ Where <u>are they going this afternoon</u>?
（他們今天下午要去哪裡？）

Q9. Celina will go to Australia this summer.
（賽琳娜今年夏天要去澳洲。）

⮡ What <u>will Celina do this summer</u>?
（今年夏天賽琳娜要做什麼？）

☞ 注意改寫句要用 What 開頭，而不是 Where，因此動詞要用 do，而不是 go。

Q10. His flight will arrive in Taipei on January 15.
（他的班機將於元月十五抵達臺北。）

⮡ When <u>will his flight arrive in Taipei</u>?
（他的班機什麼時候會抵達臺北？）

Q11. They will go to Kaohsiung by train.
（他們將搭火車到高雄。）

⮡ How <u>will they go to Kaohsiung</u>?
（他們要如何去高雄？）

Q12. Terry can speak English very well.
（泰瑞的英文講得很好。）

⮡ How well <u>can Terry speak English</u>?
（泰瑞的英文講得多好？）

Q13. Danny has spent NT$10,000 on fixing up his motorcycle.

（丹尼已經花了一萬元修理他的摩托車。）

↳ How much <u>has Danny spent on fixing up his motorcycle</u>?

（丹尼已經花了多少錢修理他的摩托車？）

☞ 提示用 How much 開頭來問，顯然是針對金額數字的部分，也就是題目中的 NT$10,000。

Q14. He has eaten <u>4 pieces of fried chicken</u>.

（他已經吃了四塊炸雞。）

↳ How many <u>pieces of fried chicken has he eaten</u>?

（他已經吃了幾塊炸雞？）

Q15. They have lived here for twenty years.

（他們已經在此地居住了二十年。）

↳ How long <u>have they lived here</u>?

（他們已經在此地居住了多久？）

☞ 提示用 How long 開頭來問，顯然是針對多久時間的部分，也就是題目中的 twenty years，因此將助動詞 have 移至主詞 they 前面，過去分詞 lived 後面接地方副詞 here，但記得要將介系詞 for 拿掉。

直述句／疑問句切換：
一般動詞型

Focus 解題焦點：

> 將一般動詞直述句轉換成疑問句時，一定要使用助動詞 **do**，這一類型主要是測驗助動詞 do 需隨著時態、人稱、數量、語態而變化，共分為三種情形：
> 一、Does 型／二、Did 型／三、Do 型。
> 注意在加入助動詞之後，應將動詞恢復為原形。

一、DOES 型（用於現在式第三人稱單數）

S + V-(e)s… → 疑問詞 + does + S + V 原形…?

例 She walks to school every day.

☞ How does she go to school every day?

二、DID 型（用於過去式）

S + V-ed… → 疑問詞 + did + S + V 原形…?

例 I went to New York last summer vacation.

☞ Where did you go last summer vacation?

三、DO 型（用於第三人稱單數以外的類型）

S + V… → 疑問詞 + do + S + V 原形…?

例 They usually eat hamburgers for lunch.

☞ What do they usually eat for lunch?

重點文法 快速查!!

一般動詞字尾變化一覽表

動詞字尾	第三人稱單數現在式字尾變化	過去式字尾變化
-ch, -sh, -x, -o,-s	+ es	+ ed
子音 + y	去 y + ies	去 y + ied
其他	+ s	+ d

助動詞 do 的變化一覽表

時態	單複數 & 人稱		助動詞	例句
現在簡單式	單數	第一人稱	do	You speak English very well. → How well do I speak English?
		第二人稱		I usually read in the morning → When do you usually read?
		第三人稱	does	It takes one hour to get there. → How long does it take to get there?
	複數	第一人稱	do	You all go to school by train. → How do we go to school?
		第二人稱		We go to see a movie once a week. → How often do you go to see a movie?
		第三人稱		They live in New York. → Where do they live?
過去簡單式	單數	第一人稱	did	You earned a thousand dollars. → How much did I earn?
		第二人稱		I danced in the room. → Where did you dance?
		第三人稱		Jean went to Paris by airplane. → How did Jean go to Paris?
	複數	第一人稱	did	You all got up at ten o'clock this morning. → What time did we get up this morning?
		第二人稱		We studied English in the classroom. → Where did you study English?
		第三人稱		Ariel and William got married in October. → When did Ariel and William get married?

 **實戰**演練

考驗你的改寫能力！

Q1. Irene goes to work by subway.

↳ How _____?

Q2. She usually buys her clothes at the department store.

↳ Where _____?

Q3. They go to school at 9:30 a.m.

↳ What time _____?

Q4. Sarah and her boyfriend like to go to the movies on weekends.

↳ What _____?

Q5. They play baseball for one hour after school.

↳ How long _____?

Q6. Vincent goes to the gym once a week.

↳ How often _____?

Q7. Tommy likes to travel with his family.

↳ With whom _____?

Q8. David went to Paris for business in March.

↳ When _____?

Q9. Jason cleaned the floor with a mop.

↳ With what _____?

Part 1 · 單句寫作 ▶▶ 01 句子改寫

Q10. Rita stayed in Hualien for three days.

↳ How long ______________________?

Q11. Jeff enjoyed his vacation at the beach last summer.

↳ Where ______________________________________?

Q12. Frank paid 120 thousand dollars for a second-hand car.

↳ How much ________________________________?

Q13. Wesley went to a doctor because he had a stomachache.

↳ Why _______________________________________?

Q14. Mr. James made a long speech to the staff in today's meeting.

↳ To whom __________________________________?

Q15. The mayor married 100 couples at the City Hall this Sunday morning.

↳ How many _________________________________?

示範 解答

中英文對照大解析

Q1. Irene goes to work by subway.
（愛琳搭地鐵上班。）

↳ How does Irene go to work?
（愛琳怎麼去上班？）

Q2. She usually buys her clothes at the department store.
（她通常都在百貨公司買衣服。）

↳ Where <u>does she usually buy her clothes</u>?
（她通常都在哪裡買衣服？）

Q3. They go to school at 9:30 a.m.
（他們早上九點半上學。）

↳ What time <u>do they go to school</u>?
（他們幾點上學？）

Q4. Sarah and her boyfriend like to go to the movies on weekends.
（莎拉和她的男友週末時喜歡去看電影。）

↳ What <u>do Sarah and her boyfriend like to do on weekends</u>?
（莎拉和她的男友週末時喜歡做什麼？）

Q5. They play baseball for one hour after school.
（他們放學後打一小時的棒球。）

↳ How long <u>do they play baseball after school</u>?
（他們放學後打多久的棒球？）

Q6. Vincent goes to the gym once a week.
（文生每週去一次健身房。）

↳ How often <u>does Vincent go to the gym</u>?
（文生多久去一次健身房？）

☞ 提示用 How often 開頭來問，顯然是針對多久一次的部分，也就是題目中的 once a week（一週一次），原句主詞是 Vincent，因此助動詞要用 does 並移至主詞 Vincent 前面，後面動詞要將原來的 goes 改為原形的 go。

29

Q7. Tommy likes to travel with his family.
（湯米喜歡和家人一起旅行。）

⤷ With whom <u>does Tommy like to travel</u>?
（湯米喜歡和誰一起旅行？）

Q8. David went to Paris for business in March.
（大衛三月份時去巴黎出差。）

⤷ When <u>did David go to Paris for business</u>?
（大衛什麼時候去巴黎出差？）

Q9. Jason cleaned the floor with a mop.
（傑森用拖把清理地板。）

⤷ With what <u>did Jason clean the floor</u>?
（傑森用什麼清理地板？）

☞ 開頭提示用 With what，可以對照原句的 with a map，後面接 "Jason cleaned the floor" 改成的疑問句 "did Jason clean the floor"，並注意時態（過去式）一致即可。

Q10. Rita stayed in Hualien for three days.
（莉塔在花蓮待了三天。）

⤷ How long <u>did Rita stay in Hualien</u>?
（莉塔在花蓮待了多久？）

Q11. Jeff enjoyed his vacation at the beach last summer.
（去年夏天傑夫在海邊度過愉快的假期。）

⤷ Where <u>did Jeff enjoy his vacation last summer</u>?
（去年夏天傑夫在哪裡度過愉快的假期？）

Q12. Frank paid 120 thousand dollars for a second-hand car.
（法蘭克花了十二萬元買了一部中古車。）

⤷ How much <u>did Frank pay for a second-hand car</u>?
（法蘭克花了多少錢買了一部中古車？）

Q13. Wesley went to a doctor because he had a stomachache.

（衛斯理去看醫生是因為他肚子痛。）

↳ Why <u>did Wesley go to a doctor</u>?

（衛斯理為什麼去看醫生？）

☞ 開頭提示用 Why，正好對照原句的 because... ，後面接 "Wesley went to a doctor" 的疑問句 "did Wesley go to a doctor"，並注意時態一致即可。

Q14. Mr. James made a long speech to the staff in today's meeting.

（詹姆士先生在今天的會議中對員工們長篇大論了一番。）

↳To whom <u>did Mr. James make a long speech in today's meeting</u>?

（詹姆士先生在今天的會議中對什麼人長篇大論了一番？）

☞ 開頭提示用 To whom，可以對照原句的 to the staff，後面接 "Mr. James made a long speech in today's meeting" 的疑問句 "did Mr. James make a long speech in today's meeting"，並注意時態一致即可。

Q15. The mayor married 100 couples at the City Hall this Sunday morning.

（星期天早上市長在市政府為一百對新人證婚。）

↳ How many couples <u>did the mayor marry at the City Hall this Sunday morning</u>?

（星期天早上市長在市政府為幾對新人證婚？）

Focus 解題焦點：

很多考生看見句首的疑問詞，就會以為這個題目是要把直述句改成疑問句，要注意題目早在句尾擺上一個驚嘆號，顯然是感嘆句的典型考題。感嘆句可分為三種句型：
一、形容詞類／二、副詞類／三、名詞類。

一、形容詞類

S + be 動詞 + (very/so) + 形容詞 → How + <u>形容詞 + S + be 動詞</u>

例 You are so beautiful.

☞ How <u>beautiful you are</u>!

二、副詞類

S + V(+ very/so) + 副詞 → How + <u>副詞 + S + V</u>

例 Time flies so fast.

☞ How <u>fast time flies</u>!

三、名詞類

S + be 動詞／V (+ very/so/such) + 名詞
→ What + <u>名詞 + S + be 動詞／V</u>

例 You sang such a beautiful song.

☞ What a <u>beautiful song you sang</u>!

重點文法 快速查!!

	感嘆句三大類型	
	直述句型	感嘆句型
形容詞類	S + be 動詞 (+ very/so) + 形容詞	How + 形容詞 + S + be 動詞
副詞類	S + V(+ very/so) + 副詞	How + 副詞 + S + V
名詞類	S + be 動詞／V (+ very/so/such) + 名詞	What + 名詞 + S + be 動詞／V

GRAMMAR

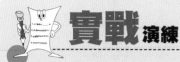

Q1. He comes very late.

↳ How _____!

Q2. Time flies so fast.

↳ How _____!

Q3. The girl is so thin.

↳ How _____!

Q4. I am so happy.

↳ How _____!

Q5. You are a very good friend.

↳ What _____!

Q6. That was a terrible accident.

↳ What _____!

Q7. You have such wonderful ideas.

↳ What _____!

Q8. It is a very expensive pen.

↳ What _____!

Q9. This is such a lovely flower.

↳ What _____!

Q10. You are making such a noise.

↳ What _____!

Q11. You've cooked very nice food.

↳ What _____!

Q12. We've been having so terrible weather these days.

↳ What _____!

Q13. It was such a lively and interesting class.

↳ What _____!

Q14. It is so pleasant to travel by boat on a hot summer night.

↳ How _____!

Q15. It caused her much pain to lose her family.

↳ How much pain _____!

示範 解答 ----------------------------------- 中英文對照大解析

Q1. He comes very late.

↳ How <u>late he comes</u>!
   （他真晚到！）

Q2. Time flies so fast.

↳ How <u>fast time flies</u>!
   （時光飛逝！）

34

Q3. The girl is so thin.

↳ How <u>thin the girl is</u>!
（這個女孩真瘦！）

Q4. I am so happy.

↳ How <u>happy I am</u>!
（我真高興！）

Q5. You are a very good friend.

↳ What <u>a good friend you are</u>!
（你真是個好朋友！）

Q6. That was a terrible accident.

↳ What <u>a terrible accident that was</u>!
（那真是場可怕的意外！）

Q7. You have such wonderful ideas.

↳ What <u>wonderful ideas you have</u>!
（你的想法真棒！）

☞ 提示用 What 開頭且句尾是驚嘆號（！），所以緊接在 What 後面要擺名詞（片語），也就是 wonderful ideas，接著是「主詞 + 動詞」的肯定句結構，也就是 you have。要注意的是，原句中 such（這麼的…）已經被改寫句句首的 How（多麼的…）取代，所以改寫句不能再出現 such！

Q8. It is a very expensive pen.

↳ What <u>an expensive pen it is</u>!
（這真是支昂貴的筆！）

Q9. This is such a lovely flower.

↳ What <u>a lovely flower this is</u>!
（這真是朵美麗的花！）

Q10. You are making such a noise.

↳ What <u>a noise you are making</u>!

（你真的很吵！）

Q11. You've cooked very nice food.

↳ What <u>nice food you've cooked</u>!

（你煮的食物真好吃！）

Q12. We've been having so terrible weather these days.

↳ What <u>terrible weather we've been having these days</u>!

（這幾天的天氣真糟糕！）

Q13. It was such a lively and interesting class.

↳ What <u>a lively and interesting class it was</u>!

（那堂課真是活潑又有趣！）

Q14. It is so pleasant to travel by boat on a hot summer night.

↳ How <u>pleasant it is to travel by boat on a hot summer night</u>!

（在仲夏的夜晚搭船遊歷真快意！）

☞ 提示用 How 開頭且句尾是驚嘆號（！），所以緊接在 How 後面要擺形容詞或副詞（片語），也就是題目中的 pleasant，接著是「虛主詞 it + be 動詞」的肯定句結構，且後面照抄即可。要注意的是，原句中 so（如此的…）已經被改寫句句首的 How（多麼的…）取代，所以改寫句不能再出現 so！

Q15. It caused her much pain to lose her family.

↳ How much pain <u>it caused her to lose her family</u>!

（失去家人讓她多麼傷痛啊！）

主題 5 | 主詞的切換

Focus 解題焦點：

> 主詞改變時，動詞和主詞補語也要跟著主詞的單複數型態一
> 起改變，可區分為四大類型：
> 一、be 動詞型／二、助動詞 do 型／三、助動詞 have 型／
> 四、一般動詞型。

一、be 動詞型

be 動詞和主詞補語都要跟著主詞變動。

例 She is a good girl.

☞ They <u>are good girls</u>.

二、助動詞 do 型

助動詞 do 隨著主詞變動。

例 My mother doesn't allow me to come home late.

☞ My parents <u>don't allow me to come home late</u>.

三、助動詞 have 型

助動詞 have 隨著主詞變動。

例 They have lived here for a long time.

☞ The old man <u>has lived here for a long time</u>.

四、一般動詞型

一般動詞隨著主詞變動。

例 I look at the window.

☞ He <u>looks at the window</u>.

 快速查!!

be 動詞、助動詞 do、助動詞 have、一般動詞 的動詞變化一覽表

GRAMMAR

動詞種類	時態	單數		複數	
be 動詞	現在式	第一人稱	am	第一人稱	are
		第二人稱	are	第二人稱	
		第三人稱	is	第三人稱	
	過去式	第一人稱	was	第一人稱	were
		第二人稱	were	第二人稱	
		第三人稱	was	第三人稱	
一般動詞（規則變化）	現在式	第一人稱	原形	第一人稱	原形
		第二人稱	原形	第二人稱	
		第三人稱	-s/-es/-ies	第三人稱	
	過去式	第一人稱	-d/-ed/-ied	第一人稱	-d/-ed/-ied
		第二人稱		第二人稱	
		第三人稱		第三人稱	
助動詞 do	現在式	第一人稱	do	第一人稱	do
		第二人稱	do	第二人稱	
		第三人稱	does	第三人稱	
	過去式	第一人稱	did	第一人稱	did
		第二人稱		第二人稱	
		第三人稱		第三人稱	
助動詞 have	現在式	第一人稱	have + p.p.	第一人稱	have + p.p.
		第二人稱	have + p.p.	第二人稱	
		第三人稱	has + p.p.	第三人稱	
	過去式	第一人稱	had + p.p.	第一人稱	had + p.p.
		第二人稱		第二人稱	
		第三人稱		第三人稱	

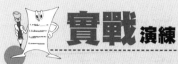
實戰演練

考驗你的改寫能力！

Q1. You are a good student.

↳ Your sister _____.

Q2. My father is not tall.

↳ I _____.

Q3. He is a nice person.

↳ They _____.

Q4. I like to jog in the morning.

↳ My grandfather _____.

Q5. Joanne usually gets up late on holidays.

↳ They usually _____.

Q6. You are very beautiful and look like a model.

↳ Your aunt _____.

Q7. You were out when John came yesterday.

↳ I _____.

Q8. She was my classmate in junior high school.

↳ They _____.

Q9. I was watching TV while the doorbell rang.

↳ We _____.

Part 1 · 單句寫作 ▶▶ 01 句子改寫

Q10. Our son has played on-line games for two hours.

↳ They _____.

Q11. They have lived here for a long time.

↳ The old man _____.

Q12. She has been to many countries.

↳ Lily and Tina _____.

Q13. That isn't mine.

↳ Those _____.

Q14. My mother doesn't allow me to come home late.

↳ My parents _____.

Q15. The school hasn't caught the burglar.

↳ The police _____.

示範 解答

中英文對照大解析

Q1. You are a good student.
（你是好學生。）

↳ Your sister is a good student.
（你姐姐是好學生。）

Q2. My father is not tall.

（我父親不高。）

↳ I <u>am not tall</u>.

（我不高·）

Q3. He is a nice person.

（他是個好人。）

↳ They <u>are nice people</u>.

（他們是好人。）

Q4. I like to jog in the morning.

（我喜歡晨跑。）

↳ My grandfather <u>likes to jog in the morning</u>.

（我祖父喜歡晨跑。）

Q5. Joanne usually gets up late on holidays.

（假日時喬安娜通常都會晚起。）

↳ They usually <u>get up late on holidays</u>.

（假日時他們通常都會晚起。）

Q6. You are very beautiful and look like a model.

（你很漂亮，而且看起來像個模特兒。）

↳ Your aunt <u>is very beautiful and looks like a model</u>.

（你的阿姨很漂亮，而且看起來像個模特兒。）

Q7. You were out when John came yesterday.

（昨天約翰來時你不在。）

↳ I <u>was out when John came yesterday</u>.

（昨天約翰來時我不在。）

Q8. She was my classmate in junior high school.
（她是我高中時的同學。）

↳ They were my classmates in junior high school.
（他們是我高中時的同學。）

Q9. I was watching TV while the doorbell rang.
（門鈴響的時候我正在看電視。）

↳ We were watching TV while the doorbell rang.
（門鈴響的時候我們正在看電視。）

Q10. Our son has played on-line games for two hours.
（我們兒子已經玩了兩個小時的線上遊戲。）

↳ They have played on-line games for two hours.
（他們已經玩了兩個小時的線上遊戲。）

Q11. They have lived here for a long time.
（他們已經在此住了很長一段時間。）

↳ The old man has lived here for a long time.
（這名老人已經在此住了很長一段時間。）

Q12. She has been to many countries.
（她去過很多國家。）

↳ Lily and Tina have been to many countries.
（莉莉和緹娜去過很多國家。）

Q13. That isn't mine.
（那不是我的。）

↳ Those aren't mine.
（那些不是我的。）

Q14. My mother doesn't allow me to come home late.

（我媽媽不准我晚回家。）

↳ My parents <u>don't allow me to come home late</u>.

（我父母不准我晚回家。）

Q15. The school hasn't caught the burglar.

（校方還沒抓到竊賊。）

↳ The police <u>haven't caught the burglar</u>.

（警方還沒抓到竊賊。）

☞ the police（警方）是複數形，必須搭配複數的助動詞 haven't，如果要用單數表示的話，可以用 policeman，它的複數形是 policemen 或 the police。

主題 6 | 原級／比較級／最高級切換

Focus 解題焦點：

> 這個主題最常要求考生活用各種句型，來表達最高級的概念，最高級的表達方式可分為三大類：
> 一、以原級表示／二、以比較級表示／三、以最高級表示。

一、以原級表示最高級

No one / Nothing is as + 形容詞原級 + as N.

No one / Nothing V as + 副詞原級 + as N.

例 William is the best.

☞ No one is as good as William.

二、以比較級表示最高級

- N is 形容詞比較級 than any other 單數名詞.
  N + V + 副詞比較級 than any other 單數名詞.

例 Of all the girls in this town, Ariel sings the best.

☞ Ariel sings better than any other girl in this town.

- IN is 形容詞比較級 than all the other 複數名詞.
  N + V + 副詞比較級 than all the other 複數名詞.

例 Of all the girls in this town, Ariel sings the best.

☞ Ariel sings better than all the other girls in this town.

- No one / Nothing is + 形容詞比較級 + than N.
  No one / Nothing V + 副詞比較級 + than N.

例 Health is the most important.

☞ Nothing is more important than health.

三、以最高級表示

N is 形容詞最高級

N + V + 副詞最高級

例 No other girl in the world is more beautiful than Belle.

☞ Belle is <u>the most beautiful girl</u> in the world.

重點文法 快速查!!

比較級、最高級變化法則

形容詞或副詞	比較級	最高級
單音節和雙音節	原級字尾 + er	the 原級字尾 + est
三音節和多音節	more + 原級	the most + 原級

不規則變化形容詞舉例

原級	比較級	最高級
good	better	the best
bad	worse	the worst
much	more	the most
many	more	the most
little	less	the least

原級和比較級轉換為最高級的思考邏輯

A > B > C	A 的層級最高
沒有人的層級和 A 一樣高	A 的層級最高
沒有人的層級比 A 高	A 的層級最高
A 的層級比其他所有人還高	A 的層級最高
A 的層級比其他任何一個人還高	A 的層級最高

Q1. Nothing is as exciting as riding the roller coaster.

↳ Nothing is _____ than riding the roller coaster.

Q2. No other precious stone is as hard as diamond.

↳ Diamond is _____ than all the other precious stones.

Q3. No one can eat as much as he does.

↳ He can eat _____ than anyone else.

Q4. No other animals run as quickly as cheetahs.

↳ Cheetahs run _____ than any other animal.

Q5. Charlie studies harder than any of my children.

↳ None of my children study _____ Charlie does.

Q6. Adam plays the guitar better than all the others on the band.

↳ No one on the band plays the guitar _____ Adam does.

Q7. No student in my class is as smart as John.

↳ John is _____ student in my class.

Q8. No other animal in the sea is as big as whales.

↳ Whales are _____ animals in the sea.

Q9. No date on calendar is as important as tomorrow.

↳ Tomorrow is _____ date on calendar.

Q10. No other person in my life is as precious as my mother.

↳ My mother is _____ person in my life.

Q11. No place I've ever been to is as beautiful as this city.

↳ This city is _____ place I've ever been to.

Q12. No one in my family is as tall as I am.

↳ I'm _____ in my family.

Q13. No game is more boring than this one.

↳ This is _____ game ever.

Q14. No other in the golf club plays worse than he does.

↳ He plays worse _____ in the golf club.

Q15. Finn is the most careful worker in the factory.

↳ All the workers in the factory are _____ than Finn.

示範 解答　　　　　　　　　　　　　　　　　　　　　　　中英文對照大解析

Q1. Nothing is as exciting as riding the roller coaster.

↳ Nothing is **more exciting** than riding the roller coaster.
（沒有比坐雲霄飛車更刺激的事了。）

Q2. No other precious stone is as hard as diamond.

↳ Diamond is <u>harder</u> than all the other precious stones.
（鑽石比所有其他寶石更堅硬。）

Q3. No one can eat as much as he does.

↳ He can eat <u>more</u> than anyone else.
（他可以比任何人吃更多東西。）

Q4. No other animals run as quickly as cheetahs.

↳ Cheetahs run <u>more quickly</u> than any other animal.
（花豹是跑得最快的動物。）

Q5. Charlie studies harder than any of my children.

↳ None of my children study <u>as hard as</u> Charlie does.
（我的孩子中查理是最用功的。）

Q6. Adam plays the guitar better than all the others on the band.

↳ No one on the band plays the guitar <u>as well as</u> Adam does.
（亞當是樂團中吉他彈最好的。）

Q7. No student in my class is as smart as John.

↳ John is <u>the smartest</u> student in my class.
（約翰是我班上最聰明的學生。）

Q8. No other animal in the sea is as big as whales.

↳ Whales are <u>the biggest</u> animals in the sea.
（鯨魚是海中最大的動物。）

Q9. No date on calendar is as important as tomorrow.

↳ Tomorrow is <u>the most important</u> date on calendar.
（明天是一年當中最重要的日子。）

Q10. No other person in my life is as precious as my mother.

↳ My mother is <u>the most precious</u> person in my life.

（母親是我生命中最珍貴的人。）

Q11. No place I've ever been to is as beautiful as this city.

↳ This city is <u>the most beautiful</u> place I've ever been to.

（這是我到過最美麗的城市。）

☞ place 是名詞，後面省略關係代名詞 which/that，所以 been 後面必須再加介系詞 to。

Q12. No one in my family is as tall as I am.

↳ I'm <u>the tallest</u> in my family.

（我是家中身高最高的人。）

Q13. No game is more boring than this one.

↳ This is <u>the most boring</u> game ever.

（這是有史以來最無聊的比賽。）

☞ "no… is more than…" 表示「沒有…比…更加…」，因此也具有最高級的意味。

Q14. No other in the golf club plays worse than he does.

（他是高爾夫俱樂部裡球技最差的。）

↳ He plays worse <u>than any other member</u> in the golf club.

（這是有史以來最無聊的比賽。）

☞ " than any other…" 表示「比任何其他…更加…」，因此也具有最高級的意味。

Q15. Finn is the most careful worker in the factory.

↳ All the workers in the factory are <u>less careful</u> than Finn.

（工廠裡所有工人都不如芬來得謹慎小心。）

解題焦點：

> 時態改變，動詞也會隨著改變。改寫時態的題型各有其特殊
> 的解題方式，可歸納為四類：
> 一、特殊連接詞／二、動詞同步轉換／三、特定時間片語／
> 四、頻率副詞。

一、特殊連接詞

　　某些連接詞本身含有時態的意義，例如：since 通常出現在完成
　　式當中。

　　例 She worked in the firm after she graduated from school.

　　☞ **She has been working in the firm** since she graduated from
　　　school.

二、動詞同步轉換

　　此種類型的句子前後各有一個動詞，同步轉換兩個動詞的時態即
　　可。下面例題中的句子，前後各有一個動詞，動詞 arrive 從現在
　　式轉換為過去式，所以同樣把 has run 從現在完成式轉換成過去
　　完成式，就可以輕鬆得到答案。

　　例 The robber has run away every time when the police arrive.

　　☞ The robber had run away before the police arrived.

三、特定時間片語

　　時間片語和時態有絕對的相關，例如：for ten years 經常出現在
　　完成式的句子當中；several years ago、yesterday、last night 經
　　常出現在過去式的句子中；tomorrow、this summer、next year
　　通常會配合未來式使用；every day、every week、on Sundays
　　一般則用於現在式。

　　例 Mary went to the movies last week.

　　☞ Mary will go to the movies tomorrow.

四、頻率副詞

　　頻率副詞 often、always、usually、sometimes、once、twice、seldom... 等副詞通常會配合現在簡單式使用。

例 He studied in the library yesterday.

☞ He <u>always studies</u> in the library.

重點文法 快速查!!

常用不規則變化動詞一覽表

原形	過去式	過去分詞	中文字義
arise	arose	arisen	上升；產生
awake	awoke	awoken	喚醒，覺醒
be	was / were	been	是；存在
bear	bore	borne	承擔，忍受
beat	beat	beaten	打、擊；跳動
become	became	become	變成
begin	began	begun	開始
behold	beheld	beheld	看，注視
bend	bent	bent	彎曲
bet	bet, betted	bet, betted	打賭，斷言
bind	bound	bound	
bite	bit	bitten	叮咬
bleed	bled	bled	流血
bless	blessed / blest	blessed / blest	祝福，賜福
break	broke	broken	打破，弄壞
bring	brought	brought	帶來
broadcast	broadcast	broadcast	廣播
build	built	built	建立，設立
burn	burned / burnt	burned / burnt	燃燒，燒焦
burst	burst	burst	爆炸，爆破
buy	bought	bought	購買
cast	cast	cast	扔，投擲

catch	caught	caught	得到，捉住，趕上，染上
choose	chose	chosen	選擇
come	came	came	到來
cost	cost	cost	花費，值……（多少錢）
cut	cut	cut	裁切
deal	dealt	dealt	經營
dig	dug	dug	挖掘
do	did	done	做
draw	drew	drawn	畫圖
dream	dreamed, dreamt	dreamed, dreamt	作夢
drink	drank	drunk	喝
drive	drove	driven	駕駛
dwell	dwelt	dwelt	居住
eat	ate	eaten	吃
fall	fell	fallen	掉落
feed	fed	fed	餵食
feel	felt	felt	感覺
fight	fought	fought	打架，打仗
find	found	found	找到
fly	flew	flown	飛
forget	forgot	forgotten	忘記
forgive	forgave	forgiven	原諒
forsake	forsook	forsaken	放棄，拋棄，離棄
freeze	froze	frozen	結冰，凍僵
get	got	got, gotten	得到
give	gave	given	給予
go	went	gone	去
grow	grew	grown	生長
have	had	had	擁有
hear	heard	heard	聽
hit	hit	hit	打，打擊
hold	held	held	抓住
hurt	hurt	hurt	使受傷，疼痛

p

keep	kept	kept	保持，保留；飼養（動物）
know	knew	known	知道，認識
lay	laid	laid	放置；下蛋
lead	led	led	領導
learn	learned, learnt	learned, learnt	學習
leave	left	left	離開；留下
lend	lent	lent	借出
let	let	let	讓，允許
lie	lay	lain	躺臥
lose	lost	lost	失去
make	made	made	使得；製造
mean	meant	meant	意謂
meet	met	met	遇見，碰見
mistake	mistook	mistaken	誤解，誤認
overcome	overcame	overcome	克服
pay	paid	paid	支付
prove	proved	proved, proven	證明
put	put	put	放置
quit	quit, quitted	quit, quitted	停止；離職，離開
read	read	read	閱讀
ride	rode	ridden	騎乘
ring	rang	rung	鈴響；打電話
rise	rose	risen	上升，上漲
run	ran	run	跑
say	said	said	說
see	saw	seen	看
seek	sought	sought	尋找
sell	sold	sold	賣
send	sent	sent	寄送，發送，傳送
set	set	set	擺放，設置
shake	shook	shaken	搖動，震動；發抖
show	showed	shown, showed	顯示，顯露
shut	shut	shut	關上，闔上

sing	sang	sung	唱
sit	sat	sat	坐
sleep	slept	slept	睡覺
smell	smelt, smelled	smelt, smelled	聞，嗅
speak	spoke	spoken	說（語言）
spend	spent	spent	花費
spoil	spoilt, spoiled	spoilt, spoiled	腐敗；破壞；寵壞
spread	spread	spread	擴散，展開
stand	stood	stood	站
steal	stole	stolen	偷
swear	swore	sworn	發誓；詛咒
sweep	swept	swept	打掃
swim	swam	swam	游泳
take	took	taken	拿，取
teach	taught	taught	教導
tear	tore	torn	撕開
tell	told	told	告訴
think	thought	thought	想，思考
throw	threw	thrown	投擲，丟
understand	understood	understood	懂，明白
undo	undid	undone	打開，復原
upset	upset	upset	打翻，打亂
wake	woke	woken	醒來
wear	wore	worn	穿戴
wed	wed, wedded	wed, wedded	結婚，嫁，娶
weep	wept	wept	哭泣，流淚
wet	wet, wetted	wet, wetted	弄濕
win	won	won	贏，得勝，成功
wind	wound	wound	蜿蜒，盤旋，纏燒
write	wrote	written	寫

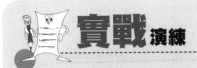
Q1. I'm baking cookies right now.

↳ _____ while he came.

Q2. We are usually in sound sleep while the burglar breaks in.

↳ We _____ while the burglar broke in.

Q3. Vincent lives in Yilan.

↳ Vincent _____ several years ago.

Q4. Bob never fights in school.

↳ Bob _____ yesterday.

Q5. Frank will not come home until midnight.

↳ Frank _____ yesterday.

Q6. Nancy went on a tour to Hawaii last summer.

↳ Nancy _____ this summer.

Q7. May is studying abroad in the UK.

↳ May _____ next year.

Q8. I did warm-ups before running in the race.

↳ I always _____ before running.

Q9. Emily spent a lot of time on her homework yesterday.

↳ Emily _____ every day.

Q10. Angela is gaining some weight.

↳ Angela _____ since she graduated.

Q11. J.K. Rowling writes stories.

↳ J.K. Rowling _____ since she was a child.

Q12. Kevin worked for Microsoft ten years ago.

↳ Kevin _____ for ten years before he retired.

Q13. The robber has run away every time before the police arrive.

↳ The robber _____ before the police arrived.

Q14. The lifeguard will save the drowning swimmer if an accident happens.

↳ The lifeguard _____ as the accident happened.

Q15. Wendy divorced Bill because he had cheated on her.

↳ Wendy _____ if he cheats on her.

示範 解答   中英文對照大解析

Q1. I'm baking cookies right now.
（我現在正在烤餅乾。）

↳ I was baking cookies while he came.
（他來的時候我正在烤餅乾。）

「過去進行式」必須有一個過去的時間參考點，本題是「他來的時候（while he came）」，所以如果只有 "I was baking cookies." 這樣的句子是錯誤的。

Q2. We are usually in sound sleep while the burglar breaks in.
（竊賊闖入時我們通常都在熟睡中。）

↳ We <u>were in sound sleep</u> while the burglar broke in.
（竊賊闖入時我們正熟睡中。）

Q3. Vincent lives in Yilan.
（文生住在宜蘭。）

↳ Vincent <u>lived in Yilan</u> several years ago.
（數年前文生住在宜蘭。）

Q4. Bob never fights in school.
（鮑伯在校從沒與人打架。）

↳ Bob <u>fought in school</u> yesterday.
（鮑伯昨天在學校與人打架。）

Q5. Frank will not come home until midnight.
（法蘭克要到半夜才會回家。）

↳ Frank <u>did not come home until midnight</u> yesterday.
（法蘭克昨天一直到半夜才回家。）

Q6. Nancy went on a tour to Hawaii last summer.
（南西去年去夏威夷旅行。）

↳ Nancy <u>will go on / is going on a tour to Hawaii</u> this summer.
（南西今年夏天會去夏威夷旅行。）

☞ this summer 這個時間副詞表示未來，所以動詞應用 will go，也可以用進行式（is going）代替未來。

Part 1 · 單句寫作 ▶▶ 01 句子改寫

Q7. May is studying abroad in the UK.
（梅正在海外的英國讀書。）

↳ May <u>will / is going to study abroad in the UK</u> next year.
（梅明年將到英國留學。）

Q8. I did warm-ups before running in the race.
（我在賽跑前先做了暖身。）

↳ I always <u>do warm-ups</u> before running.
（我在跑步前總會先做暖身。）

Q9. Emily spent a lot of time on her homework yesterday.
（艾蜜莉昨天花了很多時間做功課。）

↳ Emily <u>spends a lot of time on her homework</u> every day.
（艾蜜莉每天都花很多時間在做功課。）

Q10. Angela is gaining some weight.
（安琪拉變胖了。）

↳ Angela <u>has gained some weight</u> since she graduated.
（安琪拉自從畢業後就已經胖了。）

Q11. J.K. Rowling writes stories.
（J.K.Rowling 從事故事寫作。）

↳ J.K. Rowling <u>has written stories</u> since she was a child.
（J.K. Rowling 從小就已經開始寫故事。）

Q12. Kevin worked for Microsoft ten years ago.
（凱文十年前在微軟工作過。）

↳ Kevin <u>had worked for Microsoft</u> for ten years before he retired.
（凱文在退休前已經在微軟工作了十年。）

Q13. The robber has run away every time before the police arrive.

（每次在警方抵達前擒匪就都已經跑掉了。）

↳ The robber <u>had run away</u> before the police arrived.

（警方抵達前搶匪就已經跑掉了。）

☞ 因為 before（在…之前）後面句子動詞用過去簡單式，所以前面主要子句要用「過去完成式」（had run away），表示這個動作比 before 的那個動作發生得更早。

Q14. The lifeguard will save the drowning swimmer if an accident happens.

（如果有意外發生，救生員會去救溺水的泳客。）

↳ The lifeguard <u>saved the drowning swimmer</u> as the accident happened.

（意外發生時救生員救了溺水的泳客。）

Q15. Wendy divorced Bill because he had cheated on her.

（溫蒂和比爾離婚，因為他背叛了她。）

↳ Wendy <u>will divorce Bill</u> if he cheats on her.

（如果比爾背叛她，溫蒂會和他離婚。）

☞ if 子句的動詞是現在式（cheats），所以這是「假設直述句」，主要子句動詞要用「未來式」。

解題焦點：

> 疑問句改寫成名詞子句的竅門在於主詞和動詞的位置。在疑問句中，be 動詞或助動詞置於主詞之前；在名詞子句中，be 動詞或助動詞置於主詞之後，其擺放順序與肯定句型相同。疑問詞引導的名詞子句可分為三種類型：
> 一、be 動詞型／二、情態助動詞型／三、助動詞 do 型。

一、be 動詞型

疑問詞 + be 動詞 + S? → 疑問代名詞 + <u>S + be 動詞</u>

例 Where is my pencil?

☞ I do not know where <u>my pencil is</u>.

二、情態助動詞型

疑問詞 + 情態助動詞 + S + V? → 疑問詞 + <u>S + 助動詞 + V</u>

例 When will she go to Paris?

☞ Tell me when <u>she will go</u> to Paris.

三、助動詞 do 型

疑問詞 + do / does + S + V? → 疑問詞 + <u>S + V</u>

例 What do you want?

☞ I don't know what <u>you want</u>.

· 疑問詞 + does + S + V? → 疑問詞 + <u>S + V-es</u> (或-s/-ies)

例 Why does he go to the place every day?

☞ Do you know <u>why he goes to the place every day</u>?

· 疑問詞 + did + S + V? → 疑問詞 + <u>S + V-ed</u> (或-d/-ied)

例 Why did She cry?

☞ <u>Can you tell me why she cried</u>?

重點文法 快速查!!

疑問句 & 名詞子句（疑問詞型）對照表

	疑問句	名詞子句
be 動詞型	疑問詞 + be 動詞 + S?	疑問詞 + S + be 動詞
情態助動詞型	疑問詞 + 助動詞 + S + V?	疑問詞 + S + 助動詞 + V
Do 型	疑問詞 + do + S + V?	疑問詞 + S + V
	疑問詞 + does + S + V?	疑問詞 + S + V-es (或-s/-ies)
	疑問詞 + did + S + V?	疑問詞 + S + V-ed（或-d/-ied）

名詞子句的四大作用

名詞子句的作用	舉例說明
當主詞	What you just said is ridiculous.
當受詞	Do you know who the woman is?
當補語	The dress is what I want.
當同位語	The reason why she left remains a mystery.

實戰演練 考驗你的改寫能力！

Q1. What is your name?

↪ Tell me _____.

Q2. How is his new computer?

↪ Ask him _____.

Q3. Who was the winner?

↪ Did you notice _____?

Q4. Where were they going?

↳ Didn't they say _____?

Q5. What can the cat do?

↳ You won't believe _____.

Q6. When will they arrive?

↳ Go make sure _____.

Q7. Who should I invite?

↳ I'm not sure _____.

Q8. What would you like for dessert?

↳ You may choose _____.

Q9. What have you bought?

↳ Can I see _____?

Q10. Why has she been upset these few days?

↳ Who knows _____?

Q11. What do you want?

↳ Just tell us _____.

Q12. Why does he always make mistakes?

↳ We don't get it _____.

Q13. How much does this diamond cost?

↳ Don't worry about _____.

Q14. How did that happen?

↳ Nobody knows _____.

Q15. When did you last see Dan?

↳ They're asking _____.

示範 解答 中英文對照大解析

Q1. What is your name?
（你叫什麼名字？）

↳ Tell me <u>what your name is</u>.
（告訴我你叫什麼名字。）

Q2. How is his new computer?
（他的新電腦如何？）

↳ Ask him <u>how his new computer is</u>.
（問他看看他的新電腦如何。）

Q3. Who was the winner?
（誰是贏家？）

↳ Did you notice <u>who the winner was</u>?
（你有注意到誰是贏家嗎？）

Q4. Where were they going?
（他們去哪裡了？）

↳ Didn't they say <u>where they were going</u>?
（他們沒說他們要去哪裡嗎？）

Q5. What can the cat do?

（這隻貓能做什麼？）

↳ You won't believe <u>what the cat can do</u>.

（你不會相信這隻貓能做什麼。）

Q6. When will they arrive?

（他們何時會抵達？）

↳ Go make sure <u>when they will arrive</u>.

（去確定一下他們何時會抵達。）

Q7. Who should I invite?

（我該邀請誰呢？）

↳ I'm not sure <u>whom I should invite</u>.

（我不確定我該邀請誰。）

☞ be sure 或 make sure 後面都可以直接接名詞子句，表示「確定…（某件事）」，如果是以 who 引導的名詞子句，要注意它是當主詞或受詞，如果是受詞就要用 whom。

Q8. What would you like for dessert?

（你想吃什麼點心？）

↳ You may choose <u>what you would like for dessert</u>.

（你可以選擇要吃什麼點心。）

Q9. What have you bought?

（你買了什麼？）

↳ Can I see <u>what you have bought</u>?

（我可以看看你買了什麼嗎？）

Q10. Why has she been upset these few days?

（為什麼這幾天她一直悶悶不樂的？）

↳ Who knows <u>why she has been upset these few days</u>?

（誰知道這幾天她為什麼一直悶悶不樂的嗎？）

Q11. What do you want?

（你想要什麼？）

↳ Just tell us <u>what you want</u>.

（儘管告訴我們你想要什麼。）

Q12. Why does he always make mistakes?

（為什麼他總是犯錯？）

↳ We don't get it <u>why he always makes mistakes</u>.

（我們不懂為什麼他總是犯錯。）

☞ 注意名詞子句的動詞要用第三人稱單數（makes），因為原句的助動詞用 does。

Q13. How much does this diamond cost?

（這顆鑽石多少錢？）

↳ Don't worry about <u>how much this diamond costs</u>.

（不需要擔心這顆鑽石要多少錢。）

Q14. How did that happen?

（那是怎麼發生的？）

↳ Nobody knows <u>how that happened</u>.

（沒人知道那是怎麼發生的。）

☞ 注意名詞子句的動詞要用過去式（happened），因為原句的助動詞用 did。

Q15. When did you last see Dan?

（你最後一次見到丹是什麼時候？）

↳ They're asking <u>when you last saw Dan</u>.

（他們在問你最後一次見到丹是什麼時候。）

解題焦點：

Yes/No 疑問句改為名詞子句時，必須加入 if 或 whether (or not) 使其句意完整，其句型可分為三種類型：
一、be 動詞型／二、情態助動詞型／三、助動詞 do 型。

一、be 動詞型

be 動詞 + S...? → if + S + be 動詞…

(例) Is this my pencil?

☞ I do not know if this is my pencil.

二、情態助動詞型

助動詞 + S + V? → if + S + 助動詞 + V…

(例) Will she go to Paris?

☞ Tell me whether she will go to Paris (or not).

三、助動詞 do 型

· Do + S + V? → if + S + V

(例) Do you want something to eat?

☞ I don't know whether you want something to eat (or not).
Does + S + V? → if + S + V-s （或-es/-ied）

(例) Does he go to the place every day?

☞ Do you know if he goes to the place every day?
· Did + S + V? → if + S + V-ed （或-d/-ied）

(例) Did She cry?

☞ Can you tell me whether she cried (or not)?

重點文法 快速查!!

疑問句 & 名詞子句（Yes/No 疑問句型）對照表

	疑問句	名詞子句
be 動詞型	be 動詞 + S?	if + S + be 動詞
情態助動詞型	助動詞 + S + V?	whether/if + S + 助動詞 + V
Do 型	Do + S + V?	whether/if + S + V
	Does + S + V?	whether/if + S + V-s（或-es/-ies）
	Did + S + V?	whether/if + S + V-ed（或-d/-ied）

名詞子句在句中扮演四大角色

名詞子句的角色	舉例說明
當主詞	Whether she is a thief remains unknown.
當受詞	I don't know if she will go to the party.
當補語	My question is if cats can understand what I say.
當同位語	The question whether she is dead remains a mystery.

實戰演練

考驗你的改寫能力！

Q1. Is Eric in his room?

↳ Mom asks _____.

Q2. Is there life on the moon?

↳ The scientists want to know _____.

Q3. Are we going to have a test tomorrow?

↳ Do you know _____?

Q4. Should I buy this dress?

↳ Tell me _____.

Q5. Will there be another rainy day tomorrow?

↳ I wonder _____.

Q6. Can a dog swim?

↳ Children often ask _____.

Q7. Will Kevin go with his girlfriend?

↳ They wonder _____.

Q8. Has the baseball team ever won a game?

↳ The new coach doubts _____.

Q9. Have her parents accepted Andrew?

↳ Do you know _____?

Q10. Do fish talk to each other?

↳ My question is _____.

Q11. Does Molly like you?

↳ Go find out _____.

Q12. Did you go to the disco pub last night?

↳ Answer me _____.

Q13. Did he say anything?

↳ Can you tell me _____?

Q14. Did anybody write down the plate number?

↳ It'll be great _____.

Q15. Did July bring an umbrella with her this morning?

↳ Do you remember _____?

示範 解答　　　　　　　　　　　　　中英文對照大解析

Q1. Is Eric in his room?
（艾瑞克在他房裡嗎？）

↳ Mom asks if Eric is in his room.
（媽媽問艾瑞克是不是在他房裡。）

☞ 可以用 whether 取代 if，但 whether 附帶的 or not 可有可無，可置於 whether 後面，也可置於句尾。

Q2. Is there life on the moon?
（月球上有生物嗎？）

↳ The scientists want to know if there is life on the moon.
（科學家們想知道月球上是不是有生物。）

Q3. Are we going to have a test tomorrow?
（我們明天有考試嗎？）

↳ Do you know if we are going to have a test tomorrow?
（你知道我們明天是不是有考試嗎？）

Q4. Should I buy this dress?
（我應該買下這件洋裝嗎？）

↳ Tell me if I should buy this dress.
（告訴我，我是不是應該買下這件洋裝。）

Q5. Will there be another rainy day tomorrow?
（明天還會是個下雨天嗎？）

↳ I wonder <u>if there will be another rainy day tomorrow</u>.
（我想知道明天還會不會是個雨天。）

Q6. Can a dog swim?
（狗會游泳嗎？）

↳ Children often ask <u>if a dog can swim</u>.
（孩子們常問狗會不會游泳。）

Q7. Will Kevin go with his girlfriend?
（凱文會和他的女友去嗎？）

↳ They wonder <u>if Kevin will go with his girlfriend</u>.
（他們想知道凱文會不會和他的女友去。）

Q8. Has the baseball team ever won a game?
（這支棒球隊可曾贏過一場比賽？）

↳ The new coach doubts <u>if the baseball team has ever won a game</u>.
（新來的教練懷疑這支棒球隊是否曾經贏過一場比賽。）

Q9. Have her parents accepted Andrew?
（她父母接受安德魯了嗎？）

↳ Do you know <u>if her parents have accented Andrew</u>?
（你知道她父母是否接受安德魯了嗎？）

Q10. Do fish talk to each other?
（魚會彼此交談嗎？）

↳ My question is <u>if fish talk to each other</u>.
（我的問題是魚會不會彼此交談。）

Q11. Does Molly like you?

（茉莉喜歡你嗎？）

↳ Go find out if <u>Molly likes you</u>.

（去了解一下茉莉是否喜歡你。）

Q12. Did you go to the disco pub last night?

（你昨晚有沒有去迪司可舞廳？）

↳ Answer me <u>if you went to the disco pub last night</u>.

（回答我，你昨晚有沒有去迪司可舞廳。）

Q13. Did he say anything?

（他有沒有說什麼？）

↳ Can you tell me <u>if he said anything</u>?

（你能告訴我他有沒有說什麼嗎？）

Q14. Did anybody write down the plate number?

（有任何人寫下車牌照號碼嗎？）

↳ It'll be great <u>if anybody wrote down the plate number</u>.

（如果有任何人寫下車牌照號碼的話就太好了。）

☞ 改寫句提示以 It'll be great 開頭，表示這是個以虛主詞 it 為首，代替後面名詞子句的真主詞。因為題目句是個「Yes/No 問句」，所以改為名詞子句要用 if 或 whether 引導，答案也可以寫成 whether anybody wrote down the plate number (or not) 或是 whether (or not) anybody wrote down the plate number。

Q15. Did July bring an umbrella with her this morning?

（今早茱莉有沒有帶傘？）

↳ Do you remember <u>if July brought an umbrella with her this morning</u>?

（你記得今早茱莉有帶傘嗎？）

直接引述句／間接引述句切換：直述型

解題焦點：

「直接引述句」前後有引號（"..."），引用主詞（當時）所說的話，而「間接引述句」是將直接引述句的引號去掉，所以改寫重點在於前後主詞與動詞的一致。

一、「直接引述句」改寫為「間接引述句」的重點在於前後主詞與動詞的一致。

S1 + V1, "S2 + V2..." → S1 + V1 (+ that) S2 + V2...

例 Tom said, "I am the king of the world!"

☞ Tom said (that) he was the king of the world.

重點文法 快速查!!

直接引述句和間接引述句的句型比較

直接引述句	間接引述句
直接引述	間接引述
S1 + V1, "S2 + V2...	S1 + V1 + S2 + V2...
句子中有引號，直接引述主詞的說話內容。	句子中沒有引號，間接引述主詞的說話內容。
V1 和 V2 時態通常不一致。	V1 和 V2 時態必須一致。

GRAMMAR

實戰演練

考驗你的改寫能力！

Q1. I said, "I am hungry."

↳ I said _____.

Q2. He said, "I am doing my homework."

↳ He said _____.

Q3. They said, "We are not married."

↳ They said _____.

Q4. She told me, "I will do it."

↳ She told me _____.

Q5. His parents told him, "We will go to Paris for vacation."

↳ His parents told him _____.

Q6. The man said, "I won't accept it."

↳ The man said _____.

Q7. You told the boss, "I can do it by myself."

↳ You told the boss _____.

Q8. The woman said, "I can not tell a lie."

↳ The woman said _____.

Q9. He wrote, "I can't speak."

↳ He wrote _____.

Q10. Mr. Lee said, "I have to leave early."

↳ Mr. Lee said _____.

Q11. They said, "We have already paid."

↳ They said _____.

Q12. You said, "I haven't read that book."

↳ You said _____.

Q13. He said, "I don't want to go."

↳ He said _____.

Q14. My son said, "I plan to study abroad."

↳ My son said _____.

Q15. She told me, "I know your mother very well."

↳ She told me _____.

示範 解答 ⸻⸻⸻⸻⸻ 中英文對照大解析

Q1. I said, "I am hungry."
（我說：「我餓了。」）

↳ I said <u>I was hungry</u>.
（我說我餓了。）

Q2. He said, "I am doing my homework."
（他說：「我正在做功課。」）

↳ He said <u>he was doing his homework</u>.
（他說他正在做功課。）

Q3. They said, "We are not married."
（他們說：「我們沒有結婚。」）

↳ They said <u>they were not married</u>.
（他們說他們沒有結婚。）

Q4. She told me, "I will do it."
（她告訴我：「我會去做」。）

↳ She told me <u>she would do it</u>.
（她告訴我說她會去做。）

☞ 因為全句的動詞 told 是過去式，因此名詞子句內的時態也應用過去式，所以將原本 will 改成 would。

Q5. His parents told him, "We will go to Paris for vacation."
（他父母告訴他：「我們要去巴黎度假。」）

↳ His parents told him <u>they would go to Paris for vacation</u>.
（他父母告訴他說他們會去巴黎度假。）

Q6. The man said, "I won't accept it."
（那個男人說：「我不會接受。」）

↳ The man said <u>he wouldn't accept it</u>.
（那個男人說他不會接受。）

Q7. You told the boss, "I can do it by myself."
（你告訴老：「我自己可以處理。」）

↳ You told the boss <u>you could do it by yourself</u>.
（你告訴老闆說你自己可以處理。）

Q8. The woman said, "I cannot tell a lie."
（那個女人說：「我不能說謊。」）

↳ The woman said <u>she could not tell a lie</u>.
（那個女人說她不能說謊。）

Q9. He wrote, "I can't speak."
（他寫著：「我不能講話。」）

↳ He wrote <u>he couldn't speak</u>.
（他寫說他不能講話。）

Q10. Mr. Lee said, "I have to leave early."

（李先生說：「我必須早點離開。」）

↳ Mr. Lee said <u>he had to leave early</u>.

（李先生說他必須早點離開。）

Q11. They said, "We have already paid."

（他們說：「我們已經付錢了。」）

↳ They said <u>they had already paid</u>.

（他們說他們已經付錢了。）

☞ 改為間接引述句時，動詞應為「過去完成式」（had paid），因為「付錢」的動作比「說」這件事時更早發生。

Q12. You said, "I haven't read that book."

（你說：「我還沒看過那本書。」）

↳ You said <u>you hadn't read that book</u>.

（你說過你還沒看過那本書。）

Q13. He said, "I don't want to go."

（他說：「我不想去。」）

↳ He said <u>he didn't want to go</u>.

（他說他不想去。）

Q14. My son said, "I plan to study abroad."

（我兒子說：「我打算出國念書。」）

↳ My son said <u>he planned to study abroad</u>.

（我兒子說他打算出國念書。）

Q15. She told me, "I know your mother very well."

（她告訴我說：「我和你媽媽很熟。」）

↳ She told me <u>she knew my mother very well</u>.

（她告訴我說她和我媽媽很熟。）

主題 11 直接引述句/間接引述句切換: 疑問句型

Focus 解題焦點:

本題型的解題技巧相當類似「問句/名詞子句的切換:疑問詞型」。解題重點是將引號去掉、把疑問句轉換成名詞子句,並使前後主詞及動詞時態一致。

※直接引述句改寫為間接引述句的重點在於前後主詞及動詞時態的一致。

S1 + V1,"疑問詞 + V2 + S2..." → S1 + V1 + 疑問詞 + S2 + V2...

例 Tony asked, "Where is my pencil?"

☞ Tony asked where his pencil was.

重點文法 快速查!!

直接引述句和間接引述句的句型比較(疑問詞型)	
直接引述句	間接引述句
直接引述	間接引述
S1 + V1, "疑問詞 + S2 + V2...?"	S1 + V1 + 疑問詞 + S2 + V2...
句子中有引號,直接引述主詞的說話內容。	句子中沒有引號,間接引述主詞的說話內容。
V1 和 V2 時態通常不一致。	V1 和 V2 時態必須一致。

GRAMMAR

實戰演練

考驗你的改寫能力!

Q1. John said, "Why is Maria here?"

↳ John said _____.

Q2. Neil asked, "Whose house is that?"

↳ Neil asked _____.

Q3. The student asked, "When does the semester begin?"

↳ The student asked _____.

Q4. Jason asked her, "What are you doing?"

↳ Jason asked her _____.

Q5. They asked me, "When will you leave?"

↳ They asked me _____.

Q6. The children asked, "What can we play with?"

↳ The children asked _____.

Q7. William asked, "Who may go?"

↳ William asked _____.

Q8. They said, "What have humans done to the earth?"

↳ They wanted us to think _____.

Q9. Michael asked his brothers, "Where have you been?"

↳ Michael asked his brothers _____.

Q10. The boss asked him, "How many times have you been late for work?"

↳ The boss asked him _____.

Q11. The boy asked, "Why can birds fly?"

↳ The boy asked _____.

Q12. He asked me, "Where do you live?"

↳ He asked me _____.

Q13. I asked her, "What do you need?"

↳ I asked her _____.

Q14. His friend asked him, "How long do you study a day?"

↳ His friend asked him _____.

Q15. The driver asked them, "Where do you want to go?"

↳ The driver asked them _____.

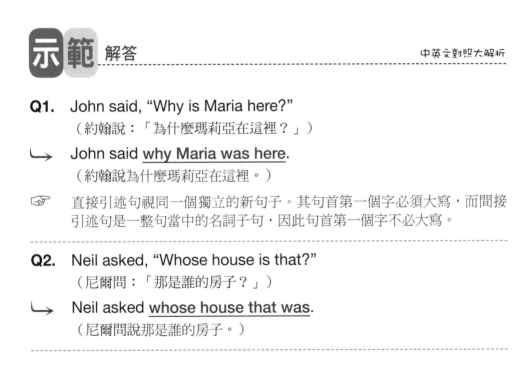

示範 解答　　　　　　　　　　　　　　　　　中英文對照大解析

Q1. John said, "Why is Maria here?"
（約翰說：「為什麼瑪莉亞在這裡？」）

↳ John said <u>why Maria was here</u>.
（約翰說為什麼瑪莉亞在這裡。）

☞ 直接引述句視同一個獨立的新句子。其句首第一個字必須大寫，而間接引述句是一整句當中的名詞子句，因此句首第一個字不必大寫。

Q2. Neil asked, "Whose house is that?"
（尼爾問：「那是誰的房子？」）

↳ Neil asked <u>whose house that was</u>.
（尼爾問說那是誰的房子。）

Q3. The student asked, "When does the semester begin?"
(學生問：「這學期什麼時候開始？」)

↳ The student asked <u>when the semester began</u>.
(學生問說這學期什麼時候開始。)

☞ 原則上名詞子句與主要子句的動詞時態一致，但本句也可以寫成 " The student asked when the semester will begin."，也就是「在說話的當下，學校尚未開學」的時候。

Q4. Jason asked her, "What are you doing?"
(傑森問她：「你在做什麼？」)

↳ Jason asked her <u>what she was doing</u>.
(傑森問她說她在做什麼。)

Q5. They asked me, "When will you leave?"
(他們問我：「你何時會離開？」)

↳ They asked me <u>when I would leave</u>.
(他們問我說我何時會離開。)

Q6. The children asked, "What can we play with?"
(孩子們問：我們可以玩什麼？)

↳ The children asked <u>what they could play with</u>.
(孩子們問他們可以玩什麼。)

Q7. William asked, "Who may go?"
(威廉問：「誰可以去？」)

↳ William asked <u>who might go</u>.
(威廉問誰可以去。)

Q8. They said, "What have humans done to the earth?"
(他們說：「人類對地球做了什麼？」)

↳ They wanted us to think <u>what humans have done to the earth</u>.
(他們要我們想想人類對地球做了什麼。)

Q9. Michael asked his brothers, "Where have you been?"
（麥克問他的哥哥們：「你們去哪裡了？」）

↳ Michael asked his brothers <u>where they had been</u>.
（麥克問他的哥哥們去了哪裡。）

☞ "ask sb. sth." 是個「授予動詞＋間接受詞（IO）＋直接受詞（DO）」的句型，IO 是「人」，DO 是「事情」。而原句的 "Where have you been?" 是個問句，轉換成間接引述的名詞子句時，除了要改成肯定句，主詞與動詞時態也須一致，也就是 you 改成 they，have been 改成 had been。

Q10. The boss asked him, "How many times have you been late for work?"
（老闆問他：「你上班遲到幾次了？」）

↳ The boss asked him <u>how many times he had been late for work</u>.
（老闆問他上班遲到幾次。）

Q11. The boy asked, "Why can birds fly?"
（男孩問：「為什麼鳥會飛？」）

↳ The boy asked <u>why birds could fly</u>.
（男孩問為什麼鳥會飛。）

Q12. He asked me, "Where do you live?"
（他問我：「你住哪裡？」）

↳ He asked me <u>where I lived</u>.
（他問我我住哪裡。）

☞ 原則上名詞子句與主要子句的動詞時態一致，但本句也可以寫成 " He asked me where I am living/live."，也就是「在說話的當下，要表達的是自己目前住的地方」的時候。

Q13. I asked her, "What do you need?"
（我問她：「你需要什麼？」）

↳ I asked her <u>what she needed</u>.
（我問她需要什麼。）

Q14. His friend asked him, "How long do you study a day?"
（他的朋友問他：「你一天念多久的書？」）

↳ His friend asked him <u>how long he studied a day</u>.
（他的朋友問他一天念書的時間多久。）

Q15. The driver asked them, "Where do you want to go?"
（司機問他們：「你們要去哪裡？」）

↳ The driver asked them <u>where they wanted to go</u>.
（司機問他們要去哪裡。）

Focus 解題焦點：

> 本單元的解題技巧相當類似「問句和／名詞子句的切換：
> Yes/No 問句句型」。解題重點是，將引號去掉、把 Yes/
> No 問句轉換成名詞子句，並使前後主詞及動詞時態一致。

※直接引述句改寫為間接引述句的重點在於前後主詞及動詞時態的一
致。

S1 + V1, "V2 + S2..." → S1 + V1 + <u>if + S2 + V2…</u>.

例 Tony asked, "Are you Mr. Lin?"

☞ Tony asked <u>if / whether he was Mr. Lin</u>.

重點文法 快速查!!

直接引述句和間接引述句的句型比較（Yes/No 問句）	
直接引述句	間接引述句
直接引述	間接引述
S1 + V1, "V2 + S2...?"	S1 + V1 + whether/if + S2 + V2...
句子中有引號，直接引述主詞的說話內容。	句子中沒有引號，間接引述主詞的說話內容。
V1 和 V2 時態通常不一致。	V1 和 V2 時態必須一致。

GRAMMAR

實戰演練 考驗你的改寫能力！

Q1. The teacher asked, "Is Fred absent?"

↳ The teacher asked _____.

Q2. Sam asked me, "Are you afraid?"

↳ Sam asked me _____.

Q3. The Student asked, "Will there be a test on the 20th?"

↳ The Student asked _____.

Q4. Victor asked, "Will there be a meeting today?"

↳ Victor asked _____.

Q5. He asked his girlfriend, "Will you marry me?

↳ He asked his girlfriend _____.

Q6. The tourists said, "Will we go to the palace?"

↳ The tourists wondered _____.

Q7. Anna asked, "Do you know Eric?"

↳ Anna wondered _____.

Q8. I asked her, "Does your cat like scratching furniture?"

↳ I asked her _____.

Q9. The managers said, "Do we have to bring a laptop?"

↳ The managers wondered _____.

Q10. The customer asked, "Can it be fixed by Sunday?"

↳ The customer wanted to know _____.

Q11. They asked the boy, "Can your dog do any tricks?"

↳ They asked the boy _____.

Q12. The woman asked the man, "Can you help me?"

↳ The woman asked the man _____.

Q13. The girl asked, "May I have another cookie?"

↳ The girl asked _____.

Q14. Sue asked her husband, "Can you drive me to the office?"

↳ Sue wanted to know _____.

Q15. She asked her father, "May I borrow your car?"

↳ She wanted to know _____.

示範 解答

中英文對照大解析

Q1. The teacher asked, "Is Fred absent?"
（老師問：「弗瑞德不在嗎？」）

↳ The teacher asked <u>if / whether Fred was absent</u>.
（老師問弗瑞德是不是不在。）

☞ Yes/No 疑問句改間接問句時，要用疑問詞 whether 或 if 來引導名詞子句，都表示「是否」，而如果用 whether 的話，可以加上 "or not" 在句尾，或是緊接在 whether 後面。例如這句可以寫成：The teacher asked whether Fred was absent or not. 或是 The teacher asked whether or not Fred was absent. 。

Q2. Sam asked me, "Are you afraid?"
（山姆問我：「你會怕嗎？」）

↳ Sam asked me <u>if I was afraid</u>.
（山姆問我是不是會怕。）

Q3. The student asked, "Will there be a test on the 20th"?"
（學生問：「20 號有考試嗎？」）

↳ The student asked <u>if there will be a test on the 20th</u>.
（學生問 20 號是不是有考試。）

☞ if 字句內的助動詞可以用 will 也可以用 would，但意思不同。前者所指的 20 號這個日期還沒到，後者表示 20 號這個日期已經過去了。

Q4. Victor asked, "Will there be a meeting today?"
（維克特問：「今天要開會嗎？」）

↳ Victor asked <u>if there would / will be a meeting today</u>.
（維克特問今天要不要開會。）

Q5. He asked his girlfriend, "Will you marry me?
（他問他的女友:「嫁給我好嗎？」）

↳ He asked his girlfriend <u>if she would marry him</u>.
（他問他的女友是不是要嫁給他。）

☞ will 和 would 也不是只有未來與過去時態的差別。在語氣上，would 會比 will 更客氣一些。

Q6. The tourists asked, "Will we go to the palace?"
（觀光客問：「我們會去皇宮嗎？」）

↳ The tourists wondered <u>if they would / will go to the palace</u>.
（觀光客問他們是不是會去皇宮。）

Q7. Anna asked, "Do you know Eric?"
（安娜問：「你認識艾瑞克嗎？」）

↳ Anna wondered <u>if I knew Eric</u>.
（安娜想知道我是不是認識艾瑞克。）

☞ 記住改寫成間接問句時，主要子句與名詞子句的動詞時態須一致（wondered 與 knew）。

Q8. I asked her, "Does your cat like scratching furniture?"
（我問她：「你的貓喜歡在傢俱上磨爪子嗎？」）

↳ I asked her if her cat liked scratching furniture.
（我問她她的貓是不是喜歡在傢俱上磨爪子。）

☞ 除了要注意動詞動詞時態一致之外，「人稱代名詞」的轉換也要留意（your → her）。

Q9. The managers said, "Do we have to bring a laptop?"
（經理們說：「我們必須帶手提電腦嗎？」）

↳ The managers wondered if they had to bring a laptop.
（經理們想知道他們是不是必須帶手提電腦。）

Q10. The customer asked, "Can it be fixed by Sunday?"
（顧客問：「星期天以前可以修好嗎？」）

↳ The customer wanted to know if it could be fixed by Sunday.
（顧客想知道星期天前是不是可以修好。）

Q11. They asked the boy, "Can your dog do any tricks?"
（他們問男孩：「你的狗會做什麼特技嗎？」）

↳ They asked the boy if his dog could do any tricks.
（他們問男孩他的狗會不會做什麼特技。）

Q12. The woman asked the man, "Can you help me?"
（女子問男子：「你可以幫我嗎？」）

↳ The woman asked the man if he could help her.
（女子問男子是不是可以幫她。）

Q13. The girl asked, "May I have another cookie?"
（女孩問：「我可以再吃一塊餅乾嗎？」）

↳ The girl asked if she might have another cookie.
（女孩問她是不是可以再吃一塊餅乾。）

☞ 改寫句中，if 後面的助動詞也可以用 could。

Q14. Sue asked her husband, "Can you drive me to the office?"

（蘇問她丈夫：「你可以載我去上班嗎？」）

↳ Sue wanted to know <u>if her husband could drive her to the office</u>.

（蘇想知道她丈夫是不是可以載她去上班。）

Q15. She asked her father, "May I borrow your car?"

（她問她父親：「我可以借你的車嗎？」）

↳ She wanted to know <u>if she could borrow her father's car</u>.

（她想知道她是不是可以借她父親的車。）

解題焦點：

虛主詞的句型可分為三大類型：
一、肯定直述句／二、否定直述句／三、Yes/No 問句。

一、肯定直述句
- · S + be 動詞 + 形容詞
☞ <u>It + is + 形容詞</u> + 不定詞（to + V）片語
- · S + V-es（或-s）
☞ <u>It + V-es</u>（或-s）+ 不定詞（to + V）片語
- · S + V-ed
☞ <u>It + V-ed</u> + 不定詞（to + V）片語

NOTE：這裡的 V-es 或 V-ed 都可能是及物或不及物動詞。

例 Singing is interesting.
☞ It is interesting to sing.

二、否定直述句
- · S + 助動詞 + not + V
☞ It's not + 形容詞 + <u>for S</u> + 不定詞（to + V）片語

NOTE：這裡的 S 為一般名詞或代名詞。
「not + 形容詞」可能會以否定形容詞如 impossible、difficult、unnecessary…替換。

例 She can't speak French.
☞ It is impossible <u>for her to speak French.</u>

三、Yes/No 問句
- · be 動詞 + S + 形容詞？
☞ <u>Is it + 形容詞</u> + 不定詞（to + V）片語
- · 助動詞 + S + V？
☞ <u>Does it + V</u> + 不定詞（to + V）片語？

89

NOTE：這裡的 S = 不定詞（to + V）或動名詞（V-ing）。be 動詞 可能為各種
　　　時態，或前面加助動詞。

例 Is cooking difficult?

☞ <u>Is it difficult to cook?</u>

重點文法 快速查!!

虛主詞三大句型一覽表

	原句	虛主詞為首
肯定 直述句	S + is + 形容詞	It + is + 形容詞 + 不定詞（to + V）
	S + V-es（或-s）	It + V-s（或-es）+ 不定詞（to + V）
	S + V-ed（或-d）	It + V-ed（或-d）+ 不定詞（to + V）
否定 直述句	S + 助動詞 + not + V	It's not + 形容詞 + for S + 不定詞（to + V）
Yes/No 問句	Is + S + 形容詞？	Is it + 形容詞 + 不定詞（to + V）？
	Does + S + V？	Does it + V + 不定詞（to + V）？
	Did + S + V？	Did it + V + 不定詞（to + V）？

GRAMMAR

實戰演練

考驗你的改寫能力！

Q1. To quit smoking is hard.

↳ It _____.

Q2. To wish to be rich is not a sin.

↳ It _____.

Q3. To travel around the world has been my dream.

↳ It _____.

Q4. To live on Mars might be possible in the future.

↳ It _____.

Q5. Walking alone at night is dangerous.

↳ It _____.

Q6. Learning how to play piano is not easy.

↳ It _____.

Q7. Is driving a car difficult ?

↳ Is _____.

Q8. Is living in a big city expensive ?

↳ Is _____.

Q9. Spending money is easier than making money.

↳ It _____.

Q10. Diving in the sea is more exciting than swimming in a pool.

↳ It _____.

Q11. Making new friends takes time.

↳ It _____.

Q12. Spending the whole day at home almost drove me crazy.

↳ It almost _____.

Q13. A fish can't live out of water.

↳ It's impossible _____.

Q14. Young kids usually can't sit still for a long time.

↳ It's difficult _____.

Q15. We don't have to do this.

↳ It isn't necessary _____.

示範 解答

中英文對照大解析

Q1. To quit smoking is hard.

↳ It <u>is hard to quit smoking</u>.
（要戒菸很難。）

Q2. To wish to be rich is not a sin.

↳ It <u>is not a sin to wish to be rich</u>.
（想致富並不是種罪過。）

Q3. To travel around the world has been my dream.

↳ It <u>has been my dream to travel around the world</u>.
（環遊世界一直是我的夢想。）

Q4. To live on Mars might be possible in the future.

↳ It <u>might be possible to live on Mars in the future</u>.
（未來要生活在火星上也許是可能的。）

Q5. Walking alone at night is dangerous.

↳ It is dangerous to walk alone at night.
（夜晚獨行很危險。）

Q6. Learning how to play piano is not easy.

↳ It is not easy to learn how to play piano.
（學彈鋼琴並不容易。）

Q7. Is driving a car difficult?

↳ Is it difficult to drive a car?
（開車難嗎？）

Q8. Is living in a big city expensive?

↳ Is it expensive to live in a big city?
（住在大都市貴／花費高嗎？）

Q9. Spending money is easier than making money.

↳ It is easier to spend money than to make money.
（花錢比賺錢容易。）

☞ 提示 It 開頭，就是要用虛主詞 it 來代替真主詞。原句的主詞是 spending money，在改寫句中要轉換成 to-V 的 to spend money，而 than 前後結構須一致，所以 than 後面也要用 to-V 的 to make money。

Q10. Diving in the sea is more exciting than swimming in a pool.

↳ It is more exciting to dive in the sea than to swim in a pool.
（在海裡潛水比在泳池游泳更刺激。）

Q11. Making new friends takes time.

↳ It takes time to make new friends.
（交新朋友需要一些時間。）

Q12. Spending the whole day at home almost drove me crazy.

↳ It almost <u>drove me crazy to spend the whole day at home</u>.
（整天待在家裡幾乎把我逼瘋了。）

Q13. A fish can't live out of water.

↳ It's impossible <u>for a fish to live out of water</u>.
（魚不可能存活在沒有水的地方。）

☞ 提示 It's impossible 開頭，就是要將原句「魚不能活出水面。」改成「對魚來說，活在沒有水的地方是不可能的。」因此，impossible 後面要先接「對魚來說（for a fish）」再接不定詞片語 to live out of water。

Q14. Young kids usually can't sit still for a long time.

↳ It's difficult <u>for young kids to sit still for a long time</u>.
（要小孩子長時間乖乖坐好是困難的。）

Q15. We don't have to do this.

↳ It isn't necessary <u>for us to do this</u>.
（我們沒必要做這件事。）

句子改寫

主題 **14** | 對話／單句切換： **不定詞型**

Focus 解題焦點：

> 對話／單句切換不定詞型的句型可分為兩大類：
> 一、當受詞／二、當受詞補語。

一、當受詞

S + <u>V</u> (+ not) + <u>to + V</u>

例 Man: What is your decision?

Woman: I will quit my job.

☞ The woman decides **to quit her job**.

二、當受詞補語

S + <u>V + O</u> (+ not) + <u>to + V</u>

例 Jim: What's this box for?

Celin: I need it to pack my books.

☞ Celin needs the box **to pack her books**.

重點文法 快速查!!

單句切換不定詞型的兩種類型

類型		句型	這一類型的動詞
當受詞	肯定	S + V + to + V	aim, fail, decide...
	否定	S + V + not + to + V	
當受詞補語	肯定	S + V + O + to + V	tell, call, need...
	否定	S + V + O + not + to + V	

GRAMMAR

 實戰演練

考驗你的改寫能力！

Q1. Clair: Why do you spend so much time on computer?

Melvin: My aim is to become a computer expert.

↳ Melvin aims to _____.

Q2. Nancy: Did you pass the college entrance exams?

John: No. I failed.

↳ John failed to _____.

Q3. Jim: What's this box for?

Celin: I need it to pack my books.

↳ Celin needs the box to _____.

Q4. Man: What is your decision?

Woman: I will quit my job.

↳ The woman decides _____.

Q5. John: Are you going to visit Rome?

Amanda: Yes, and I can't wait.

↳ Amanda can't wait _____.

Q6. Susie: Let's go see a movie.

Oliver: Why not?

↳ Oliver agreed _____.

Q7. Woman: Can you fix the car yourself?

Man: I'll try.

↳ The man will try _____.

Q8. Sam: Did you lock the door?

Melody: Oh, I forgot.

↳ Melody forgot _____.

Q9. Jessica: Why are we stopping here?

Mary: I'm hungry. Let's go eat something.

↳ Mary and Jessica stopped _____.

Q10. Anthony: What's your plan?

Phillip: I will move out.

↳ Phillip plans _____.

Q11. Kyle: Would you like to go shopping?

Daisy: No, I have to do my homework.

↳ Daisy doesn't want _____.

Q12. Kelly: Why has Gina gone to Paris?

Hillary: She will study for her master degree.

↳ Gina has gone to Paris _____.

Q13. Daniel: Did you call Michael?

Peter: Yes, he'll come to help us.

↳ Peter has called _____.

Q14. Mother: What did I just say?

Son: "Don't go away."

↳ The mother told the son _____.

Q15. Jack: Don't be late for the dinner.

Tammy: I won't.

↳ Tammy promised _____.

 示 範 解答　　　　　　　　　　　　　　　中英文對照大解析

Q1. Clair: Why do you spend so much time on computer?
（克萊兒：你為什麼花這麼多時間在電腦上？）

Melvin: My aim is to become a computer expert.
（邁爾文：我的目標是成為一位電腦專家。）

↳ Melvin aims to <u>become a computer expert</u>.
（邁爾文致力於成為一位電腦專家。）

☞ aim 當動詞時，後面要接不定詞（to-V）。

Q2. Nancy: Did you pass the college entrance exams?
（南西：你通過大學入學考試了嗎？）

John: No, I failed.
（約翰：不，我沒通過。）

↳ John failed to <u>pass the college entrance exams</u>.
（約翰未能通過大學入學考試。）

☞ 動詞 fail 表示「未能做到…」，後面要接不定詞（to-V）。所以 to 後面要接原形動詞 pass。

Q3. Jim: What's this box for?
（吉米：這箱子是做什麼用的？）

Celin: I need it to pack my books.
（瑟琳：我需要它來打包我的書。）

↳ Celin needs the box to <u>pack her books</u>.
（瑟琳需要這箱子來打包她的書。）

Q4. Man: What is your decision?
（男子：你有什麼決定？）

Woman: I will quit my job.
（女子：我會辭掉工作。）

↳ The woman decides <u>to quit her job</u>.
（女子決定要辭掉她的工作。）

☞ 動詞 decide 後面要接不定詞（to-V）。

Q5. John: Are you going to visit Rome?
（約翰：你打算去羅馬玩嗎？）

Amanda: Yes, and I can't wait.
（阿曼達：是啊，我真等不及了呢。）

↳ Amanda can't wait <u>to visit Rome</u>.
（阿曼達等不及要去羅馬玩。）

Q6. Susie: Let's go see a movie.
（蘇珊：我們去看電影吧。）

Oliver: Why not?
（奧立佛：好啊。）

↳ Oliver agreed <u>to go see a movie</u>.
（奧立佛同意去看電影。）

☞ 動詞 agree 後面要接不定詞（to-V）。

Q7. Woman: Can you fix the car yourself?

（女子：你可以自己修車嗎？）

Man: I'll try.

（男子：我試試。）

↳ The man will try to fix the car himself.

（男子會試著自己修車。）

Q8. Sam: Did you lock the door?

（山姆：你有鎖門嗎？）

Melody: Oh, I forgot.

（美樂蒂：喔，我忘了。）

↳ Melody forgot to luck the door.

（美樂蒂忘了鎖門。）

☞ 「忘記去做某事」的 forget 後面要接不定詞（to-V）；如果是「忘記已經做了某事」的 forget，後面要動名詞（Ving）。

Q9. Jessica: Why are we stopping here?

（潔西卡：我們為什麼停在這兒？）

Mary: I'm hungry. Let's go eat something.

（瑪莉：我餓了。我們去吃點東西吧。）

↳ Mary and Jessica stopped to eat something.

（瑪莉和潔西卡停下來去吃點東西。）

☞ 「停下來去做別的事」的 stop，後面要接不定詞（to-V）；如果是「停止做某事」的 stop，後面要動名詞（Ving）。

Q10. Anthony: What's your plan?

（安東尼：你有什麼計畫?）

Phillip: I will move out.

（菲力普：我會搬出去·）

↳ Phillip plans to move out.

（菲力普打算要搬出去。）

Q11. Kyle: Would you like to go shopping?

（凱爾：你要去購物嗎？）

Daisy: No, I have to do my homework.

（黛西：不，我得做功課。）

↳ Daisy doesn't want **to go shopping**.

（黛西不想去購物。）

Q12. Kelly: Why has Gina gone to Paris?

（凱莉：吉娜為什麼到巴黎去了？）

Hillary: She will study for her master degree.

（希拉蕊：她要攻讀她的碩士學位。）

↳ Gina has gone to Paris **to study for her master degree**.

（吉娜已經到巴黎去攻讀她的碩士學位了。）

Q13. Daniel: Did you call Michael?

（丹尼爾：你有打電話給麥可嗎？）

Peter: Yes, he'll come to help us.

（彼得：有，他會來幫我們。）

↳ Peter has called **Michael to help them**.

（彼得已經打電話請麥可來幫他們。）

Q14. Mother: What did I just say?

（媽媽：我剛才說什麼？）

Son: "Don't go away."

（兒子：不要離開。）

↳ The mother told the son **not to go away**.

（媽媽叫兒子不要離開。）

Q15. Jack: Don't be late for the dinner.

（傑克：晚餐別遲到了。）

Tammy: I won't.

（黛咪：不會的。）

↳ Tammy promised <u>not to be late for the dinner.</u>

（黛咪答應晚餐不會遲到。）

☞ promise（答應）後面用不定詞（to-V）作為其受詞，若該受詞為「否定意義的不定詞」，只要在 to 前面加 not 即可。

句子改寫

主題 **15** 對話／單句切換：

「動詞-ing」型

Focus 解題焦點：

「對話／單句切換」的「動詞-ing」型可分為兩大類：
一、接動名詞／二、接現在分詞。

一、接動名詞

S + V + 動詞-ing

例 Brian: Do you like travelling?

Sue: Yes, I like to travel around the world.

☞ Sue enjoys travelling around the world.

二、接現在分詞

S + V + O + 動詞-ing

例 Sean: Your child is crying.

Erin: I know, but I'm very busy now.

☞ Erin had to leave her child crying for a while.

重點文法 快速查!!

對話切換單句中帶有動詞-ing 的兩種類型

類型	句型	這一類型的動詞
接動名詞	S + V + 動詞-ing	enjoy, finish, apologize for …
接現在分詞	S + V + O + 動詞-ing	see, keep, leave, find … (+O+Ving)

GRAMMAR

Part 1・單句寫作 ▶ 01 句子改寫

Q1. Irene: You've being laughing for a while. When are you going to stop?

Wayne: I just can't. It's so funny.

↳ Wayne can't stop _____.

Q2. Rose: Will you play soccer after school?

Sam: Yes, I will.

↳ Sam will go _____.

Q3. Tina: You shouldn't smoke.

Ernie: I know and I'm trying to quit.

↳ Ernie wants to quit _____.

Q4. Man: Are you still painting the room?

Woman: It's almost done.

↳ The woman hasn't finished _____.

Q5. Brian: Do you like reading?

Sue: Yes, I like to read all kinds of book.

↳ Sue enjoys _____.

Q6. Alex: I talked to you at Julia's party. Don't you remember?

Winnie: Sorry, I don't.

↳ Winnie doesn't remember _____.

Q7. Joy: I'm sorry to bother you.

Carol: It's fine.

↳ Carol doesn't mind _____ by Joy.

Q8. Caroline: Sorry, how long have you been waiting?

Calvin: It's alright-just an hour.

↳ Caroline kept Calvin _____.

Q9. Patricia: I don't think we can make a movie.

Ben: Don't give up.

↳ Patricia is about to give up on _____.

Q10. Lily: Will you stop laughing at me?

Sarah: I can't control myself.

↳ Sarah can't help _____.

Q11. Police officer: What did you see?

Mike: The man was hitting the woman.

↳ Mike saw the man _____.

Q12. Woman: Will you sell your old car?

Man: Maybe.

↳ The man is thinking about _____.

Q13. Woman: Are you still leaving your hometown?

Man: Yes. I've made up my mind.

↳ The man insists on _____.

Q14. Sean: Let me help you carry the box.

Erin: Oh, thank you.

↳ Erin thanked Sean for _____.

Q15. Batty: You're late again.

Rick: I'm sorry.

↳ Rick apologized for _____ to Batty.

 解答   中英文對照大解析

Q1. Irene: You've being laughing for a while. When are you going to stop?

（愛琳：你已經笑很久了，你什麼時候才要停啊？）

Wayne: I just can't. It's so funny.

（律恩：我就是停不下來，太好笑了！）

↳ Wayne can't stop <u>laughing</u>.

（偉恩無法不笑。）

☞ 「stop + Ving」表示「停止正在做的事情」，而「stop + to-V」表示「停止下來去做別的事」。

Q2. Rose: Will you play soccer after school?

（蘿絲：放學後你會去踢足球嗎？）

Sam: Yes, I will.

（山姆：是的，我會。）

↳ Sam will go <u>playing soccer after school</u>.

（山姆放學後會去踢足球。）

☞ 「go + Ving」表示從事某種休閒活動。例如 go shopping（購物）. go jogging（慢跑）……等。

Q3. Tina: You shouldn't smoke.

（提娜：你不應該抽煙·）

Ernie: I know and I'm trying to quit.

（爾尼：我知道，我正試著要戒。）

↳ Ernie wants to quit <u>smoking</u>.

（爾尼想要戒煙。）

Q4. Man: Are you still painting the room?

（男子：你還在油漆房間嗎？）

Woman: It's almost done.

（女子：快好了。）

↳ The woman hasn't finished <u>painting the room</u>.

（女子還沒把房間漆好。）

Q5. Brian: Do you like reading?

（布萊恩：你喜歡閱讀嗎？）

Sue: Yes, I like to read all kinds of book.

（蘇：是，我喜歡閱讀各類書籍。）

↳ Sue enjoys <u>reading all kinds of book</u>.

（蘇喜歡閱讀各類書籍。）

Q6. Alex: I talked to you at Julia's party. Don't you remember?

（艾立克斯：我在茱莉雅的宴會上和你說過話，你不記得嗎？）

Winnie: Sorry, I don't.

（溫妮：對不起，我不記得。）

↳ Winnie doesn't remember **talking to the Alex at Julia's party**.

（溫妮不記得在茱莉雅的宴會上和艾力克斯說過話。）

☞ 「remember + Ving」表示「記得做過某事」，而「remember + to-V」表示「記得要去做某事」。

Q7. Joy: I'm sorry to bother you.

（喬依：很抱歉打擾你·）

Carol: It's fine.

（凱若：沒關係。）

↳ Carol doesn't mind <u>being bothered</u> by Joy.

（凱若不介意被喬依打擾。）

Q8. Caroline: Sorry, how long have you been waiting?

（凱若琳：對不起，你等多久了？）

Calvin: It's alright–just an hour.

（凱文：沒關係，只等了一個小時。）

↳ Caroline kept Calvin <u>waiting for an hour</u>.

（凱若琳讓凱文等了一個小時。）

☞ 「keep + O. + Ving」是固定句型，表示「讓…一直…」，因為有「（等待）動作持續」的意味，所以要用現在分詞 waiting，作為受詞 Calvin 的補語。

Q9. Patricia: I don't think we can make a movie.

（派翠西亞：我不認為我們可以拍一部電影。）

Ben: Don't give up.

（班：別放棄。）

↳ Patricia is about to give up on <u>making a movie</u>.

（派翠西亞快要放棄拍電影了。）

Q10. Lily: Will you stop laughing at me?

（莉莉：你可以不要笑我了嗎？）

Sarah: I can't control myself.

（莎拉：我控制不了我自己。）

↳ Sarah can't help <u>laughing at Lily</u>.

（莎拉忍不住取笑莉莉。）

☞ 「can't help + Ving」是固定句型，表示「忍不住…，不得不…」。也可以轉換成「can't help but+ to-V」。所以答案也可以寫成 but to laugh at Lily。

Q11. Police officer: What did you see?

（員警：你看到了什麼？）

Mike: The man was hitting the woman.

（麥可：那名男子在毆打那名女子。）

↳ Mike saw the man <u>hitting the woman</u>.

（麥可看到那名男子在毆打那名女子。）

☞ 「see + O. + Ving」是感官動詞的用法之一，表示「看見…（正在做…）」，因為有「強調當時正在進行的動作（毆打）」的意味，所以要用現在分詞 hitting，作為受詞 the man 的補語。

Q12. Woman: Will you sell your old car?

（女子：你會賣掉你的舊車嗎？）

Man: Maybe.

（男子：或許吧。）

↳ The man is thinking about <u>selling his old car</u>.

（男子考慮要賣掉他的舊車。）

☞ 介系詞後面如果不是接名詞，就一定是「動名詞」。

Q13. Woman: Are you still leaving your hometown?

（女子：你還是要離開家鄉嗎？）

Man: Yes. I've made up my mind.

（男子：是的，我已經下定決心了。）

↳ The man insists on <u>leaving his hometown</u>.

（男子堅持要離開家鄉。）

Q14. Sean: Let me help you carry the box.

（史恩：我來幫你搬這個箱子。）

Erin: Oh, thank you.

（愛倫：喔，謝謝你。）

↳ Erin thanked Sean for <u>helping her carry the box</u>.

（愛倫謝謝史恩幫她搬箱子。）

Q15. Batty: You're late again.

（貝蒂：你又遲到了。）

Rick: I'm sorry.

（瑞克：對不起。）

↪ Rick apologized for <u>being late again</u> to Batty.

（瑞克因為再度遲到而向貝蒂道歉。）

句子合併

❶ 句子合併的題目中有兩個完整的英文句子，考生必須將這兩個句子合併為一句，並使其結構完整，且語意涵蓋前面的兩個句子。

❷ 本書針對句子合併的命題趨向，將考題歸納為 19 個文法主題，百分之百的嚴選內容，提供考生有系統的學習。

本書嚴選

句子合併的 19 個文法主題

主題 16 | 問句 + 答句合併

 解題焦點：

問句／答句的合併，跟直述句／疑問句的切換有異曲同工之妙，唯一不同的是要加進答句的元素，例如：主詞、時間副詞、地方副詞、肯定及否定…等。可分為：
一、主詞類／二、副詞類／三、Yes／No 問句類。

一、主詞類

這一類的問句通常以 who 開頭，句子的主詞是合併的重點。

例 Who made the mistake?

Bill did

☞ Bill made the mistake.

二、副詞類

這一類的問句經常以 where，when，what time…等開頭，答句的地方副詞、時間副詞一類的元素是合併的重點。

例 Where can we buy a cake?

At a bakery.

☞ We can buy a cake at a bakery.

三、Yes／No 問句類

合併這一類句子的重點，在於將否定或肯定的語意加進句子中。

例 Can we go swimming this afternoon?

No, you can't.

☞ You can not go swimming this afternoon.

重點文法 快速查!!

問句／答句的合併，句型可分為三類

類型	問句句型	答句句型	合併句型
主詞類	Who + V + O?	S + 助 V	S + V + O
副詞類	Where + 助 V + S + V + O?	地方副詞	S + V + O + 地方副詞
	What time + 助 V + S + V + O?	時間副詞	S + V + O + 時間副詞
Yes/No 問句類	助 V + S + V + O + 地方副詞？ 助 V + S + V + O + 時間副詞？	Yes, S + 助 V. No, S + 助 V + not.	S + 助 V + (not) + V + O + 地方副詞. S + 助 V (+ not) + V + O + 時間副詞.
	助 V + S + V + (that) + 子句.	Yes, S + 助 V. No, S + 助 V + not.	S + 助 V (+ not) + V + (that) + 子句.
	Have + S + p.p. + ...? Has + S + p.p. + ...?	Yes, S + have/has. No, S + have/has + not.	S + have/has (+ not) + p.p. …

實戰演練

考驗你的合併能力！

Q1. Who made the decision?

Bill did.

↳ Bill _____.

Q2. Who runs the fastest?

Rick does.

↳ Rick _____.

Q3. Who has seen the movie?

I have.

↳ I _____ .

Q4. Where can we buy a cake?

At a bakery.

↳ We can _____ .

Q5. What time is Ted's piano lesson?

At three o'clock.

↳ Ted's piano lesson _____ .

Q6. What day does Terry play basketball every week?

On Tuesday.

↳ Terry _____ .

Q7. Can we go swimming this afternoon?

Yes, you can.

↳ You can _____ .

Q8. Will it rain tomorrow?

No, it won't.

↳ It will _____ .

Q9. Did Bob say he would come?

No, he didn't.

↳ Bob did _____ .

Q10. Don't you want to have a piece of cake?

Yes, I do.

↳   I _____.

Q11. Didn't they win the game?

No, they didn't.

↳   They did _____.

Q12. Has Lydia gone to America?

No, she hasn't.

↳   Lydia has _____.

Q13. Is the king sick in bed?

No, he isn't.

↳   The king is _____.

Q14. Doesn't Peter work for this company?

Yes, he does.

↳   Peter _____.

Q15. Where does Carol come from?

Japan.

↳   Carol _____.

 解答 中英文對照大解析

Q1. Who made the decision?
（誰做的決定？）

Bill did.
（比爾。）

↳ Bill <u>made the decision</u>.
（比爾做的決定。）

Q2. Who runs the fastest?
（誰跑得最快？）

Rick does.
（瑞克。）

↳ Rick <u>runs the fastest</u>.
（瑞克跑得最快。）

Q3. Who has seen the movie?
（誰看過這部電影？）

I have.
（我看過。）

↳ I <u>have seen the movie</u>.
（我看過這部電影。）

Q4. Where can we buy a cake?
（我們可以在哪兒買蛋糕?）

At a bakery.
（在麵包店。）

↳ We can <u>buy a cake at a bakery</u>.
（我們可以在麵包店買蛋糕。）

☞ 地方副詞 "At a bakery" 置於句尾。

Q5. What time is Ted's piano lesson?

（泰德的鋼琴課是幾點？）

At three o'clock.

（三點。）

↳ Ted's piano lesson is at three o'clock.

（泰德的鋼琴課是在三點。）

Q6. What day does Terry play basketball every week?

（泰瑞每個星期的哪天打籃球?）

On Tuesday.

（在星期二。）

↳ Terry plays basketball on Tuesday.

（泰瑞在星期二打籃球。）

☞ 句子提示開頭為 Terry，為第三人稱單數的主詞，因此動詞 play 應用第三人稱單數的 plays。因為句尾有 every week，因此 Tuesday 不必加 s。on Tuesdays = on Tuesday every week。

Q7. Can we go swimming this afternoon?

（我們今天下午可以去游泳嗎？）

Yes, you can.

（是的，你們可以。）

↳ You can go swimming this afternoon.

（你們今天下午可以去游泳。）

Q8. Will it rain tomorrow?

（明天會下雨嗎？）

No, it won't.

（不，不會。）

↳ It will not rain tomorrow.

（明天不會下雨。）

117

Q9. Did Bob say he would come?

（鮑伯有說他會來嗎？）

No, he didn't.

（沒有。）

↳ Bob did <u>not say he would come</u>.

（鮑伯沒有說他會來。）

☞ 題目只給 Bob did，因為 didn't = did not，所以空格要以 not 開頭。

Q10. Don't you want to have a piece of cake?

（你不吃塊蛋糕嗎？）

Yes, I do.

（不，我要吃。）

↳ I <u>want to have a piece of cake</u>.

（我想要吃一塊蛋糕。）

☞ 回答中的 I do = I want to...。

Q11. Didn't they win the game?

（他們沒有贏得比賽嗎？）

No, they didn't.

（是的，他們沒有。）

↳ They did <u>not win the game</u>.

（他們沒有贏得比賽。）

☞ 針對否定問句的回答，No 要翻成「是」，而 Yes 要翻成「不」（例如 Q10 的答句）。

Q12. Has Lydia gone to America?

（莉迪亞已經去美國了嗎？）

No, she hasn't.

（還沒。）

↳ Lydia has <u>not gone to the America</u>.

（莉迪亞還沒去美國。）

Q13. Is the king sick in bed?

（國王臥病在床嗎？）

No, he isn't.

（沒有。）

↳ The king is <u>not sick in bed</u>.

（國王沒有臥病在床。）

Q14. Doesn't Peter work for this company?

（彼得不是在這家公司上班嗎？）

Yes, he does.

（不，他是。）

↳ Peter <u>works for this company</u>.

（彼得是在這家公司上班。）

Q15. Where does Carol come from?

（凱若來自哪裡？）

Japan.

（日本。）

↳ Carol <u>comes from Japan</u>.

（凱若來自日本。）

主題 17 | 副詞合併

Focus 解題焦點：

副詞的合併可分為三類：
一、合併時間副詞／二、合併地方副詞／三、合併地方副詞
＋時間副詞。

一、合併時間副詞

S＋V → S＋V＋時間副詞

例 The president was shot yesterday afternoon.

The time was four o'clock.

☞ The president was shot at four o'clock yesterday afternoon.

二、合併地方副詞

S＋V → S＋V＋地方副詞

例 The dog jumped.

It jumped over the fence.

☞ The dog jumped over the fence.

三、合併地方副詞＋時間副詞

S＋V＋時間副詞 → S＋V＋地方副詞＋時間副詞
S＋V＋地方副詞 → S＋V＋地方副詞＋時間副詞

例 The year was 1945.

He was born in a small town.

☞ He was born in a small town in 1945.

重點文法 快速查!!

副詞並排時順序必須由小到大排列

	時間副詞	地方副詞
小 ↓ 大	at ten o'clock	at home
	in the afternoon	in a tall building
	on Monday	in a small town
	in June	in Taipei
	in spring	in Taiwan
	in 1981	in Asia

多種副詞同時使用時,必須依副詞的種類排列

副詞的種類	副詞舉例說明	例句
情狀副詞	slowly, quietly, sadly...	Robert sings sadly in the house every day lately.（羅伯最近每天都在那間房子裡傷心地唱歌。）
地方副詞	here, home, abroad...	
頻率副詞	every day, once a week...	
時間副詞	soon, tomorrow, lately...	

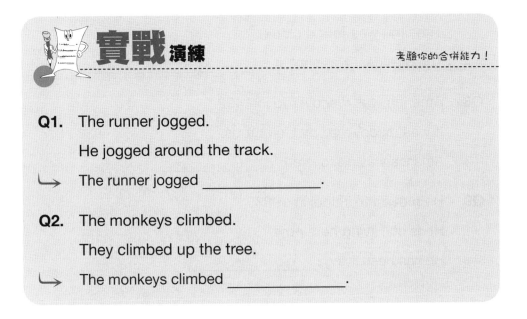

實戰演練

考驗你的合併能力!

Q1. The runner jogged.

He jogged around the track.

↳ The runner jogged _____.

Q2. The monkeys climbed.

They climbed up the tree.

↳ The monkeys climbed _____.

Q3. The dog jumped.

It jumped over the fence.

⤷ The dog jumped _____.

Q4. Donna stayed in Hilton Hotel.

She stayed there for three days.

⤷ Donna stayed in _____.

Q5. The year was 1945.

He was born in a small town.

⤷ He was born in _____.

Q6. Mr. Douglas will arrive in Taipei tomorrow.

He will arrive at 9 o'clock.

⤷ Mr. Douglas will arrive in _____.

Q7. The president was shot yesterday afternoon.

The time was four o'clock.

⤷ The president was shot at _____.

Q8. America was discovered in 1492.

It was discovered by Columbus.

⤷ America was discovered _____.

Q9. He moved to Taipei in 1983.

He is still living here now.

⤷ He has been living _____.

Q10. We arrived in Tokyo on Monday.

We left there on Thursday.

↳ We stayed in Tokyo from _____.

Q11. Molly sits in front of me.

Lora sits behind me.

↳ I sit between _____.

Q12. Neo lives in Main Street.

His door number is 303.

↳ Neo lives at _____.

Q13. There are three boys.

John is the tallest.

↳ John is _____ the three boys.

Q14. The ice cream was in the freezer.

Gina took the ice cream out.

↳ Gina took the ice cream out _____.

Q15. We went to the beach last Saturday.

We stayed there whole day.

↳ We spent the whole day at _____.

Q1. The runner jogged.
（跑者在慢跑。）

He jogged around the track.
（他沿著跑道慢跑。）

↳ The runner jogged <u>around the track</u>.
（跑者沿著跑道在慢跑。）

Q2. The monkeys climbed.
（猴子在攀爬。）

They climbed up the tree.
（牠們爬上了樹。）

↳ The monkeys climbed <u>up the tree</u>.
（猴子爬上了樹。）

Q3. The dog jumped.
（狗跳了起來。）

It jumped over the fence.
（牠跳過了柵欄。）

↳ The dog jumped <u>over the fence</u>.
（狗跳過了柵欄。）

Q4. Donna stayed in Hilton Hotel.
（唐娜住在希爾頓飯店。）

She stayed there for three days.
（她在哪裡住了三天。）

↳ Donna stayed <u>in Hilton Hotel for three days</u>.
（唐娜在希爾頓飯店住了三天。）

Q5. The year was 1945.

（那一年是 1945 年。）

He was born in a small town.

（他出生在一個小鎮。）

↳ He was born in <u>a small town in 1945</u>.

（他於 1945 年出生在一個小鎮。）

☞ 「何時出生在何地」，英文習慣上先寫「在某地」，再寫「在某一年」。因此本題 in 後面要先寫 a small town 再寫 in 1945。

Q6. Mr. Douglas will arrive in Taipei tomorrow.

（道格拉斯先生明天會抵達臺北。）

He will arrive at 9 o'clock.

（他會在九點抵達。）

↳ Mr. Douglas will arrive in <u>Taipei at 9 o'clock tomorrow</u>.

（道格拉斯先生明天會在九點抵達臺北。）

Q7. The president was shot yesterday afternoon.

（總統昨天下午遭到槍擊。）

The time was four o'clock.

（時間是四點鐘。）

↳ The president was shot at <u>four o'clock yesterday afternoon</u>.

（總統昨天下午四點遭到槍擊。）

☞ 一個句子同時有兩個時間副詞要表達時，先寫「小時間」，再寫「大時間」。因此本題 at 後面要先寫 four o'clock 再寫 yesterday afternoon。

Q8. America was discovered in 1492.

（美洲是在 1492 年被發現的。）

It was discovered by Columbus.

（它是被哥倫布發現的。）

↳ America was discovered <u>by Columbus in 1492</u>.

（美洲是在 1492 年被哥倫布發現的。）

☞ 「何時被誰…」，英文習慣上先寫「被誰」，再寫「何時」。因此本題 was discovered 後面要先寫 by Columbus 再寫 in 1492。

Q9. He moved to Taipei in 1983.

（他在 1983 年時就搬去臺北了。）

He is still living here now.

（他現在還住在這裡。）

↳ He has been living <u>in Taipei since 1983</u>.

（他從 1983 年起就一直住在臺北了。）

Q10. We arrived in Tokyo on Monday.

（我們在星期一抵達東京。）

We left there on Thursday.

（我們星期四離開那裡。）

↳ We stayed in Tokyo from <u>Monday to Thursday</u>.

（我們星期一到星期四在東京停留。）

☞ 這是「時間副詞合併」的題型。題目第一句是「何時抵達」，第二句是「何時離開」，而合併句提示用 from，顯然就是要表達「從什麼時候到什麼時候」，所以是 <u>from Monday to Tuesday</u>。

Q11. Molly sits in front of me.

（茉莉坐在我前面。）

Lora sits behind me.

（蘿拉坐在我後面。）

↳ I sit between <u>Molly and Lora</u>.

（我坐在茉莉和蘿拉中間。）

Q12. Neo lives in Main Street.

（尼歐住在「大街」。）

His door number is 303.

（他的門牌號碼是 303。）

↳ Neo lives at <u>(number) 303 Main Street</u>.

（尼歐住在「大街」303 號。）

Q13. There are three boys.

（有三個男孩。）

John is the tallest.

（約翰最高。）

↳ John is <u>the tallest among</u> the three boys.

（約翰是三個男孩中最高的。）

Q14. The ice cream was in the freezer.

（冰淇淋在冰箱裡。）

Gina took the ice cream out.

（吉娜把冰淇淋拿了出來。）

↳ Gina took the ice cream out <u>from the freezer</u>.

（吉娜把冰淇淋從冰箱拿了出來。）

Q15. We went to the beach last Saturday.

（我們上星期六去海邊。）

We stayed there whole day.

（我們在那兒待了一整天。）

↳ We spent the whole day at <u>the beach last Saturday</u>.

（我們上星期六在海邊待了一整天。）

句子合併

主題 **18** | **形容詞合併**

 解題焦點：

形容詞一般放在名詞前面，有時候只用單一形容詞修飾名詞，有時候則用多個形容詞修飾一個名詞，此時需特別注意形容詞的擺放順序。

一、單一形容詞

例 The girl sings very well.

She is tall.

☞ The <u>tall girl</u> sings very well.

二、多個形容詞

例 The tall woman is her mother.

Her mother is very beautiful.

☞ The <u>beautiful tall woman</u> is her mother.

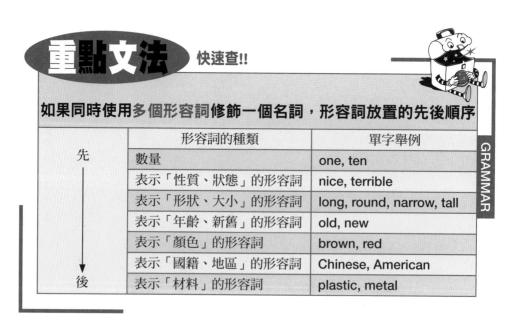

重點文法 快速查!!

如果同時使用多個形容詞修飾一個名詞，形容詞放置的先後順序

	形容詞的種類	單字舉例
先	數量	one, ten
↓	表示「性質、狀態」的形容詞	nice, terrible
	表示「形狀、大小」的形容詞	long, round, narrow, tall
	表示「年齡、新舊」的形容詞	old, new
	表示「顏色」的形容詞	brown, red
	表示「國籍、地區」的形容詞	Chinese, American
後	表示「材料」的形容詞	plastic, metal

GRAMMAR

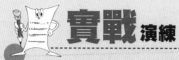

Q1. She met a man.

The man is blind.

↳ She met ＿＿＿＿＿＿＿ man.

Q2. The dog is an animal.

It is faithful.

↳ The dog is ＿＿＿＿＿＿＿ animal.

Q3. This is a cat.

The cat is white and black.

↳ This is ＿＿＿＿＿＿＿ cat.

Q4. A man talked to her.

The man is young.

↳ A ＿＿＿＿＿＿＿ man talked to her.

Q5. The balloon is big.

It's green.

↳ It's a ＿＿＿＿＿＿＿ balloon.

Q6. The girl has long hair.

It's brown.

↳ The girl has ＿＿＿＿＿＿＿ hair.

Q7. The man is old.

He is a nice person

↳ He is a _____ man.

Q8. We need a plastic bag.

It must be a big one.

↳ We need a _____ bag.

Q9. Look at this tall vase.

It is a Chinese vase.

↳ Look at this _____ vase.

Q10. Mary has just bought herself a cotton dress.

It's green and it's pretty.

↳ Mary has just bought herself a _____.

Q11. Danny met a French girl.

She is young and beautiful.

↳ Danny met a _____ girl.

Q12.There are red roses in the vase.

The number is twelve.

↳ There are _____ rose in the vase.

Q13. Some children will take the test.

They are nine years old.

↳ _____ children will take the test.

130

Q14. Have you ever seen a car like this?

This car has only three wheels.

↳ Have you ever seen _____ car?

Q15. The beetle-nut trees were chopped down.

All of them were chopped down.

↳ _____ trees were chopped down.

示範 解答

中英文對照大解析

Q1. She met a man.
（她遇到了一名男子。）

The man is blind.
（那名男子是瞎的。）

↳ She met <u>a blind</u> man.
（她遇到了一名瞎眼的男子。）

Q2. The dog is an animal.
（狗是一種動物。）

It is faithful.
（牠是忠心的。）

↳ The dog is <u>a faithful</u> animal.
（狗是一種忠心的動物。）

Q3. This is a cat.
（這是一隻貓。）

The cat is white and black.
（這隻貓是黑白相間的。）

↳ This is a <u>white and black</u> cat.
（這是一隻黑白相間的貓。）

Q4. A man talked to her.
（有一名男子和她說話。）

The man is young.
（這名男子是年輕的。）

↳ A <u>young</u> man talked to her.
（一名年輕的男子和她說話。）

Q5. The balloon is big.
（氣球是大的。）

It's green.
（它是綠色的。）

↳ It's a <u>big green</u> balloon.
（它是一顆綠色的大氣球。）

☞ 中文說「綠色的大氣球」，英文要說 a big green ball，這是中英文語序上的不同。

Q6. The girl has long hair.
（女孩留著長髮。）

It's brown.
（它是棕色的。）

↳ The girl has <u>long brown</u> hair.
（女孩留著棕色的長髮。）

Q7. The man is old.

（男子是老的。）

He is a nice person.

（他是個好人。）

↳ He is a <u>nice old</u> man.

（他是個好心的老人。）

Q8. We need a plastic bag.

（我們需要一個塑膠袋。）

It must be a big one.

（它必須是大的。）

↳ We need a <u>big plastic</u> bag

（我們需要一個大的塑膠袋。）

Q9. Look at this tall vase.

（看這高高的花瓶。）

It is a Chinese vase.

（它是個中國式的花瓶。）

↳ Look at this <u>tall Chinese</u> vase.

（看這高高的中國式花瓶。）

Q10. Mary has just bought herself a cotton dress.

（瑪莉剛為自己買了一件棉質洋裝。）

It's green and it's pretty.

（它是綠色的，且它很漂亮。）

↳ Mary has just bought herself a <u>pretty green cotton</u> dress.

（瑪莉剛買給自己一件漂亮的綠色棉質洋裝。）

Q11. Danny met a French girl.

（丹尼遇到了一位法國女孩。）

She is young and beautiful.

（她既年輕又美麗。）

↳ Danny met a <u>beautiful young French</u> girl.

（丹尼遇到了一位年輕貌美的法國女孩。）

☞ 中文說「年輕貌美的女孩」，英文習慣說 a beautiful young girl，這是中英文語序上的不同。

Q12. There are red roses in the vase.

（花瓶裡有紅色玫瑰。）

The number is twelve

（數量是 12。）

↳ There are <u>twelve red</u> roses in the vase.

（花瓶裡有 12 朵紅玫瑰。）

Q13. Some children will take the test.

（有些孩子會參加這場考試。）

They are nine years old.

（他們九歲。）

↳ <u>Some nine-year-old</u> children will take the test.

（有些九歲大的孩子會參加這場考試。）

☞ 合併句空格後面已經是個完整句子，因此空格處就是修飾主詞 children 的形容詞，而根據前兩句修飾 children 的有 some 以及 nine years old，因此依據前述形容詞的位置順序原則，先寫 some 再寫 nine years old，但須注意 nine years old 轉換成前置的形容詞時，應改為 nine-year-old，year 後面不可加 s。

Q14. Have you ever seen a car like this?

（見過像這樣的車嗎？）

This car has only three wheels.

（這部車只有三個輪子。）

↳ Have you ever seen <u>a three-wheel</u> car?

（你見過三輪的車子嗎？）

Q15. The beetle-nut trees were chopped down.

（檳榔樹被砍掉了。）

All of them were chopped down.

（它們全部都被砍掉了。）

↳ <u>All（of）the beetle-nut</u> trees were chopped down.

（所有檳榔樹都被砍掉了。）

> 對等連接詞可以用來連接單字、片語、句子，並且前後連接
> 的「結構」（ex. 詞性、時態）必須對等，如果前面接的是
> 名詞，後面也要接名詞。
> 本單元可分為四種題型：
> 一、and 型／二、or 型／三、but 型／四、倒裝型。

一、and 型

　　例 I have a daughter.

　　　 I have a son.

　　☞ I have a daughter and a son.

二、or 型

　　例 Do you want some tea?

　　　 Do you want some coffee?

　　☞ Do you want some tea or coffee?

三、but 型

　　例 I am not a teacher.

　　　 I am a student.

　　☞ I am not a teacher but a student.

四、倒裝型

　　例 I love reading.

　　　 He loves reading, too.

　　☞ I love reading, and so does he.

重點文法 快速查!!

對等連接詞合併的四大題型一覽表

題型	句型	中文意義
and 型	X and Y	X 和 Y
or 型	X or Y	X 或 Y
but 型	X but not Y	是 X 而不是 Y
	not X but Y	不是 X 而是 Y
	X or Y but not Z	是 X 或 Y，而不是 Z
倒裝型 so	肯定句 and so + be 動詞／助動詞+S	S 也是
倒裝型 neither	否定句 and neither + be 動詞／助動詞+S	S 也不是

對等連接詞前後連接相同的結構或詞性

用法	例句
連接名詞	You and I are good friends.
連接動詞	She washed and ironed her shirt.
連接不定詞	Do you want to go shopping or to go hiking?
連接動名詞	I love fishing and jogging.
連接形容詞	She is beautiful but not intelligent.
連接副詞	She walked along the road slowly and carefully.
連接句子	You come here or I go to your place.

實戰演練　　　考驗你的合併能力！

Q1. Johnson has a brother.

Johnson has two sisters.

↳ Johnson has _____.

Q2. Emma is young.

She is beautiful.

↳ Emma is _____.

Q3. Helen likes making cookies.

She likes eating cookies, too.

↳ Helen likes _____.

Q4. Ivy waved.

She drove away.

↳ Ivy waved and _____.

Q5. I'd like some iced tea.

Soda will also do.

↳ I'd like some _____.

Q6. Do you want to go dance?

Or maybe you want to go see a movie?

↳ Do you want to _____?

Q7. They are rich.

They aren't happy.

↳ They are _____.

Q8. Victor isn't my boyfriend.

He is my brother.

↳ Victor isn't my boyfriend but _____.

Q9. We can go by bus or train.

We can't go by plane.

↳ We can go by bus or train but _____.

Q10. Michael didn't go home.

He stayed at Jack's place.

↳ Michael didn't go home but _____.

Q11. Owen is a lawyer.

His sister is a lawyer, too.

↳ Owen is a lawyer and so _____.

Q12. You can't go.

We can't go, either.

↳ You can't go and neither _____.

Q13. You may pay by cash or credit card.

How would you like to pay?

↳ How would you like to pay, _____?

Q14. We have shoes and boots.

Which ones would you like to see?

↳ Which ones would you like to see, _____?

Q15. There is a doll and a teddy bear.

Which one would you like to buy?

↳ Which one would you like to buy, _____?

Q1. Johnson has a brother.
（強生有一個弟弟。）

Johnson has two sisters.
（強生有兩個妹妹。）

↳ Johnson has <u>a brother and two sisters</u>.
（強生有一個弟弟和兩個妹妹。）

Q2. Emma is young.
（愛瑪很年輕。）

She is beautiful.
（她很漂亮。）

↳ Emma is <u>young and beautiful</u>.
（愛瑪年輕又漂亮。）

Q3. Helen likes making cookies.
（海倫喜歡做餅乾。）

She likes eating cookies, too.
（她也喜歡吃餅乾。）

↳ Helen likes <u>making and eating cookies</u>.
（海倫喜歡做和吃餅乾。）

Q4. Ivy waved.
（艾薇揮手。）

She drove away.
（她開車離開。）

↳ Ivy waved and <u>drove away</u>.
（艾薇揮揮手並開車離開。）

Q5. I'd like some iced tea.

（我想喝冰紅茶。）

Soda will also do.

（汽水也可以。）

↳ I'd like some <u>iced tea or soda</u>.

（我想喝冰紅茶或汽水。）

☞ 題目第二句 "Soda will also do." 要表達的意思是，喝汽水也可以，並不是 iced tea 和 soda 都要喝，所以合併句要用對等連接詞 or 而非 and。

Q6. Do you want to go dance?

（你想去跳舞嗎？）

Or maybe you want to go see a movie?

（或者你想去看電影？）

↳ Do you want to <u>go dance or see a movie</u>?

（你想去跳舞或是去看電影？）

Q7. They are rich.

（他們很富有。）

They aren't happy.

（他們不快樂。）

↳ They are <u>rich but not happy</u>.

（他們富有但並不快樂。）

Q8. Victor isn't my boyfriend.

（艾維特不是我男朋友。）

He is my brother.

（他是我哥哥。）

↳ Victor isn't my boyfriend but <u>my brother</u>.

（艾維特不是我男友，而是我哥哥。）

Q9. We can go by bus or train.

（我們可以搭巴士或火車去。）

We can't go by plane.

（我們不能搭飛機去。）

↳ We can go by bus or train but <u>not plane</u>.

（我們可以搭巴士或搭計程車，但不能搭飛機。）

Q10. Michael didn't go home.

（麥可沒回家。）

He stayed at Jack's place.

（他待在傑克的住處。）

↳ Michael didn't go home but <u>stayed at Jack's place</u>.

（麥可沒有回家而是待在傑克的住處。）

Q11. Owen is a lawyer.

（歐文是律師。）

His sister is a lawyer, too.

（他妹妹也是律師。）

↳ Owen is a lawyer and so <u>is his sister</u>.

（歐文是律師，他妹妹也是。）

☞ 空格前是 and so，表示要填入的是倒裝句「so + be動詞 + S」。這樣的句型在文法中又稱為「附和句」，且是「肯定附和句」。

Q12. You can't go.

（你不能去。）

We can't go, either

（我們也不能去。）

↳ You can't go and neither <u>do we</u>.

（你不能去，我們也不能。）

142

Q13. You may pay by cash or credit card.
（您可以用現金或信用卡付費。）

How would you like to pay?
（您想怎麼付費呢？）

↳ How would you like to pay, <u>by cash or credit card</u>?
（您想怎麼付費，用現金或信用卡？）

☞ 空格前是個完整句子，所以空格處應為修飾動詞 pay 的副詞片語，所以
可以將第一句的 "by cash or credit card" 擺進去即可。

Q14. We have shoes and boots.
（我們有鞋子和靴子。）

Which ones would you like to see?
（您想看那一種？）

↳ Which ones would you like to see, <u>shoes or boots</u>?
（你想看那一種，鞋子或靴子?）

Q15. There is a doll and a teddy bear.
（有一個洋娃娃和一隻泰迪熊。）

Which one would you like to buy?
（您想買那一個？）

↳ Which one would you like to buy, <u>the doll or the teddy bear</u>?
（您想買那一個，洋娃娃還是泰迪熊？）

句子合併

主題 **20** | # 對等相關連接詞合併

Focus 解題焦點：

所謂「對等相關連接詞」其實就是「連接詞詞組」，它的句
型可分為四大類：
一、兩者皆是／二、兩者皆非
三、兩者擇其一／四、不只…也…。

一、兩者皆是
both X and Y

例 You are my friend.

He is my friend, too.

☞ Both you and he are my friends.

二、兩者皆非
neither X nor Y

例 I do not drink coffee.

I do not drink tea, either.

☞ I drink neither coffee nor tea.

三、兩者擇其一
either X or Y

例 I might go to New York.

I might go to Paris

☞ I might go to either New York or Paris.

四、不只…也…
not only X but also Y

例 He is cute

He is also smart

☞ He is not only cute but also smart.

重點文法 快速查!!

對等相關連接詞用法一覽表

對等相關連接詞	中文意義	用法
both X and Y	X 和 Y 都是…	意義上為複數
neither X nor Y	X 和 Y 都不是…	意義上為單數
either X or Y	X 或 Y 其中一個	意義上為單數
not only X but also Y	不只 X 而且也 Y	意義上為複數

對等相關連接詞前後連接相同的結構

用法	例句
連接名詞	Both you and I are singers.
連接動詞	She not only washed but also ironed her shirt.
連接不定詞	Do you prefer either to sleep or to chat?
連接動名詞	I love both fishing and jogging.
連接形容詞	She is not only beautiful but also intelligent.
連接副詞	She typed the article both rapidly and correctly.

實戰演練

考驗你的合併能力！

Q1. Jack is my friend.

Theresa is my friend, too.

↳ Both ＿＿＿＿＿＿＿ my friends.

Q2. Neil likes Batty.

So does Henry.

↳ Both ＿＿＿＿＿＿＿＿＿.

Q3. Zoe wishes for a watch.

She thinks a necklace was also fine.

↳ Zoe wishes for either a watch _____.

Q4. We accept cash.

We also accept credit card.

↳ We accept either cash _____.

Q5. My family may go on a trip to Mt. Ali.

We think Kenting maybe a good idea, too.

↳ My family may go on a trip to either _____.

Q6. Dogs are good pets.

So are cats.

↳ Not only dogs _____.

Q7. Reading is a good habit.

So is doing sports.

↳ Not only reading _____.

Q8. Chris doesn't know what happened.

Brian doesn't know it, either.

↳ Neither Chris _____.

Q9. Wayne speaks English well.

He also speaks German well.

↳ Wayne speaks not only English _____.

Q10. Dannie has a full time job.

He also goes to college in the evening.

↳ Dannie not only has a full time job _____.

Q11. The little girl doesn't like green beans.

She doesn't like mushrooms, either.

↳ The little girl likes neither green beans _____.

Q12. They shouldn't leave now.

Neither do we.

↳ Neither they _____.

Q13. His parents don't support his decision.

Neither does his girlfriend.

↳ Neither his parents _____.

Q14. Jackie isn't good at math.

He isn't good at English, either.

↳ Jackie is good at _____.

Q15. I can't swim.

Not to mention dive.

↳ I can neither _____.

Q1. Jack is my friend.
（傑克是我的朋友。）

Theresa is my friend, too.
（泰瑞莎也是我的朋友。）

↳ Both **Jack and Theresa are** my friends.
（傑克和泰瑞莎都是我的朋友。）

Q2. Neil likes Batty.
（尼爾喜歡貝蒂。）

So does Henry.
（亨利也是。）

↳ Both **Neil and Henry like Batty**.
（尼爾和亨利兩人都喜歡貝蒂。）

Q3. Zoe wishes for a watch.
（若伊想要一支手錶。）

She thinks a necklace was also fine.
（她覺得項鍊也不錯。）

↳ Zoe wishes for either a watch **or a necklace**.
（若伊想要一支手錶或一條項鍊。）

Q4. We accept cash.
（我們接受現金。）

We also accept credit card.
（我們也接受信用卡。）

↳ We accept either cash **or credit card**.
（我們接受現金或信用卡。）

Q5. My family may go on a trip to Mt. Ali.

（我們一家人可能會去阿里山旅遊。）

We think Kenting maybe a good idea, too.

（我們認為墾丁可能也是不錯的主意。）

⮡ My family may go on a trip to either <u>Mt. Ali or Kenting</u>.

（我們一家人可能會去阿里山或是墾丁旅遊。）

Q6. Dogs are good pets.

（狗是好寵物。）

So are cats.

（貓也是。）

⮡ Not only dogs <u>but also cats are good pets</u>.

（不只是狗，貓也是好寵物。）

Q7. Reading is a good habit.

（閱讀是一種好習慣。）

So is doing sports.

（運動也是。）

⮡ Not only reading <u>but also doing sports is a good habit</u>.

（不只是閱讀，運動也是一種好習慣。）

☞ not only...but also... 連接兩個主詞時，後面的動詞只配合最接近的主詞，也就是 but also 後面的主詞。

Q8. Chris doesn't know what happened.

（克里斯不知道發生了什麼事。）

Brian doesn't know it, either.

（布萊恩也不知道。）

⮡ Neither Chris <u>nor Brian knows what happened</u>.

（克里斯和布萊恩都不知道發生了什麼事。）

☞ neither...nor... 連接兩個主詞時，後面的動詞只配合最接近的主詞，也就是 nor 後面的主詞。

Q9. Wayne speaks English well.

（偉恩英文說得好。）

He also speaks German well.

（他德文也說得好。）

→ Wayne speaks not only English <u>but also German well</u>.

（偉恩不只英文說得好，連德文也很棒。）

Q10. Dannie has a full time job.

（丹尼有一份全職的工作。）

He also goes to college in the evening.

（他晚上還要去大學念書。）

→ Dannie not only has a full time job <u>but also goes to college in the evening</u>.

（丹尼不僅有一份全職的工作，晚上還要上大學念書。）

Q11. The little girl doesn't like green beans.

（小女孩不喜歡綠豆。）

She doesn't like mushrooms, either.

（她也不喜歡香菇。）

→ The little girl likes neither green beans <u>nor mushrooms</u>.

（這小女孩既不喜歡豆子，也不喜歡香菇。）

☞ neither...nor... 本身就具有否定意義，因此 do/does not like A and B = like neither A nor B。

Q12. They shouldn't leave now.

（他們現在不該離開。）

Neither do we.

（我們也不應該。）

→ Neither they <u>nor we should leave now</u>.

（他們和我們都不該現在離開。）

Q13. His parents don't support his decision.

（他的父母不支持他的決定。）

Neither does his girlfriend.

（他的女朋友也不支持。）

↳ Neither his parents <u>nor his girlfriend supports his decision</u>.

（他的父母和他的女朋友都不支持他的決定。）

Q14. Jackie isn't good at math.

（傑奇不擅長數學。）

He isn't good at English, either.

（他也不擅長英文。）

↳ Jackie is good at <u>neither math nor English</u>.

（傑奇既不擅長數學，也不擅長英文。）

Q15. I can't swim.

（我不會游泳。）

Not to mention dive.

（更別說潛水了。）

↳ I can neither <u>swim nor dive</u>.

（我既不會游泳，也不會潛水。）

句子合併 | 名詞子句合併：

主題 **21** | **that 型**

「名詞子句 that 型」在句子中扮演以下四種角色：
一、當主詞／二、當受詞／三、當補語／四、當同位語。

一、當主詞

> 例 Judy is a dancer.
>
> This is incredible.

☞ <u>That Judy is a dancer</u> is incredible

NOTE：that 子句當主詞時，若字數過多，可以虛主詞 it 代替，以避免閱讀上的困難，故本句亦可寫成：It is incredible that Judy is a dancer.

二、當受詞

> 例 We cannot eat in this room.
>
> I do not know about the rule.

☞ I do not know <u>that we cannot eat in this room</u>.

三、當補語

> 例 She doesn't like you
>
> This is the reason.

☞ The reason is <u>that she doesn't like you</u>.

四、當同位語

> 例 He got cancer.
>
> The fact is sad.

☞ The fact <u>that he got cancer</u> is sad.

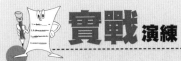
Q1. There's a problem.

I don't have her phone number.

↳ The problem is that _____.

Q2. There's a rumor.

Kyle was beaten by his father.

↳ The rumor is that _____.

Q3. You must rewrite your report.

This is the answer.

↳ The answer is that _____.

Q4. I don't like him.

This is the reason.

↳ The reason is that _____.

Q5. William is fired.

The news surprises me.

↳ It surprises me that _____.

Q6. Actually, he is a thief.

The fact is surprising.

↳ The fact that _____ is surprising.

Q7. She has given birth to a baby.

I don't know about it.

↳ I don't know the news that _____.

Q8. They can't wear jeans to work.

The workers are told about the rule.

↳ The workers are told that _____.

Q9. The factory boss has promised to solve the problem.

They will fix the water pollution.

↳ The factory boss has promised that _____.

Q10. They say Tony has changed.

We all think it's impossible.

↳ We all think it impossible that _____.

Q11. Kelly was killed.

The truth is shocking.

↳ It is shocking that _____.

Q12. A horse runs faster than a car.

The fact is unbelievable.

↳ It's unbelievable that _____.

Q13. Something is true.

Swimming helps one relax.

↳ That _____ is true.

Q14. Something is hard to believe.

Having too much fish is harmful.

↳ That _____ is hard to believe.

Q15. Something sounds weird.

He collects Teddy bears.

↳ That _____ sounds weird.

示範 解答

中英文對照大解析

Q1. There's a problem.

（有個問題。）

I don't have her phone number.

（我沒有她的電話號碼。）

↳ The problem is that I don't have her phone number.

（問題是我沒有她的電話號碼。）

Q2. There's a rumor.

（有一個謠傳。）

Kyle was beaten by his father.

（凱爾被他爸爸打。）

↳ The rumor is that Kyle was beaten by his father.

（謠傳說凱爾被他爸爸打。）

Q3. You must rewrite your report

（你必須重寫你的報告。）

This is the answer.

（這是答案。）

↳ The answer is that <u>you must rewrite your report</u>.

（答案是你必須重寫你的報告。）

Q4. I don't like him.

（我不喜歡他。）

This is the reason.

（這是理由。）

↳ The reason is that <u>I don't like him</u>.

（理由是我不喜歡他。）

Q5. William is fired.

（威廉被開除了。）

The news surprises me.

（這個消息使我震驚。）

↳ It surprises me that <u>William is fired</u>.

（我很震驚威廉被開除了。）

Q6. Actually, he is a thief.

（事實上他是個小偷。）

The fact is surprising.

（這是個令人驚訝的事實。）

↳ The fact that <u>he is a thief</u> is surprising

（他是小偷的這事實令人驚訝。）

Q7. She has given birth to a baby.
（她已經生下一個寶寶。）

I don't know about it.
（我不曉得件事。）

↳ I don't know the news that <u>she has given birth to a baby</u>.
（我不知道她生了一個寶寶的消息。）

Q8. They can't wear jeans to work.
（他們不能穿牛仔褲去上班。）

The workers are told about the rule.
（員工們被告知這項規定。）

↳ The workers are told that <u>they can't wear jeans to work</u>.
（員工們被告知他們不能穿牛仔褲上班。）

Q9. The factory boss has promised to solve the problem.
（工廠老闆已答應會解決這問題。）

They will fix the water pollution.
（他們將解決水污染的情況。）

↳ The factory boss has promised that <u>they will fix the water pollution</u>.
（工廠老闆已答應他們將會解決水污染的情況。）

Q10. They say Tony has changed.
（他們說東尼已經變了。）

We all think it's impossible
（我們都認為那是不可能的·）

↳ We all think it impossible that <u>Tony has changed</u>.
（我們都認為東尼不可能改變的。）

☞ think it impossible that... 表示「認為…是不可能的」。這裡的 it 是「虛受詞」，代替後面 that 子句這個真受詞。

Q11. Kelly was killed.

（凱莉被殺了。）

The truth is shocking.

（這個事實真嚇人。）

↳ It is shocking that Kelly was killed

（凱莉被殺的這件事真是嚇人。）

Q12. A horse runs faster than a car.

（馬跑得比車快。）

The fact is unbelievable

（這事實讓人無法置信。）

↳ It's unbelievable that a horse runs faster than a car.

（馬跑得比車快這件事讓人無法置信。）

Q13. Something is true.

（有件事是真的。）

Swimming helps one relax.

（游泳可以讓人放鬆。）

↳ That swimming helps one relax is true.

（游泳可以讓人放鬆是真的。）

☞ 合併句提示以 That 開頭，且後面有動詞 is，顯然句子是以 that 引導的名詞子句當主詞，也就是指「游泳可以讓人放鬆」這件事，因此只要把第二句照抄填入空格即可。

Q14. Something is hard to believe.

（有件事令人難以置信。）

Having too much fish is harmful.

（吃太多魚是有害的。）

↳ That having too fish is harmful is hard to believe.

（吃太多魚是有害的這件事令人難以置信。）

158

Q15. Something sounds weird.

（有件事聽起來怪怪的。）

He collects Teddy bears.

（他收藏泰迪熊。）

↳ That <u>he collects Teddy bears</u> sounds weird.

（他收藏泰迪熊這件事聽起來怪怪的。）

關係代名詞隨形容詞子句修飾的對象而改變，先行詞為「人」時，關係代名詞為 who；先行詞為「事物」時，關係代名詞為 which。一般情況下，who 或 which 都可以用 that 代替。

一、先行詞為「人」
  使用關係代名詞 who 或 that

  例 I know the girl.

   The girl stands in front of the house.

  ☞ I know the girl <u>who stands in front of the house</u>.

二、先行詞為「事物」
  使用關係代名詞 which 或 that

  例 A rabbit is an animal.

   This animal has a pair of long ears.

  ☞ A rabbit is an animal <u>which has a pair of long ears</u>.

重點文法 快速查!!

形容詞子句的主詞隨先行詞而改變	
先行詞	關係代名詞主格
人	who, that
事物	which, that

GRAMMAR

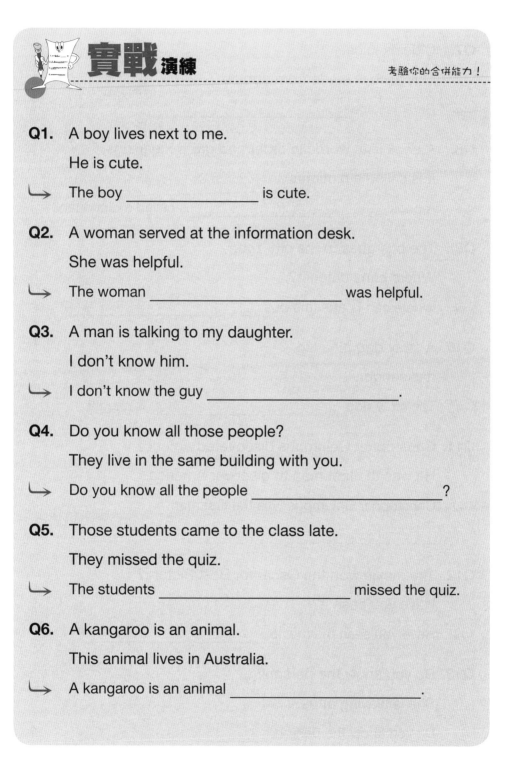

實戰演練   考驗你的合併能力！

Q1. A boy lives next to me.

He is cute.

↳ The boy _____ is cute.

Q2. A woman served at the information desk.

She was helpful.

↳ The woman _____ was helpful.

Q3. A man is talking to my daughter.

I don't know him.

↳ I don't know the guy _____.

Q4. Do you know all those people?

They live in the same building with you.

↳ Do you know all the people _____?

Q5. Those students came to the class late.

They missed the quiz.

↳ The students _____ missed the quiz.

Q6. A kangaroo is an animal.

This animal lives in Australia.

↳ A kangaroo is an animal _____.

Q7. Cider is juice.

This juice is made from apples.

↳ Cider is juice _____ .

Q8. A book lists words in order and gives meanings.

It is called a dictionary.

↳ A book _____ is called a dictionary.

Q9. The bus goes to the city zoo.

Where can I catch it?

↳ Where can I catch the bus _____ ?

Q10. A stray dog bit a kid.

It is caught.

↳ The stray dog _____ is caught.

Q11. Christopher Columbus discovered America.

He was the first man to discover America.

↳ Christopher Columbus was the first man _____

_____ .

Q12. The movie won the Oscar for Best Picture?

Have you seen it?

↳ Have you seen the movie _____ ?

Q13. Do you know the person?

She is waving at us.

↳ Do you know the person _____ ?

Q14. I have some teachers.

They ever taught my brother.

⤷ I have some teachers _____.

Q15. A person is called a photographer.

He takes photos professionally.

⤷ A person _____ is called a photographer.

示範 解答

中英文對照大解析

Q1. A boy lives next to me.
（有個男孩住在我家隔壁。）

He is cute.
（他很可愛。）

⤷ The boy who / that lives next to me is cute.
（住在我家隔壁的男孩很可愛。）

Q2. A woman served at the information desk.
（有名女子在服務台服務。）

She was helpful.
（她樂於助人。）

⤷ The woman who / that served at the information desk was helpful.
（在服務台服務的女子樂於助人。）

Q3. A man is talking to my daughter.
（一名男子正在和我女兒說話。）

I don't know him.
（我不認識他。）

↳ I don't know the guy <u>who is talking to my daughter</u>.
（我不認識那個正在和我女兒說話的男子。）

☞ 空格前是個完整句子，顯然要填入的是前面名詞 the guy 的修飾語。有兩種情況：1. 形容詞子句；2. 分詞片語。因此，本題答案可以寫 who is talking to my daughter 或 talking to my daughter 皆可。

Q4. Do you know all those people?
（你認識所有的人嗎？）

They live in the same building with you.
（他們和你住在同一棟樓裡。）

↳ Do you know all the people <u>who live in the same building with you</u>?
（你認識和你住在同一棟樓裡所有的人嗎？）

Q5. Those students came to the class late.
（那些學生上課遲到。）

They missed the quiz.
（他們錯過了小考。）

↳ The students <u>who came to the class late</u> missed the quiz.
（那些上課遲到的學生錯過了小考。）

Q6. A kangaroo is an animal.
（袋鼠是一種動物。）

This animal lives in Australia.
（這種動物生長在澳洲。）

↳ A kangaroo is an animal <u>which/that lives in Australia</u>.
（袋鼠是一種生長在澳洲的動物。）

164

Q7. Cider is juice.

（蘋果汁是一種果汁。）

This juice is made from apples.

（這種果汁是用蘋果製造的。）

↳ Cider is juice **which is made from apples**.

（蘋果汁是用蘋果製造的果汁。）

Q8. A book lists words in order and gives meanings.

（一本書照順序列出單字並給予意義。）

It is called a dictionary.

（它被稱為字典。）

↳ A book **which lists words in order and gives meanings** is called a dictionary.

（一本照順序列出單字並給予意義的書被稱為字典，）

Q9. The bus goes to the city zoo.

（這巴士往市立動物園。）

Where can I catch it?

（我要在哪裡搭車？）

↳ Where can I catch the bus **which goes to the city zoo**?

（我要在哪裡搭往市立動物園的巴士？）

Q10. A stray dog bit a kid.

（一隻流浪狗咬了一個小孩。）

It is caught.

（牠被抓了。）

↳ The stray dog **which bit a kid** is caught.

（咬了一個小孩的那隻流浪狗被抓了。）

Q11. Christopher Columbus discovered America.

（克里斯多福・哥倫布發現美洲。）

He was the first man to discover America.

（他是第一個發現美洲的人。）

↳ Christopher Columbus was the first man <u>who / that discovered American</u>.

（克里斯多福・哥倫布是第一個發現美洲的人。）

Q12. The movie won the Oscar for Best Picture?

（那部電影贏得奧斯卡最佳影片。）

Have you seen it?

（你看過嗎？）

↳ Have you seen the movie <u>which / that won the Oscar for Best Picture</u>?

（你看過那部贏得奧斯卡最佳影片的電影嗎？）

Q13. Do you know the person?

（你認識那個人嗎？）

She is waving at us.

（她正在向我們揮手。）

↳ Do you know the person <u>that is waving at us</u>?

（你認識那個正在向我們揮手的人嗎？）

Q14. I have some teachers.

（我有一些老師。）

They ever taught my brother.

（他們曾經教過我哥哥。）

↳ I have some teachers <u>that ever taught my brother</u>.

（我有幾位曾經教過我哥哥的老師。）

Q15. A person is called a photographer.
（一個人被稱為攝影師。）

He takes photos professionally.
（他專門拍照。）

↳ A person that takes photos professionally is called a photographer.
（專門拍照的人被稱為攝影師。）

句子合併
形容詞子句合併：
主題 23 | 受格型

Focus 解題焦點：

若先行詞為「人」，關係代名詞要用 whom；若先行詞為「事物」，則關係代名詞用 which。而 whom 或 which 都可以用 that 代替，或甚至予以省略。

一、先行詞為「人」

使用關係代名詞 whom 或 that 或省略

例 You met the student yesterday.

The student is the smartest one in my class.

☞ The student (whom / that) you met yesterday is the smartest one in my class.

二、先行詞為「事物」

使用關係代名 which 或 that 或省略

例 This is the dog.

We have kept it for ten years.

☞ This is the dog (which / that) we have kept for ten years.

重點文法 快速查!!

形容詞子句的受詞隨先行詞而改變	
先行詞	關係代名詞受格
人	whom / that / X (省略)
事物	which / that / X (省略)

GRAMMAR

168

Q1. Bill invited some people to his party.

I know only a few of them.

↳ I know only a few people _____ .

Q2. I talked to a man yesterday.

He is a professor.

↳ The man _____ is a professor.

Q3. I introduced a girl to you at yesterday's meeting.

Do you remember her?

↳ Do you remember the girl _____ ?

Q4. This is the dog.

We have kept it for ten years.

↳ This is the dog _____ .

Q5. Is this the book?

You are looking for it.

↳ Is this the book _____ ?

Q6. I borrowed the umbrella from my classmate.

I lost it.

↳ I lost the umbrella _____ .

Q7. My student asked me a question.

I couldn't answer it.

↳ My student asked me a question _____.

Q8. Your children gave you a gift.

Do you like it?

↳ Do you like the gift _____?

Q9. We went to the café yesterday.

What's the name of the café?

↳ What's the name of the café _____?

Q10. My brother rides a motorcycle.

It is too heavy for me.

↳ The motorcycle _____ is too heavy to me.

Q11. I talked to a man on the phone.

He was rude.

↳ The man _____ was rude.

Q12. I saw a girl crying in your office?

What's wrong with her?

↳ What's wrong with the girl _____?

Q13. You met the student this morning.

The student is the smartest one in my class.

↳ The student _____

is the smartest one in my class.

Q14. I want to own a car.

The car is very expensive.

↳ The car that _____ is very expensive.

Q15. The bride is wearing a dress.

The dress is tailor-made.

↳ The dress _____ is tailor-made.

解答 中英文對照大解析

Q1. Bill invited some people to his party.
（比爾邀請一些人參加他的宴會。）

I know only a few of them.
（我只認識其中幾位。）

↳ I know only a few people <u>whom Bill invited to his party</u>.
（比爾邀請來參加他宴會的人當中我只認識幾位。）

☞ 空格前是個完整句子，顯然要填入的是前面名詞 a few people 的修飾語。有兩種情況：1. 以當受詞的關係代名詞引導形容詞子句；2. 省略關係代名詞的形容詞子句。因此，本題答案可以寫 whom/that Bill invited to his party 或 Bill invited to his party 皆可。注意這裡 invited 是及物動詞，它的受詞是前面的 a few people。

Q2. I talked to a man yesterday.
（我昨天和一名男子交談。）

He is a professor.
（他是一位教授。）

↳ The man <u>whom I talked to yesterday</u> is a professor.
（昨天和我交談的那名男子是一位教授。）

Part 1 · 單句寫作 ▶▶ 02 句子合併

171

Q3. I introduced a girl to you at yesterday's meeting.
（昨天開會時我介紹了一位女孩子給你認識。）

Do you remember her?
（你記得她嗎?）

↳ Do you remember the girl <u>whom I introduced to you at yesterday's meeting</u>?
（你記得在昨天會議上我介紹給你認識的那位女孩子嗎？）

Q4. This is the dog.
（這就是那隻狗。）

We have kept it for ten years.
（我們養牠 10 年了。）

↳ This is the dog <u>which we have kept for ten years</u>.
（這就是我們養了 10 年的那隻狗。）

Q5. Is this the book?
（這是那本書嗎？）

You are looking for it.
（你正在找它。）

↳ Is this the book <u>which you are looking for</u>?
（這是你正在找的那本書嗎？）

Q6. I borrowed the umbrella from my classmate.
（我向同學借了這把傘。）

I lost it.
（我把它遺失了。）

↳ I lost the umbrella <u>that I borrowed from my classmate</u>.
（我遺失了向同學借的那把傘。）

Q7. My student asked me a question.
（我的學生問了我一個問題。）

I couldn't answer it.
（我無法回答。）

↳ My student asked me a question <u>that I couldn't answer</u>.
（我的學生問了一個我無法回答的問題。）

Q8. Your children gave you a gift.
（你的孩子們送你一份禮物。）

Do you like it?
（你喜歡它嗎？）

↳ Do you like the gift <u>that your children gave you</u>?
（你喜歡你孩子們送你的那份禮物嗎？）

Q9. We went to the café yesterday.
（我們昨天去了這家咖啡廳。）

What's the name of the café?
（那家咖啡廳叫什麼？）

↳ What's the name of the café <u>that we went to yesterday</u>?
（我們昨天去的那家咖啡廳叫什麼？）

Q10. My brother rides a motorcycle.
（我哥哥騎一輛摩托車。）

It is too heavy for me.
（那對我而言太重了。）

↳ The motorcycle <u>that my brother rides</u> is too heavy to me.
（我哥哥騎的那輛摩托車對我而言太重了。）

Q11. I talked to a man on the phone.

（我和一名男子在講電話。）

He was rude.

（他很粗魯。）

⮡ The man that I talked to on the phone was rude.

（和我通話的那名男子很粗魯。）

Q12. I saw a girl crying in your office?

（我看到一個女孩在你辦公室裡哭。）

What's wrong with her?

（她怎麼了？）

⮡ What's wrong with the girl that I saw crying in your office?

（我在你辦公室裡看到在哭的那個女孩怎麼了？）

Q13. You met the student this morning.

（你今天早上遇見那個學生。）

The student is the smartest one in my class.

（那個學生是我班上最聰明的。）

⮡ The student you met this morning is the smartest one in my class.

（你今天早上遇到的那個學生是我班上最聰明的。）

Q14. I want to own a car.

（我想擁有一部車。）

The car is very expensive.

（這部車很貴。）

⮡ The car that I want to own is very expensive.

（我想擁有的那部車很貴。）

Q15. The bride is wearing a dress.
（新娘正在穿一件洋裝。）

The dress is tailor-made.
（這件洋裝是訂製的。）

↳ The dress <u>the bride is wearing</u> is tailor-made.
（新娘正在穿的那件洋裝是訂製的。）

句子合併

主題 **24** 形容詞子句合併：
所有格型

Focus 解題焦點：

> 不論先行詞是人還是事物，形容詞子句的所有格一律用
> **whose**。

一、先行詞為「人」
   使用關係代名詞所有格 whose

   例 I have a friend.

   His mother is an actress.

   ☞ I have a friend <u>whose mother is an actress</u>.

二、先行詞為「事物」
   使用關係代名所有格 whose

   例 The house is ours.

   Its roof is red.

   ☞ The house <u>whose roof is red</u> is ours.

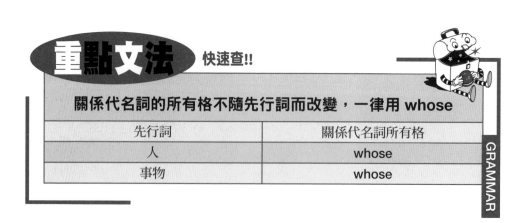

重點文法 快速查!!

關係代名詞的所有格不隨先行詞而改變，一律用 whose

先行詞	關係代名詞所有格
人	whose
事物	whose

GRAMMAR

 **實戰演練**　　　　　　　　　　考驗你的合併能力！

Part 1 · 單句寫作 ▶▶ 02 句子合併

Q1. I have a friend.

His mother is an actress.

↳ I have a friend whose _____.

Q2. Here is the boy.

His parents are dead.

↳ Here is the boy whose _____.

Q3. Once upon a time, there was a girl.

Her name was Cinderella.

↳ Once upon a time, there was a girl whose _____
is right there.

Q4. The winner is right there.

Her work got the first prize.

↳ The winner whose _____.

Q5. A woman called the police.

Her apartment was broken into.

↳ The woman whose _____ called the police.

Q6. They are the couple.

We bought their car.

↳ They are the couple whose _____.

Q7. I borrowed my friend's laptop.

I thanked him.

↳ I thanked my friend whose _____.

Q8. The man is famous.

I'm dating his daughter.

↳ The man _____ is famous.

Q9. The girl is a good friend of mine.

I stayed at her home last night.

↳ The girl at whose _____ is a good friend of mine.

Q10. The house is ours.

Its roof is red.

↳ The house whose _____ is ours.

Q11. The dog is mine.

Its tail is waving.

↳ The dog whose _____ is mine.

Q12. The mountain is Mt. Jade.

Its top is in the clouds.

↳ The mountain whose _____ is Mt. Jade.

Q13. The cat can't jump over the fence.

Its tail was cut off.

↳ The cat whose _____ can't jump over the fence.

Q14. The monkey was sent to the vet.

Its head was terribly damaged.

↳ The monkey _____ was sent to the vet.

Q15. The kid is upset.

His toy is broken.

↳ The kid _____ is upset.

示範 解答 中英文對照大解析

Q1. I have a friend.
（我有一位朋友。）

His mother is an actress.
（他媽媽是一位演員。）

↳ I have a friend whose **mother is an actress**.
（我有一位媽媽在當演員的朋友。）

Q2. Here is the boy.
（這就是那個男孩。）

His parents are dead.
（他父母雙亡。）

↳ Here is the boy whose **parents are dead**.
（這就是父母雙亡的那個男孩。）

Q3. Once upon a time, there was a girl.
（很久以前有一個女孩。）

Her name was Cinderella.
（她的名字叫作「灰姑娘」。）

↳ Once upon a time, there was a girl whose <u>name was Cinderella</u>.
（很久以前有一個名叫「灰姑娘」的女孩。）

Q4. The winner is right there.
（獲勝者在此。）

Her work got the first prize.
（她的作品贏得首獎。）

↳ The winner whose <u>work got the first prize</u> is right there.
（其作品贏得首獎的那位獲勝者在此。）

Q5. A woman called the police.
（一名女子打電話報警。）

Her apartment was broken into.
（她的公寓被闖入了。）

↳ The woman whose <u>apartment was broken into</u> called the police.
（一名公寓被闖入的女子打電話報警。）

Q6. They are the couple.
（他們就是那對夫妻。）

We bought their car.
（我們買了他們的車。）

↳ They are the couple whose <u>car we bought</u>.
（他們就是我們買他們車的那對夫妻。）

Q7. I borrowed my friend's laptop.
（我借了我朋友的筆電。）

I thanked him.
（我感謝他。）

↳ I thanked my friend whose <u>laptop I borrowed</u>.
（我感謝我那位借我筆電的朋友。）

Q8. The man is famous.
（這男人很有名。）

I'm dating his daughter.
（我和他女兒正在交往。）

↳ The man <u>whose daughter I'm dating</u> is famous.
（我正在和他女兒交往的那名男子很有名氣。）

Q9. The girl is a good friend of mine.
（那女孩是我的一個好朋友。）

I stayed at her home last night.
（我昨晚住她家。）

↳ The girl at whose <u>home I stayed last night</u> is a good friend of mine.
（我昨晚住在她家的那女孩是我一個好朋友。）

☞ 空格前是關係代名詞所有格 whose，所以要在題目中找有「所有格」的句子：I stayed at her home last night.。whose home 是這個形容詞子句動詞 stayed at 的受詞。注意這裡的 at 已經出現在 whose 前面了，因此子句中 stay 後面可別再加上 at 了。

Q10. The house is ours.
（那棟房子是我們的。）

Its roof is red.
（它的屋頂是紅色的。）

↳ The house whose <u>roof is red</u> is ours.
（屋頂紅色的那棟房子是我們的。）

Q11. The dog is mine.

（那隻狗是我的。）

Its tail is waving.

（牠的尾巴在搖著。）

↳ The dog whose <u>tail is waving</u> is mine.

（尾巴在搖的那隻狗是我的。）

Q12. The mountain is Mt. Jade.

（那座山是玉山。）

Its top is in the clouds.

（它的山頂在雲裡面。）

↳ The mountain whose <u>top is in the clouds</u> is Mt. Jade.

（山頂在雲裡的那座山是玉山。）

Q13.The cat can't jump over the fence.

（那隻貓無法跳過柵欄。）

Its tail was cut off.

（牠的尾巴被剪斷了。）

↳ The cat whose <u>tail was cut off</u> can't jump over the fence.

（尾巴被剪斷的那隻貓無法跳過柵欄。）

Q14. The monkey was sent to the vet.

（那隻猴子被送到獸醫那兒。）

Its head was terribly damaged.

（牠的頭受到重創。）

↳ The monkey <u>whose head was terribly damaged</u> was sent to the vet.

（頭部受到重創的那隻猴子被送到獸醫那兒。）

Q15. The kid is upset.

（那小孩很不開心。）

His toy is broken.

（他的玩具壞了。）

↳ The kid <u>whose toy is broken is upset</u>.

（他玩具壞掉的那小孩很不開心。）

形容詞子句合併：關係副詞型

解題焦點：

關係副詞可依先行詞的內容分為四類：
一、表時間／二、表地點／三、表原因／四、表方法，分別
使用關係副詞 when、where、why、how。

一、表時間
表示時間的關係副詞是 when

例 I remember that day.

On that day we first met.

☞ I remember the day <u>when we first met</u>.

二、表地點
表示地點的關係副詞是 where

例 This is the town.

In this town he grew up.

☞ This is the town <u>where he grew up</u>.

三、表原因
表示原因的關係副詞是 why

例 Do you know the reason?

He came so late because of the reason.

☞ Do you know (the reason) <u>why he came so late</u>?

四、表方法
表示方法的關係副詞是 how

例 Bees communicate in some way.

That way is an interesting thing to study.

☞ <u>The way how bees communicate</u> is an interesting thing to study.

實戰演練

考驗你的合併能力！

Q1. I remember that day.

On that day we first met.

↳ I remember the day _____.

Q2. Kenny was taking a picture at the time.

The bomb explored then.

↳ Kenny was taking a picture _____.

Q3. The year is 1981.

In that year I was born.

↳ The year _____ is 1981.

Q4. Chinese New Year is the holiday.

Families get together during the holiday.

↳ Chinese New Year is the holiday _____.

Q5. This is the town.

In this town he grew up.

↳ This is the town _____.

Q6. The map marks the place.

At that place we buried the treasures.

↳ The map marks the place _____.

Part 1 · 單句寫作 ▶▶ 02 句子合併

185

Q7. The island is paradise.

I can swim in the river there.

↪ The island _____ is a paradise.

Q8. The place has changed a lot.

I visited here ten years ago.

↪ The place _____ has changed a lot.

Q9. Do you know the reason?

He came so late because of the reason.

↪ Do you know (the reason) _____ ?

Q10. No doctor can tell the reason.

The patient suddenly died because of the reason.

↪ No doctor can tell (the reason) _____ ?

Q11. Judy is absent because of the reason.

The reason is that she is sick.

↪ _____ is that she is sick.

Q12. Many ships disappeared in that area because of the reason.

The reason remains a mystery.

↪ _____ is still a mystery.

Q13. I don't know the way.

He works for three jobs in that way.

↪ I don't know _____ .

Q14. Can you tell me the way?

You learn English so quickly in that way.

↳ Can you tell _____?

Q15. Bees communicate in some way.

That way is an interesting thing to study.

↳ _____ is an interesting thing to study.

示範 解答   中英文對照大解析

Q1. I remember that day.
（我記得那一天。）

On that day we first met.
（那天我們第一次相遇。）

↳ I remember the day <u>when we first met</u>.
（我記得我們第一次相遇的那一天。）

☞ 空格前是個完整句子，顯然要填入的是前面名詞 the day 的修飾語。主要有兩種情況：1. 以關係副詞 when 引導形容詞子句；2. 以關係代名詞 which/that 引導形容詞子句。因此，本題答案可以寫 when we first met 或 (which/that) we first met on或 on which we first met 皆可。這裡的 on which 等於 when，也就是說，關係副詞 = 介系詞 + 關係代名詞。但須注意的是，沒有 on that 的用法喔！

Q2. Kenny was taking a picture at the time.
（肯尼當時正在拍照。）

The bomb explored then.
（炸彈在那時候爆炸。）

↳ Kenny was taking a picture <u>when the bomb explored</u>.
（炸彈爆炸的當時肯尼正在拍照。）

187

Q3. The year is 1981.
（那年是 1981 年。）

In that year I was born.
（那年我出生。）

↳ The year <u>when I was born</u> is 1981.
（我出生的那年是 1981 年。）

Q4. Chinese New Year is the holiday.
（中國新年是假日。）

Families get together during the holiday.
（家人們在這假日期間相聚。）

↳ Chinese New Year is the holiday <u>when families get together</u>.
（中國新年是家人們相聚的假日。）

Q5. This is the town.
（就是這個城鎮。）

In this town he grew up.
（他在這個城鎮長大。）

↳ This is the town <u>where he grew up</u>.
（這是他從小生長的城鎮。）

Q6. The map marks the place.
（這張地圖標示出這地方。）

At that place we buried the treasures.
（在那地方我們埋藏了寶藏。）

↳ The map marks the place <u>where we buried the treasures</u>.
（這張地圖上標示出我們埋藏寶藏的地方。）

188

Q7. The island is paradise.
（這座島是個人間天堂。）

I can swim in the river there.
（我可以在那裡的河流中游泳。）

↳ The island <u>where I can swim in the river</u> is a paradise.
（我可以在河流中游泳的那座島是個人間天堂。）

Q8. The place has changed a lot.
（這地方已經變了很多。）

I visited here ten years ago.
（我十年前造訪過這裡。）

↳ The place <u>where I visited ten years ago</u> has changed a lot.
（我十年前造訪過的這地方已經變了很多。）

Q9. Do you know the reason?
（你知道理由嗎？）

He came so late because of the reason.
（他這麼晚到就是因為這理由。）

↳ Do you know (the reason) <u>why he came so late</u>?
（你知道為什他這麼晚到的理由嗎？）

Q10. No doctor can tell the reason.
（沒有一位醫生說得出原因。）

The patient suddenly died because of the reason.
（病人突然死亡因為這原因而死亡。）

↳ No doctor can tell (the reason) <u>why the patient suddenly died</u>.
（沒有一位醫生能說得出這病人為何突然死亡。）

Q11. Judy is absent because of the reason.

（茱蒂因為這理由而缺席。）

The reason is that she is sick.

（這理由就是她生病了。）

↳ <u>Why Judy is absent</u> is that she is sick.

（茱蒂為何缺席的原因是她生病了。）

☞ 空格後面是「be動詞 + 補語」，顯然要填入的是句子的主詞。主要有兩種情況：1. 名詞子句當主詞；2.「名詞 + 形容詞子句」當主詞。因此答案也可以寫成 The reason why/that Judy is absent。

Q12. Many ships disappeared in that area because of the reason.

（很多船因為這原因而消失在那個區域。）

The reason remains a mystery.

（原因仍是個謎。）

↳ <u>Why many ships disappeared in that area</u> is still a mystery.

（為何許多船消失在那區域仍是個謎。）

Q13. I don't know the way.

（我不知道方法。）

He works for three jobs in that way.

（他用那方法身兼三職。）

↳ I don't know <u>how he works for three jobs</u>.

（我不知道他如何身兼三份工作。）

☞ 空格要填入的是 know 的受詞。主要有兩種情況：1. 名詞子句當受詞；2.「名詞 + 形容詞子句」當受詞。因此答案也可以寫成 the way (how/that) he works for three jobs。the way 後面的 how 或 that 都可省略。

Q14. Can you tell me the way?
（你可以告訴我方法嗎？）

You learn English so quickly in that way.
（你用那方法學英文學得這麼快。）

↳ Can you tell <u>how you learn English so quickly</u>?
（你可以告訴我你如何學英文學得這麼快嗎？）

Q15. Bees communicate in some way.
（蜜蜂以某種方式溝通。）

The way is an interesting thing to study.
（這種方式是一件可研究且有趣的東西。）

↳ <u>How bees communicate</u> is an interesting thing to study.
（蜜蜂如何溝通是一件可研究且有趣的東西。）

句子合併 | 主題 **26**

副詞子句合併：表時間

Focus 解題焦點：

合併表時間的副詞子句，可依連接詞分為六種題型：
一、when／二、as soon as／三、before／
四、after／五、since／六、until。

一、when（在⋯時候）

例 We were in Sydney.

During that time, we went to the opera every night.

☞ We went to the opera every night <u>when</u> we were in Sydney.

二、as soon as（一⋯就⋯）

例 The speaker entered the auditorium.

At the sight of the speaker, the audience clapped.

☞ The audience clapped <u>as soon as</u> the speaker entered the auditorium.

三、before（在⋯之前）

例 Sara spent a long time dressing up.

Then she went out with her boyfriend.

☞ Sara spent a long time dressing up <u>before</u> she went out with her boyfriend.

四、after（在⋯之後）

例 Tom arrived at the station late.

The train had left.

☞ Tom arrived at the station <u>after</u> the train had left.

192

五、since（自從）

例 The rain started when I got up this morning.

The rain lasts until now.

☞ **It has been raining** since **I got up this morning**.

六、until（直到）

例 The dog will move.

You must tell him to move.

☞ **The dog will not move** until **you tell him to do so**.

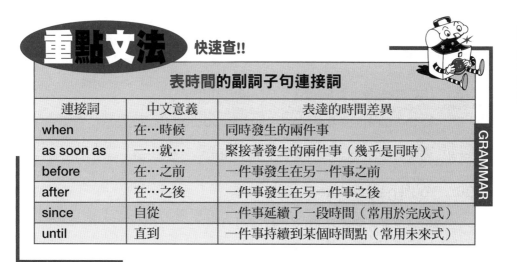

重點文法 快速查!!

表時間的副詞子句連接詞

連接詞	中文意義	表達的時間差異
when	在…時候	同時發生的兩件事
as soon as	一…就…	緊接著發生的兩件事（幾乎是同時）
before	在…之前	一件事發生在另一件事之前
after	在…之後	一件事發生在另一件事之後
since	自從	一件事延續了一段時間（常用於完成式）
until	直到	一件事持續到某個時間點（常用未來式）

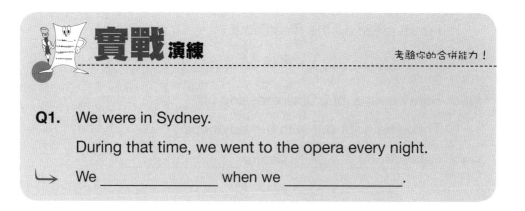

實戰演練

考驗你的合併能力！

Q1. We were in Sydney.

During that time, we went to the opera every night.

↳ We _____ when we _____.

Q2. I came into the room.

At that moment, he was writing a letter.

↳ When _____, _____.

Q3. The fire broke out.

James was taking a bath at that time.

↳ _____ when _____.

Q4. We reached the mountaintop.

It began to rain at that very moment.

↳ As soon as _____, _____.

Q5. The speaker entered the auditorium.

At the sight of the speaker, the audience clapped.

↳ _____ as soon as _____.

Q6. You'll get back to the office.

Give me a call right away.

↳ _____ as soon as _____.

Q7. My mother will come back soon.

I must clean up the mess now.

↳ _____ before _____.

Q8. Sara spent a long time dressing up.

Then she went out with her boyfriend.

↳ Sara _____ before _____.

Q9. I'll get his reply first.

I'll make the final decision next.

↳ _____ after _____.

Q10. Tom arrived at the station late.

The train had left.

↳ Tom _____ after _____.

Q11. It was two years ago.

He left home in that year.

↳ _____ since he left home.

Q12. The rain started when I got up this morning.

The rain lasts until now.

↳ It _____ since I got up this morning.

Q13. The show will start.

The mayor must arrive first.

↳ _____ until the mayor arrives.

Q14. The dog will move.

You must tell him to move.

↳ _____ until you tell him to do so.

Q15. The workers will leave.

They have to get the money first.

↳ _____ until they get the money.

Q1. We were in Sydney.
（我們在雪梨。）

During that time, we went to the opera every night.
（在那期間，我們每晚都上劇院。）

↳ We <u>went to the opera every night</u> when we <u>were in Sydney</u>.
（我們在雪梨時每晚都上劇院。）

Q2. I came into the room.
（我進到房裡。）

At that moment, he was writing a letter.
（當時他正在寫信。）

↳ When <u>I came into the room</u>, <u>he was writing a letter</u>.
（當我進到房裡時，他正在寫信。）

Q3. The fire broke out.
（失火了。）

James was taking a bath at that time.
（詹姆士當時正在洗澡。）

↳ <u>James was taking a bath</u> when <u>the fire broke out</u>.
（火災發生時詹姆士正在洗澡。）

Q4. We reached the mountaintop.
（我們抵達山頂。）

It began to rain at that very moment.
（就在那時候開始下起雨來。）

↳ As soon as <u>we reached the mountain</u>, <u>it began to rain</u>.
（我們一抵達山頂時，就開始下起雨來了。）

Q5. The speaker entered the auditorium.
（演講者進入講堂。）

At the sight of the speaker, the audience clapped.
（觀眾一見到這位演說家就鼓掌。）

↳ <u>The audience clapped</u> as soon as <u>the speaker entered the auditorium</u>.
（觀眾一見到這位演說家進入講堂時就鼓掌。）

Q6. You'll get back to the office.
（你將回到辦公室。）

Give me a call right away.
（馬上打電話給我。）

↳ <u>Give me a call</u> as soon as <u>you get back to the office</u>.
（你一回到辦公室就馬上打電話給我。）

☞ "as soon as..." 表示「一⋯就⋯」，所以合併句要表達的是「你一回到辦公室就打電話給我」，這時候 as soon as 所引導的副詞子句必須用「現在式代替未來式」，不能寫成 as soon as you'll get back to the office。

Q7. My mother will come back soon.
（我媽媽很快就會回來了。）

I must clean up the mess now.
（我現在必須把這一團亂清理掉。）

↳ <u>I must clean up the mess</u> before <u>my mother comes back</u>.
（在我媽媽回來之前我必須把這一團亂清理掉。）

☞ 雖然原句是 "My mother will come back soon."，但合併句中，before 引導的副詞子句不必再將 soon 放進去。

Q8. Sara spent a long time dressing up.

（莎拉花了很多時間打扮。）

Then she went out with her boyfriend.

（然後她和男朋友出去。）

↳ Sara spent a long time dressing up before she went out with her boyfriend.

（莎拉和男朋友出去之前花了很多時間打扮。）

Q9. I'll get his reply first.

（我會先得到他的回覆。）

I'll make the final decision next.

（再來我會做最後決定。）

↳ I'll make the final decision after I get his reply.

（我得到他的答覆後就會做最後決定。）

Q10. Tom arrived at the station late.

（湯姆太晚抵達車站。）

The train had left.

（火車已經開走。）

↳ Tom arrived at the station after the train had left.

（火車開走後湯姆才抵達車站。）

Q11. It was two years ago.

（那是兩年前了。）

He left home in that year.

（他在那年離家。）

↳ It has been two years since he left home.

（他離家到現在已兩年了。）

198

Q12. The rain started when I got up this morning.

（在我早上起床時就開始下雨了。）

The rain lasts until now.

（雨一直持續到現在。）

↳ It **has been raining** since I got up this morning.

（從我早上起床時，雨就一直下不停。）

Q13. The show will start.

（表演將要開始。）

The mayor must arrive first.

（市長必須先抵達。）

↳ **The show will not start** until the mayor arrives.

（市長到了表演才會開始。）

Q14. The dog will move.

（這隻狗會動。）

You must tell him to move.

（你必須叫牠動。）

↳ **The dog will not move** until you tell him to do so.

（這隻狗要你叫牠動牠才會動。）

Q15. The workers will leave.

（員工們將離開。）

They have to get the money first.

（他們必須先拿到錢。）

↳ **The workers will not leave** until they get the money.

（員工們要拿到錢才會離開。）

☞ "not... until..." 是固定搭配的「連接詞片語」，表「直到…才會…」，所以在 until 前面的主要子句應為「否定句」。

199

句子合併

主題
27

副詞子句合併：
其他用法

Focus 解題焦點：

副詞子句除了表達時間之外，還有其他用法：表達讓步、原因、條件、目的。

一、表讓步

例 Jeff took a taxi to the airport.

He still missed the flight.

☞ **Although** Jeff took a taxi to the airport, he still missed the flight.

二、表原因

例 He is honest.

He is loved by all.

☞ He is loved by all **because** he is honest.

三、表條件

例 It will rain tomorrow.

She will not go to the party.

☞ She will not go to the party **if** it rains tomorrow.

四、表目的

例 My mother ate only two meals a day.

She wanted to save some money.

☞ My mother ate only two meals a day **in order that** she can save some money.

重點文法 快速查!!

副詞子句其他用法 — 常用連接詞一覽表

用法	常用連接詞	中文意義
表讓步	though / although	雖然，儘管
	even though	雖然，儘管
表原因與結果	because	因為
	so	所以
	so～that such～that	這麼…所以… 如此…以致於…
	that / in that	因為…
表目的	in order that	為了…
	so that	以便…
表條件	if	如果…
	as long as	只要…
	unless	除非…否則…

實戰演練

考驗你的合併能力！

Q1. Jeff took a taxi to the airport.

He still missed the flight.

↳ Although _____, _____.

Q2. He works from morning till night.

He is as poor as before.

↳ _____ even though _____.

Q3. He is honest.

He is loved by all.

↳ _____ because _____ .

Q4. I didn't know what to say.

I remained silent.

↳ _____ , so _____ .

Q5. It is very cold in winter.

We need a heater.

↳ It is so cold in winter _____ .

Q6. This is a very beautiful place.

I will live here forever.

↳ This is such a beautiful place _____ .

Q7. Our daughter is pregnant.

We are glad about it.

↳ We are glad that _____ .

Q8. He left home early.

He hoped he would not miss the train.

↳ _____ so that _____ .

Q9. My brother puts some money away each month.

He hoped he can buy a car in two years.

↳ _____ in order that _____ .

Q10. We will have a field trip tomorrow.

The weather must be fine.

↳ If _____ tomorrow, we will have a field trip.

Q11. It will probably rain on Sunday.

The concert will be cancelled.

↳ If _____, the concert will be cancelled.

Q12. You will enjoy it.

You must like it.

↳ As long as _____, _____.

Q13. You may stay here.

You must keep quiet.

↳ As long as _____, _____.

Q14. I will not ask him for help.

I will only ask him for help when it's necessary.

↳ _____ unless _____.

Q15. Patrick will go on a study tour.

He will not go if his parents don't lend him money.

↳ _____ unless _____.

Q1. Jeff took a taxi to the airport.

（傑夫搭計程車到機場。）

He still missed the flight.

（他還是錯過了班機。）

↳ Although <u>Jeff took a taxi to the airport</u>, <u>he still missed the flight</u>.

（雖然傑夫搭計程車到機場，但還是錯過了班機。）

Q2. He works from morning till night.

（他一天到晚都在工作。）

He is as poor as before.

（他和以前一樣窮。）

↳ <u>He is as poor as before</u> even though <u>he works from morning till night</u>.

（他還是和以前一樣窮，儘管他一天到晚都在工作。）

Q3. He is honest.

（他為人誠實。）

He is loved by all.

（他為眾人所喜歡。）

↳ <u>He is loved by all</u> because <u>he is honest</u>.

（他人見人愛，因為他為人誠實。）

Q4. I didn't know what to say.

（我不知道該說什麼。）

I remained silent.

（我保持沈默。）

↳ <u>I didn't know what to say</u>, so <u>I remained silent</u>.

（我不知道要說什麼，所以我保持沈默。）

Q5. It is very cold in winter.

（冬天很冷。）

We need a heater.

（我們需要一台暖氣。）

↳ It is so cold in winter <u>that we need a heater</u>.

（冬天如此地冷，因此我們需要一台暖氣。）

☞ "so... that..." 是固定搭配的「連接詞片語」，表「如此…以致於…」，so cold in winter 呼應第一句的 very cold in winter，因此空格先填入 that 之後，照抄第二句即可。

Q6. This is a very beautiful place.

（這是個很漂亮的地方。）

I will live here forever.

（我會一直住在這裡。）

↳ This is such a beautiful place <u>that I will live here forever</u>.

（這真是個如此美麗的地方，因此我會一直住在這裡。）

☞ "such... that..." 是固定搭配的「連接詞片語」，表「如此…以致於…」，such a beautiful place 呼應第一句的 a very beautiful place，因此空格先填入 that 之後，照抄第二句即可。

Q7. Our daughter is pregnant.

（我們女兒懷孕了。）

We are glad about it.

（我們對此感到高興。）

↳ We are glad that <u>our daughter is pregnant</u>.

（我們很高興我們的女兒懷孕了。）

Q8. He left home early.

（他很早就出門了。）

He hoped he would not miss the train.

（他希望不會錯過火車。）

↳ <u>He left home early</u> so that <u>he would not miss the train</u>.

（他很早就出門了，那麼他才不會錯過火車。）

Q9. My brother puts some money away each month.

（我哥哥每個月會存一點錢下來。）

He hoped he can buy a car in two years.

（他希望兩年內可以買車。）

↳ <u>My brother puts some money away each month</u> in order that <u>he can buy a car in two years</u>.

（我哥哥每個月存一點錢下來，這是為了兩年內可以買車。）

Q10. We will have a field trip tomorrow.

（我們明天要去踏青。）

The weather must be fine.

（天氣一定要晴朗。）

↳ If <u>the weather is fine</u> tomorrow, we will have a field trip.

（如果明天天氣晴朗，我們就會去踏青。）

Q11. It will probably rain on Sunday.

（星期天可能會下雨。）

The concert will be cancelled.

（演唱會將被取消。）

↳ If <u>it rains on Sunday</u>, the concert will be cancelled.

（如果星期天下雨，演唱會將被取消）

Q12. You will enjoy it.

（你會樂在其中。）

You must like it.

（你一定會喜歡。）

↳ As long as <u>you like it</u>, <u>you will enjoy it</u>.

（只要你喜歡，你就會樂在其中。）

Q13. You may stay here.

（你可以待在這兒。）

You must keep quiet.

（你必須保持安靜。）

↳ As long as <u>you keep quiet</u>, <u>you may stay here</u>.

（只要你保持安靜，你就可以待在這兒。）

Q14. I will not ask him for help.

（我不會請他來幫忙。）

I will only ask him for help when it's necessary.

（我只會在有必要時才會請他來幫忙。）

↳ <u>I will not ask him for help</u> unless <u>it's necessary</u>.

（我不會請他來幫忙，除非有必要。）

☞ unless 是「除非…否則不…」的意思，引導條件句，因此主要子句應為否定句，只要將第一句助動詞 will 後面加上 not 即可。

Q15. Patrick will go on a study tour.

（派崔克將參加一個遊學團。）

He will not go if his parents don't lend him money.

（如果他父母沒有借他錢，他就不會去了。）

↳ <u>Patrick will not go on a study tour</u> unless <u>his parents lend him money</u>.

（派崔克不會去參加遊學團，除非他父母借他錢）

主題 28 | 副詞片語合併

Focus 解題焦點：

> 副詞片語主要用來修飾動詞，可用來表示使用工具、搭乘交通工具的方式、心理狀態、行進方向、針對某對象、伴隨、動作執行者、手段或方法。

一、表使用工具

例 The man cut the cake.

He used a knife to cut it.（用 with）

☞ The man cut the cake <u>with a knife</u>.

二、表搭乘交通工具的方式

例 Mr. Smith will come to Taipei.

He will take a plane.（用 by）

☞ Mr. Smith will come to Taipei <u>by plane</u>.

三、表心理狀態

例 The family looked at the sick child.

They were worried about him.（用 with）

☞ The family looked at the sick child <u>with worry</u>.

四、表方向、針對某對象

例 You'll hear all the questions.

Listen carefully.（用 to 合併）

☞ Listen carefully <u>to all the questions</u>.

五、表陪伴

例 We're going to the movies.

Would you like to go together?（用 with）

☞ Would you like to go to the movies <u>with us</u>?

六、表動作者（用於被動語態）

例 The children were sleeping.

A loud thunderclap awakened them.（用 by）

☞ The children were awakened <u>by a loud thunderclap</u>.

七、表手段或方法

例 The fox left its tracks in the mud.

The hunter followed the tracks.（用 by）

☞ The hunter followed the fox <u>by its tracks in the mud</u>.

重點文法 快速查!!

副詞片語的用途	常用片語
表使用工具	with a knife 用刀子 wipe with a handkerchief 用手帕來擦 without a computer 沒有電腦 without glasses 沒有戴眼鏡
表搭乘交通工具的方式	by plane 搭飛機 by car 開車　　by taxi 搭計程車 on foot 走路
表心理狀態	without fear 無所畏懼地 in peace 心平氣和地 with worry 擔心地
表方向、針對某對象	listen carefully to the questions 仔細聽問題 a trip to Mexico 一趟墨西哥之旅
表陪伴	with us 和我們一起
表動作者 （用於被動語態）	be wakened by a loud thunder clap 被轟雷巨響吵醒
表手段或方法	by its tracks 沿著足跡

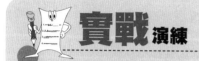

Q1. The man cut the cake.

He used a knife to cut it. （用 with）

↳ The man _____.

Q2. The woman wiped her tears.

She used a handkerchief to do so. （用 with）

↳ The woman _____.

Q3. I can't do it.

I have to use a computer. （用 without）

↳ I can't _____.

Q4. Jerry can't see anything.

He has to wear glasses. （用 without）

↳ Jerry can't _____.

Q5. Mr. Smith will come to Taipei.

He will take a plane. （用 by）

↳ Mr. Smith will _____.

Q6. My father goes to work.

He drives a car. （用 by）

↳ My father _____.

Q7. I go to school.

I walk.（用 on）

↳ I _____ .

Q8. The children climbed the mountain.

They were not fearful.（用 without）

↳ The children _____ .

Q9. I read my book.

I was peaceful.（用 in）

↳ I _____ .

Q10. The family looked at the sick child.

They were worried about him.（用 with）

↳ The family looked at the sick child _____ .

Q11. You'll hear all the questions.

Listen carefully.（用 to）

↳ Listen carefully _____ .

Q12. I took a trip.

I went to Mexico.（用 to）

↳ I _____ .

Q13. We're going to the movies.

Would you like to go together?（用 with）

↳ Would you _____ ?

Q14. The children were sleeping.

A loud thunderclap awakened them. （用 by）

↳ The children were awakened _____.

Q15. The fox left its tracks in the mud.

The hunter followed the tracks. （用 by）

↳ The hunter followed the fox _____.

示範 解答 ··· 中英文對照大解析

Q1. The man cut the cake.
（男子切了蛋糕。）

He used a knife to cut it. （用 with）
（他用刀子來切。）

↳ The man cut the cake with a knife.
（男子用刀子切了蛋糕。）

Q2. The woman wiped her tears.
（女子擦拭她的眼淚。）

She used a handkerchief to do so. （用 with）
（她用手帕來擦。）

↳ The woman wiped her tears with a handkerchief.
（女子用手帕來擦拭她的眼淚。）

Q3. I can't do it.
（我沒辦法做。）

I have to use a computer.（用 without）
（我必須使用電腦。）

↳ I can't **do it without a computer**.
（沒有電腦我沒辦法做。）

Q4. Jerry can't see anything.
（傑瑞看不到東西。）

He has to wear glasses.（用 without）
（他必須戴上眼鏡。）

↳ Jerry can't **see anything without (wearing) glasses**.
（傑瑞沒有戴上眼鏡的話看不到東西。）

Q5. Mr. Smith will come to Taipei.
（史密斯先生會到台北來。）

He will take a plane.（用 by）
（他將會搭飛機。）

↳ Mr. Smith will **come to Taipei by plane**.
（史密斯先生會搭飛機到台北來。）

Q6. My father goes to work.
（我父親去上班。）

He drives a car.（用 by）
（他開車。）

↳ My father **goes to work by car**.
（我父親開車去上班。）

☞ 題目提示用 by，也就是用「by＋交通工具」的副詞片語來合併句子。題目中的交通工具是 car，因此照抄第一句的 goes to work 後再接 by car 即可。

Q7. I go to school.
（我去上學。）

I walk.（用 on）
（我走路。）

⮡ I go to school on foot.
（我走路去上學。）

Q8. The children climbed the mountain.
（孩子們爬山。）

They were not fearful.（用 without）
（他們不害怕。）

⮡ The children climbed the mountain without fear.
（孩子們心無所懼地去爬山。）

☞ without 是介系詞，後面可以接名詞或動名詞，因此答案先寫 climbed the mountain 之後，再接 without fear 或 without being fearful 皆可。

Q9. I read my book.
（我讀我的書。）

I was peaceful.（用 in）
（我很平靜。）

⮡ I read my book in peace.
（我心平氣和地讀我的書。）

☞ 題目提示用 in，也許乍看之下會不曉得怎麼改寫，但就兩句意思來看，合併句應為「我平靜地在讀書。」所以「平靜地」除了 peacefully 之後，也可以用 in peace 來表示。

Q10. The family looked at the sick child.
（家人們看著這個生病的孩子。）

They were worried about him.（用 with）
（他們很擔心他。）

⮡ The family looked at the sick child with worry.
（家人們憂心忡忡地看著這個生病的孩子。）

Q11. You'll hear all the questions.

（你將會聽到所有的問題。）

Listen carefully.（用 to 合併）

（仔細聽。）

↳ Listen carefully <u>to all the questions</u>.

（仔細聽所有的問題。）

Q12. I took a trip.

（我去了一趟旅行。）

I went to Mexico.（用 to）

（我去了墨西哥。）

↳ I <u>took a trip to Mexico</u>.

（我去墨西哥旅行。）

Q13. We're going to the movies.

（我們要去看電影。）

Would you like to go together?（用 with）

（你要一起去嗎?）

↳ Would you <u>like to go to the movies with us</u>?

（你要和我們一起去看電影？）

Q14. The children were sleeping.

（孩子們正在睡。）

A loud thunderclap awakened them.（用 by）

（轟雷巨響吵醒了她們。）

↳ The children were awakened <u>by a loud thunderclap</u>.

（孩子們被轟雷巨響給吵醒了。）

Q15. The fox left its tracks in the mud.
（這隻狐狸在泥地上留下了足跡。）

The hunter followed the tracks.（用 by）
（獵人循著足跡。）

↳ The hunter followed the fox <u>by its tracks in the mud</u>.
（獵人沿著這隻狐狸在泥地上留下的足跡追捕牠。）

☞ 本題是考你用「by + 方法」來合併句子。答案也可以寫成 by the tracks it (had) lift in the mud。

句子合併

主題 29 | 形容詞片語合併

 解題焦點：

> 形容詞片語修飾名詞，置於名詞後面（後位修飾），可用來
> 表示：具有或帶著、穿戴、來源、作者、內容……等。

一、表具有或帶著

例 A pretty girl has big green eyes.

She sat beside me at the banquet.（用 with）

☞ A pretty girl **with big green eyes** sat beside me at the banquet.

二、表穿戴

例 The man wears a gray suit.

I know him.（用 in）

☞ I know the man **in a gray suit**.

三、表來源

例 The koalas come from Australia.

We saw them sleeping in the tree.（用 from）

☞ We saw the koalas **from Australia** sleeping in the tree.

四、表作者

例 Pat Conroy writes stories.

I have read many of them.（用 by）

☞ I have read many stories **by Pat Conroy**.

五、表內容

例 I'm looking for some books.

The books are about arts and crafts.

☞ I'm looking for some books **about arts and crafts**.

Part 1 · 單句寫作 ▼ 02 句子合併

217

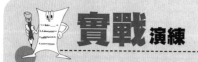

Q1. The boy has a skateboard.

He hurried down the street.（用 with）

↳ The boy _____ hurried down the street.

Q2. The man wears a gray suit.

I know him.（用 in）

↳ I know _____.

Q3. A pretty girl has big green eyes.

She sat beside me at the banquet.（用 with）

↳ A pretty girl _____ sat beside me at the banquet.

Q4. The koalas come from Australia.

We saw them sleeping in the tree.（用 from）

↳ We saw _____ sleeping in the tree.

Q5. The roses bear sharp thorns.

They hurt the gardener's finger.（用 with）

↳ The roses _____ hurt the gardener's finger.

Q6. Pat Conroy writes stories.

I have read many of them.（用 by）

↳ I have read many stories _____.

Q7. I'm looking for some books.

The books are about arts and crafts.

↳ I'm looking for some books _____.

Q8. James was absent from class.

What's his reason?（用 for）

↳ What's the reason _____?

Q9. Mary is wearing a new dress.

What's its price?（用 of）

↳ What's _____ Mary is wearing?

Q10. Walt was watching the movie.

He watched it with great interest.（用 in）

↳ Walt had a great interest _____.

Q11. These two cars are different.

I can't see the difference.（用 between）

↳ I can't see the difference _____.

Q12. Amanda is riding a bicycle.

She has never had the experience before.（用 of）

↳ Amanda has never had the experience _____.

Q13. I know little about business.

I need your advice.（用 on）

↳ I need your advice _____ (which I know little about).

Q14. We received an invitation.

We will go to Terry's birthday party. (用 to)

↳ We received an invitation _____.

Q15. Vincent has big feet.

Finding the right shoes is always a trouble to him.
(用 with)

↳ Vincent always has trouble with _____ for his
big feet.

示範 解答
中英文對照大解析

Q1. The boy has a skateboard.
(男孩有一個滑板。)

He hurried down the street. (用 with)
(他沿著這條街呼嘯而過。)

↳ The boy <u>with a skateboard</u> hurried down the street.
(溜著滑板的男孩沿著這條街呼嘯而過。)

Q2. The man wears a gray suit.
(男子穿著一件灰色西裝。)

I know him. (用 in)
(我認識他。)

↳ I know <u>the man in a gray suit</u>.
(我認識穿著灰色西裝的那名男子。)

Q3. A pretty girl has big green eyes.
（有個女孩有綠色的大眼睛。）

She sat beside me at the banquet.（用 with）
（在吃宴席中她坐在我身旁。）

↳ A pretty girl **with big green eyes** sat beside me at the banquet.
（在宴席中一個有著綠色大眼睛的漂亮女孩坐在我身旁。）

Q4. The koalas come from Australia.
（無尾熊來自澳洲。）

We saw them sleeping in the tree.（用 from）
（我們看見牠們在樹上睡覺。）

↳ We saw **the koalas from Australia** sleeping in the tree.
（我們看見來自澳洲的無尾熊在樹上睡覺。）

Q5. The roses bear sharp thorns.
（玫瑰有著尖銳的刺。）

They hurt the gardener's finger.（用 with）
（它們傷了園丁的手指。）

↳ The roses **with sharp thorns** hurt the gardener's finger.
（有著尖刺的玫瑰傷了園丁的手指。）

Q6. Pat Conroy writes stories.
（派特·康洛伊撰寫故事。）

I have read many of them.（用 by）
（我讀過其中很多故事。）

↳ I have read many stories **by Pat Conroy**.
（我讀過很多派特·康洛伊所寫的故事。）

Q7. I'm looking for some books.

（我在找一些書。）

The books are about arts and crafts.

（這些書關於藝術與工藝。）

➥ I'm looking for some books <u>about arts and crafts</u>.

（我正在找一些關於藝術與工藝的書。）

Q8. James was absent from class.

（詹姆沒有去上課。）

What's his reason?（用 for）

（他的理由是什麼？）

➥ What's the reason <u>for James' absence from class?</u>

（詹姆沒有去上課的理由是什麼？）

☞ 「reason for + 名詞」為常見固定用法，這裡要表達的是「沒有去上課的
理由」，因此要將形容詞 absent 改為名詞 absence，而原本的 "James
was" 可以改成所有格 James'，形成 James' absence 放在介系詞 for 後面。

Q9. Mary is wearing a new dress.

（瑪莉穿著一件新的洋裝。）

What's its price?（用 of）

（它的價綫是多少？）

➥ What's the price of <u>the new dress</u> Mary is wearing?

（瑪莉身上穿的那件新洋裝要多少錢？）

☞ 空格前是介系詞 of，後面是個缺了受詞的句子，顯然是個形容詞子句，
應填入名詞與受格關係代名詞（可省略），所以只有 the new dress 是最
正確的答案。但要注意的是，這裡 new dress 前面要用 the 而不能用 a。

Q10. Walt was watching the movie.

（華特正在看電影。）

He watched it with great interest.（用 in）

（他興致勃勃地看著。）

➥ Walt had a great interest <u>in watching the movie</u>.

（華特興致勃勃地看著這部電影。）

Q11. These two cars are different.

（這兩部車不一樣。）

I can't see the difference.（用 between）

（我看不出差異之處。）

↪ I can't see the difference <u>between these two cars</u>.

（我看不出這兩部車的差異之處。）

Q12. Amanda is riding a bicycle.

（阿曼達正在騎單車。）

She has never had the experience before.（用 of）

（她以前沒有過這樣的經驗。）

↪ Amanda has never had the experience <u>of riding a bicycle</u>.

（阿曼達從未有過騎單車的經驗。）

Q13. I know little about business.

（我不對於做生意一竅不通。）

I need your advice.（用 on）

（我需要你的建議。）

↪ I need your advice <u>on business</u> (which I know little about).

（我需要你給些（我一竅不通的）做生意方面的建議。）

Q14. We received an invitation.

（我們收到邀請函了。）

We will go to Terry's birthday party. （用 to）

（我們會去泰瑞的生日派對。）

↪ We received an invitation <u>to Terry's birthday party</u>.

（我們收到泰瑞生日派對的邀請函。）

Q15. Vincent has big feet

（文生有雙大腳丫。）

Finding the right shoes is always a trouble to him.（用 with）
（找到合腳的鞋對他來說很難。）

↳ Vincent always has trouble with <u>finding the right shoes for his big feet</u>.

（文生總是很難找到適合他那雙大腳丫的鞋子。）

☞ 「trouble with +（動）名詞」為常見固定用法，這裡要表達的是「找到他合適鞋子的麻煩或問題」，所以 with 後面放動名詞片語 "finding the right shoes..." 即可。

句子合併

句 子 合 併

主題 30

動詞合併：

不定詞型

Focus 解題焦點：

> 大部分的動詞合併題型都是將其中一個動詞改成不定詞或動
> 名詞的形式。這裡先探討不定詞的句型，可分為兩大類：
> 一、當動詞的受詞／二、當受詞補語。

一、當動詞的受詞

S+<u>V</u>（+not）<u>+to-V</u>

例 I go straight home after work.

I prefer to do so

☞ I <u>prefer to go straight home</u> after work.

二、當受詞補語

S+<u>V+O</u>（+not）<u>+to-V</u>

例 I take the medicine.

The doctor asked me to do so.

☞ The doctor <u>asked me to take the medicine</u>.

重點文法 快速查!!

「動詞合併：不定詞型」的兩種題型

類型		句型	這類動詞
當動詞的受詞	肯定	S + V + to-V	aim, fall, decide, prefer, like, want, try, learn, ...
	否定	S + V + not + to-V	
當受詞補語	肯定	S + V + O + to-V	tell, call, need, ask, like, want, hire, invite, teach, promise, tell, know...
	否定	S + V + O + not + to-V	

GRAMMAR

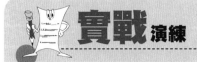

Q1. I go straight home after work.

I prefer to do so.

↳ I prefer _____.

Q2. I take the medicine.

The doctor asked me to do so.

↳ The doctor asked me _____.

Q3. We should stay in the room.

Mr. White would like us to do so.

↳ Mr. White would like us _____.

Q4. I will wait for him if he is late.

He wants me to do so.

↳ He wants me _____ if he is late.

Q5. She hired three workers.

The workers harvest crops.（用 to-V 合併）

↳ She hired three workers _____.

Q6. We are invited.

We will take part in their party.

↳ We are invited _____.

Q7. I had to shout.

I wanted to be heard among the noisy crowd.

⤷ I had to shout _____.

Q8. Try to do something.

Do not be late next time.

⤷ Try not _____.

Q9. We should learn something.

Do not waste water.

⤷ We should learn _____.

Q10. The children are taught something.

They should not play with fire.

⤷ The children are taught _____.

Q11. The husband promised his wife something.

He would never drink alcohol again.（用不定詞 to-V）

⤷ The husband promised his wife _____.

Q12. Where will he go for the holiday?

He has not decided yet.（用不定詞 to-V）

⤷ He has not decided _____.

Q13. Can you tell us something?

How can we get there?（用不定詞 to-V）

⤷ Can you tell us _____?

Q14. I haven't been told something.

Whom should I inform?（用不定詞 to-V）

⮡ I haven't been told _____.

Q15. Do you know something?

Where can I get an application form?

⮡ Do you know _____?

示範 解答   中英文對照大解析

Q1. I go straight home after work.
（我下班後直接回家。）

I prefer to do so.
（我比較喜歡這樣做。）

⮡ I prefer to go straight home after work.
（我比較喜歡下班後直接回家。）

Q2. I take the medicine.
（我吃藥。）

The doctor asked me to do so.
（醫生要我這樣做。）

⮡ The doctor asked me to take the medicine.
（醫生要求我吃藥。）

Q3. We should stay in the room.
（我們應該待在房間裡。）

Mr. White would like us to do so.
（懷特先生希望我們這樣做。）

↳ Mr. White would like us <u>to stay in the room</u>.
（懷特先生希望我們待在房間裡。）

Q4. I will wait for him if he is late.
（如果他晚到的話我會等他。）

He wants me to do so.
（他想要我這樣做。）

↳ He wants me <u>to wait for him</u> if he is late.
（如果他晚到的話，他想要我等他。）

Q5. She hired three workers.
（她雇用了三名工人·）

The workers harvest crops.（用 to-V 合併）
（這些工人將作物收成了。）

↳ She hired three workers <u>to harvest crops</u>.
（她雇用三名工人來收成作物。）

Q6. We are invited.
（我們被邀請了。）

We will take part in their party.
（我們將參加他們的宴會。）

↳ We are invited <u>to take part in their party</u>.
（我們受邀參加他們的宴會。）

Q7. I had to shout.
（我得大叫。）

I wanted to be heard among the noisy crowd.
（我想在吵雜的人群中讓人聽到我的聲音。）

↳ I had to shout <u>to be heard among the noisy crowd</u>.
（我得大叫才能在吵雜的人群中讓人聽到我的聲音。）

Q8. Try to do something.
（試著去做某事。）

Do not be late next time.
（下次不要遲到。）

↳ Try not <u>to be late next time</u>.
（試著下次不要遲到。）

Q9. We should learn something.
（我們應該學習一件事。）

Do not waste water.
（不要浪費水。）

↳ We should learn <u>not to waste water</u>.
（我們應該學著不浪費水。）

☞ 空格要填入的是 learn 的受詞，也就是「不浪費水」這件事，所以可以用否定的不定詞（to-V）來表示，也就是 not to waste water。

Q10. The children are taught something.
（孩子們被教導某件事。）

They should not play with fire.
（他們不該玩火。）

↳ The children are taught <u>not to play with fire</u>.
（孩子們被教導不要玩火。）

☞ 空格前是被動式的動詞 are taught（被教導），因此應填入不定詞，而且是否定的不定詞：not to play...。原本的肯定句 teach sb. to do sth.（教某人做某事）改為被動語態是 "sb. be taught to do sth."。

Q11. The husband promised his wife something.
（丈夫答應了他的妻子某件事。）

He would never drink alcohol again.（用不定詞 to-V）
（他不會再喝酒了。）

↳ The husband promised his wife <u>never to drink alcohol again</u>.
（丈夫答應他的妻子絕不會再喝酒了。）

Q12. Where will he go for the holiday?
（他要去哪裡度假？）

He has not decided yet.（用不定詞 to-V）
（他還沒決定。）

↳ He has not decided <u>where to go for the holiday</u>.
（他還沒決定去哪裡度假。）

☞ 空格要填入的是 decide 的受詞，也就是「去哪裡度假」這件事，所以可以用「疑問詞 + 不定詞」（= 名詞片語）來表示，也就是 where to go for the holiday。

Q13. Can you tell us something?
（你可以告訴我們某件事嗎？）

How can we get there?（用不定詞 to-V）
（我們要怎麼去那裡？）

↳ Can you tell us <u>how to get there</u>?
（你可以告訴我們要怎麼去那裡嗎？）

Q14. I haven't been told something.
（我還沒被告知某事。）

Whom should I inform?（用不定詞 to-V）
（我應該通知誰？）

↳ I haven't been told <u>whom to inform</u>.
（我還沒被告知要通知誰。）

Q15. Do you know something?

（你知道某事嗎？）

Where can I get an application form?

（我可以在哪裡拿到申請表？）

↪ Do you know **where to get an application form**?

（你知道要去哪裡拿申清表嗎？）

☞ 空格要填入的是 know 的受詞，也就是「去哪裡拿申請表」這件事，所以可以用「疑問詞 + 不定詞」（= 名詞片語）來表示，也就是 where to get an application form。另外，由於本題沒有提示用不定詞合併，因此 where to get an application form 也可以改為，或還原為 "where I can get an application form"。

句子合併

主題 **31** | 動詞合併：
原形動詞、動名詞或分詞型

Focus 解題焦點：

動詞合併除了不定詞形式的考題之外，還有一些特定動詞或
助動詞後面接原形動詞、動名詞或現在／過去分詞的考題類
型。

一、後接原形動詞

（助）V + 原形動詞

例 Find the documents

You had better do it quickly.

☞ You **had better find the documents quickly**.

二、後接動名詞

V + 動名詞

例 He has painted the wall

He isn't painting now.

☞ He has **finished painting the wall**.

三、後接（受詞後再接）分詞

V + O + 分詞

例 When he woke up, he found something.

He was badly injured.

☞ When he woke up, he **found himself badly injured**.

Part 1 · 單句寫作 ▶▶ **02** 句子合併

233

重點文法 快速查!!

特定（助）動詞後面接原形動詞或分詞	
後接原形動詞	help（幫）、had better（最好）、could not but（不得不）
後接動名詞	finish（完成）、practice（練習）、mind（介意）、enjoyed（享受）、take one's time（慢慢來，悠哉）、feel like（想要）、could not help（不禁）
後接（受詞後再接）現在／過去分詞	find（發現）、leave（留下）、keep（保持）

實戰演練

考驗你的合併能力！

Q1. Sam's father grows flowers.

Sam helps his father after school.

↳ Sam _____ after school.

Q2. When he woke up, he found something.

He was badly injured.

↳ When he woke up, he found _____.

Q3 . Find the documents.

You'd better do it quickly.

↳ You'd better _____ quickly.

Q4. It's dangerous to play balls in the street.

You'd better not do so.

↳ You'd better not _____.

Q5. We watched the movie.

We enjoyed it.

↳ We enjoyed _____.

Q6. Why don't you have some tea?

Take your time.

↳ Why don't you take your time _____.

Q7. He has painted the wall.

He isn't painting now.

↳ He has finished _____.

Q8. Bill is singing.

He started practicing from noon.

↳ Bill _____ since noon.

Q9. I will open the window.

Do you mind it?

↳ Do you mind _____?

Q10. She is supposed to prepare dinner.

She doesn't feel like doing it.

↳ She doesn't feel like _____.

Q11. He admitted that it was his fault.

He didn't want to but had to do so.

↳ He couldn't help but _____.

Q12. Martha screamed while seeing a rat.

She was unable to control herself not to scream.

↳ Martha couldn't help _____.

Q13. They left their dog at home.

They didn't want to but had to do so.

↳ They could not choose but _____.

Q14. He went shopping with his girlfriend.

He didn't want to but had to go.

↳ He could but _____.

Q15. The puppy was very cute.

I was unable to control myself not to love her.

↳ The puppy was so cute that I could not help _____.

示範 解答

Q1. Sam's father grows flowers.
（山姆的爸爸種花。）

Sam helps his father after school.
（山姆在放學後幫他爸爸的忙。）

↪ Sam <u>helps his father (to) grow flowers</u> after school.
（山姆在放學後幫他爸爸種花。）

☞ 本題屬於「後接受詞後再接原形動詞」的題型，除了 help 這個動詞之外，主要還有用於「S +V+O+OC」句型的「感官動詞」，像是 "see sb. do sth."（看見某人在做某事）的例子。因此本題合併句中的第二個動作（種花）可以用原形動詞 grow 或不定詞 to grow。

Q2. When he woke up, he found something.
（當他醒來時，他發現了某事。）

He was badly injured.
（他傷得很重。）

↪ When he woke up, he found <u>himself (to be) badly injured</u>
（當他醒來時，他發現自己傷得很重。）

Q3. Find the documents.
（找文件。）

You'd better do it quickly.
（你最好趕快做這件事。）

↪ You'd better <u>find the documents</u> quickly.
（你最好趕快找到那些文件。）

☞ had better（最好）可以和代名詞縮寫成「'd better」，一般視為「助動詞」，因此後面一定要接原形動詞，與 had 是過去式沒有任何關係喔！

Q4. It's dangerous to play balls in the street
（在街上玩球很危險。）

You'd better not do so
（你們最好不要這樣做。）

↳ You'd better not play balls in the street.
（你們最好不要在街上玩球。）

Q5. We watched the movie.
（我們看了這部電影·）

We enjoyed it.
（我們很喜歡它。）

↳ We enjoyed watching the movie.
（我們很開心地看了這部電影。）

Q6. Why don't you have some tea?
（你何不喝點茶呢？）

Take your time.
（慢慢來。）

↳ Why don't you take your time having some tea?
（你何不悠哉地喝點茶呢？）

☞ "take (one's) time + Ving" 的用法，相當於 "spend time + Ving"，其實 Ving 前面省略了介系詞 in，因此這裡的 Ving 是「動名詞」，不是「現在分詞」。

Q7. He has painted the wall.
（他漆了牆壁。）

He isn't painting now.
（他現在沒在漆油漆。）

↳ He has finished painting the wall.
（他已經把牆壁漆好了。）

Q8. Bill is singing
（比爾正在唱歌。）

He started practicing from noon.
（他從中午開始練習。）

↳ Bill <u>has been practicing singing</u> since noon.
（比爾從中午開始就一直練習唱歌。）

Q9. I will open the window.
（我會打開窗戶。）

Do you mind?
（你介意嗎？）

↳ Do you mind <u>my opening the window</u>?
（你介意我把窗戶打開嗎？）

☞ 本來 mind 後面就是得接動名詞（Ving）當受詞，但合併句要表達的是「介意我把窗戶打開」，所以 opening 前面要再加所有格 my，語意會比較清楚，如果沒有 my 的話，會變成好像要對方去開窗戶的意思。

Q10. She is supposed to prepare dinner.
（她應該要準備晚餐。）

She doesn't feel like doing it tonight.
（她今晚不想做這件事。）

↳ She doesn't feel like <u>preparing dinner tonight</u>.
（她今晚不想準備晚餐。）

Q11. He admitted that it was his fault.
（他承認那是他的錯。）

He didn't want to but had to do so.
（他並不想但還是得這麼做。）

↳ He couldn't help but <u>admit that it was his fault</u>.
（他不得不去承認過那是他的過錯。）

☞ can't/couldn't help but 等同於 can't/couldn't but，後面都是接原形動詞。

Q12. Martha screamed while seeing a rat.

（瑪莎一見到老鼠就尖叫。）

She was unable to control herself not to scream.

（她無法控制自己不尖叫。）

↳ Martha couldn't help <u>screaming while seeing a rat</u>.

（瑪莎一看到老鼠就不自禁地尖叫。）

☞ 「can't/couldn't (help) but + V」等同於 can't/couldn't help + Ving」，都是「不得不…，必須…」的意思。這往往是學習者容易混淆的句型，應多加注意！

Q13. They left their dog at home.

（他們把狗留在家裡。）

They didn't want to but had to do so.

（他們不想但還是必須這麼做。）

↳ They could not choose but <u>leave their dog at home</u>.

（他們不得不把狗留在家裡。）

Q14. He went shopping with his girlfriend.

（他和他的女朋友去逛街購物。）

He didn't want to but had to go.

（他並不想但還是得去。）

↳ He could but <u>go shopping with his girlfriend</u>.

（他不得不陪他女朋友去逛街購物。）

Q15. The puppy was very cute.

（小狗很可愛。）

I was unable to control myself not to love her.

（我無法克制自己不去喜歡牠。）

↳ The puppy was so cute that I could not help <u>loving her</u>.

（小狗太可愛了，讓我不自禁地愛上牠。）

Focus 解題焦點：

> 使役動詞接受詞之後，後面一定要再接原形動詞，感官動詞
> 也是，後面接受詞之後，可以接原形動詞，強調動作的事
> 實，或接現在分詞，強調動作的正在進行。

一、使役動詞

使役動詞 + 受詞 + 原形動詞

例 My parents don't let me do something.

I can't keep a pet.

☞ My parents don't <u>let me keep</u> a pet.

二、感官動詞

感官動詞 + 受詞 + 原形動詞／現在分詞

例 I smelt something.

The bread was burning.

☞ I <u>smelt the bread burning</u>.

三、其他用於此句型的動詞

及物動詞 + 受詞 + （現在／過去）分詞

例 I found a rat.

It ran into your room.

☞ I <u>found a rat run into your room</u>.

※ 以上這類動詞都屬於「不完全及物動詞」，後面接受詞還不夠，
必須再接受詞補語，語意才算完整。基本上，受詞補語屬於形容
詞的詞性，可能是不定詞、現在分詞、過去分詞或一般形容詞，
但如果是原形動詞的話，可視為「沒有 to」的不定詞。

重點文法　快速查!!

此類動詞的句型一覽表

	句型
使役動詞	make + O + 原形動詞 = be made to + 原形動詞
	have + O + 原形動詞
	let + O + 原形動詞
感官動詞	see + O + 原形動詞／現在分詞 = be seen to + 原形動詞
	hear + O + 原形動詞／現在分詞 = be heard to + 原形動詞
	notice + O + 原形動詞／現在分詞
	smell + O + 原形動詞／現在分詞
	watch + O + 原形動詞／現在分詞
	listen to + O + 原形動詞／現在分詞
其他動詞	find + O + 現在／過去分詞 = be found to-V / P.P.
	leave + O + 現在／過去分詞 = be left to-V / P.P.

實戰演練　考驗你的合併能力！

Q1. He made his sons do something.

They cleaned up the room.

↳ He made his sons ＿＿＿＿＿＿＿＿＿＿＿.

Q2. The teacher had the students do something.

They must read an English novel in summer vacation.

↳ The teacher had the students ＿＿＿＿＿＿＿＿＿＿＿.

Q3. My parents don't let me do something.

I can't keep a pet.

↳ My parents don't let me _____ .

Q4. He was made to do something.

He worked overtime.

↳ He was made _____ .

Q5. I saw him yesterday.

He worked in the garden.

↳ J saw him _____ yesterday.

Q6. They found their son.

He slept on the sofa

↳ They found their son _____ .

Q7. Did you notice something?

Did anyone leave the house?

↳ Did you notice _____ ?

Q8. I smelt something.

The bread was burning.

↳ I smelt _____ .

Q9. Our father sings while taking a bath.

We often hear him do so.

↳ We often hear my father _____ .

Q10. They watched the football players.

The football players practiced.

⤷   They watched _____.

Q11. You will play the drum tomorrow.

We will listen to it.

⤷   We will listen to you _____ tomorrow.

Q12. The man was knocked down by the car.

I saw it happened.

⤷   I saw the man _____.

Q13. Tom was seen to do something.

He roamed in the park after school.

⤷   Tom was seen _____.

Q14. The boy stayed in the living room.

He was seen to do so.

⤷   The boy was seen _____.

Q15. People last saw the missing boy in the park.

He was playing with other kids.

⤷   The missing boy was last seen _____ in the park.

 解答

Q1. He made his sons do something.
（他叫他兒子們做點事。）

They cleaned up the room
（他們打掃了房間。）

↳ He made his sons <u>clean up the room</u>.
（他叫他兒子們去打掃房間。）

Q2. The teacher had the students do something.
（老師叫學生們去做某事。）

They must read an English novel in summer vacation.
（他們必須在暑假時讀一本英文小說。）

↳ The teacher had the students <u>read an English novel in summer vacation</u>.
（老師要學生們在暑假時讀一本英文小說。）

Q3. My parents don't let me do something.
（我的父母不讓我做某事。）

I can't keep a pet.
（我不能養寵物。）

↳ My parents don't let me <u>keep a pet</u>.
（我的父母不讓我養寵物。）

Q4. He was made to do something
（他被叫去做某事。）

He worked overtime.
（他加班工作。）

↳ He was made <u>to work overtime</u>.
（他被叫去加班工作。）

245

Q5. I saw him yesterday.
（我昨天看到他。）

He worked in the garden.
（他在花園裡工作。）

⮑ I saw him <u>work in the garden</u> yesterday.
（我昨天看到他在花園裡工作。）

☞ 空格前有感官動詞 saw，應直接聯想到「感官動詞 + O + V/Ving」的句型，所以答案可以寫 work/working in the garden。

Q6. They found their son.
（他們發現了他們的兒子。）

He slept on the sofa.
（他睡在沙發上。）

⮑ They found their son <u>sleeping on the sofa</u>.
（他們發現他們的兒子睡在沙發上。）

☞ 空格前有動詞 found（find 的過去式），應直接聯想到「S + V + O + OC」的句型，這裡的OC只能用現在分詞，因此只要將題目中的 slept 改成 sleeping 即可。

Q7. Did you notice something?
（你有注意到某事嗎？）

Did anyone leave the house?
（有人離開房子嗎？）

⮑ Did you notice <u>anyone leaving the house</u>?
（你注意到有任何人離開房子嗎？）

Q8. I smelt something
（我聞到某種味道。）

The bread was burning.
（麵包燒焦了。）

⮑ I smelt <u>the bread burning</u>.
（我聞到麵包燒焦的味道。）

Q9. Our father sings while taking a bath.
（我們的父親在洗澡時候唱歌。）

We often hear him do so.
（我們常聽到他這麼做。）

↳ We often hear our father <u>sing while taking a bath</u>.
（我們經常聽到父親在洗澡的時唱歌。）

☞ 就「感官動詞 + O + V/Ving」的句型來說，受詞後面可以接 V 或 Ving，
但本題關鍵字在 often（經常，表示一個常態而非偶發事件，也就是單純
陳述一件事情，因此不宜用 singing。

Q10. They watched the football players.
（他們看著足球選手們。）

The football players practiced.
（足球選們做練習。）

↳ They watched <u>the football players practice / practicing</u>.
（他們看著足球選手們做練習。）

Q11. You will play the drum tomorrow.
（你明天將打鼓。）

We will listen to it.
（我們會聆聽。）

↳ We will listen to you <u>play the drum</u> tomorrow.
（我們明天會聆聽你打鼓。）

Q12. The man was knocked down by the car.
（該名男子被車撞倒了。）

I saw it happened.
（我看到這件事的發生。）

↳ I saw the man <u>(being) knocked down by the car</u>.
（我看見該名男子被車撞倒了。）

Q13. Tom was seen to do something.
（湯姆被人看到做了某事。）

He roamed in the park after school.
（他放學後在公園遊蕩。）

↳ Tom was seen <u>to roam in the park after school.</u>
（湯姆被人看到放學後在公園遊蕩。）

- -

Q14. The boy stayed in the living room.
（男孩待在客廳裡。）

He was told to do so.
（他被告知要這麼做。）

↳ The boy was told <u>to stay in the living room.</u>
（男孩被告知要待在客廳裡。）

- -

Q15. People last saw the missing boy in the park.
（有人在公園裡最後一次見到這名失蹤的男孩。）

He was playing with other kids.
（他正在和其他小朋友玩。）

↳ The missing boy was last seen <u>playing with other kids</u> in the park.
（這名失蹤的男孩最後被人看到是在公園裡和其他小朋友玩。）

- -

句子合併 | 比較句型：

主題 **33** | 原級

Focus 解題焦點：

「比較句型」中的「原級比較」廣泛運用了 as... as 的片語。原級比較的合併句型又分為 be 動詞型和一般動詞型。

一、be 動詞型
- S + be + as + Adj + as...

例 You are twenty years old.

I am twenty years old, too.

☞ I <u>am as old as</u> you.

- S + be + 倍數詞 + as + Adj + as...

例 You are 180cm tall.

I am 90cm tall.

☞ I <u>am half as tall as</u> you.

二、一般動詞型
- S + V + as + many/much + N + as...

例 I have one hundred dollars.

You have one hundred dollars, too.

☞ You <u>have as much</u> money <u>as</u> I (do).

- S + V + as + Adv + as...

例 All the boys on the team play soccer well.

Donald plays the best.

☞ No other boy on the team <u>plays</u> soccer <u>as well as</u> Donald (does).

- S + V + 倍數詞 + as + Adj + N + as...

例 I have ten pairs of shoes.

You have five pairs of shoes.

☞ I <u>have twice as</u> many shoes <u>as</u> you (do).

Part 1 · 單句寫作 ▶▼ 02 句子合併

 快速查!!

	常用的倍數詞
四分之一	quarter
一半	half
相等	as... as... / once
兩倍	twice, double
三倍	triple, three times, threefold
四倍	four times, fourfold
五倍	five times, fivefold
六倍	six times, sixfold
七倍	seven times, sevenfold
八倍	eight times, eightfold
九倍	nine times, ninefold
十倍	ten times, tenfold
十一倍	eleven times, elevenfold
十二倍	twelve times
十三倍	thirteen times
十四倍	fourteen times
十五倍	fifteen times
十六倍	sixteen times
十七倍	seventeen times
十八倍	eighteen times
十九倍	nineteen times
二十倍	twenty times
三十倍	thirty times
四十倍	forty times
五十倍	fifty times
六十倍	sixty times
七十倍	seventy times
八十倍	eighty times
九十倍	ninety times
一百倍	one hundred times

GRAMMAR

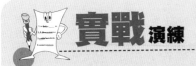

Q1. Victoria is 160cm tall.

Gloria is 160cm tall, too.

↳ Victoria is as/so _____ .

Q2. The temperature is high today. It is 36°C.

It was 36°C yesterday, too.

↳ Today's temperature is _____ yesterday's.

Q3. Kyle has three children.

Ron has three children, too.

↳ Kyle has _____ as Ron.

Q4. Mandy spent one hour on the test.

Sandy also spent one hour on the test.

↳ Sandy spent _____ as Mandy does.

Q5. She is tall.

Her sister is even taller.

↳ She is _____ as her sister.

Q6. Paul runs fast.

Ted runs even faster.

↳ Paul runs _____ as Ted.

Q7. Dolphins are smart animals.

Whales are smarter than dolphins.

↳ Dolphins are _____ as whales.

Q8. My father works for 8 hours a day.

He worked for 14 hours a day before.

↳ My father does not work for _____ as he did before.

Q9. This baby drinks little milk.

Other babies drink more than she (does).

↳ This baby doesn't drink _____ as others do.

Q10. He weighs 90kg.

Everyone in his family weighs less than 90kg.

↳ No one in his family _____ as he.

Q11. All the boys on the team plays soccer well.

Donald plays the best.

↳ No other boy on the team _____ as Donald.

Q12. This river is 300 km long.

That river is 150 km long.

↳ This river is _____ as that one.

Q13. She bought 6 dresses.

I bought 3 dresses.

↳ I bought _____ as she (did).

Q14. They own 10 cars.

We own 50 cars.

↳ We own _____ as they do.

Q15. You earn 120 thousand.

I only earn 30 thousand.

↳ You earn _____ as I do.

示範 解答

中英文對照大解析

Q1. Victoria is 160cm tall.
（維多利亞 160 公分高。）

Gloria is 160cm tall, too.
（葛莉雅也是 160 公分高。）

↳ Victoria is as/so <u>tall as Gloria</u>.
（維多利亞和葛莉雅一樣高。）

Q2. The temperature is high today. It is 36℃.
（今天氣溫很高。是攝氏 36 度。）

It was 36C yesterday, too.
（昨天也是攝氏 36 度。）

↳ Today's temperature is <u>as/so high as</u> yesterday's.
（今天溫度和昨天一樣高。）

Q3. Kyle has three children.
（凱爾有三個孩子。）

Ron has three children, too.
（羅恩也有三個孩子。）

↳ Kyle has <u>as many children</u> as Ron.
（凱爾的孩子和羅恩的一樣多。）

Q4. Mandy spent one hour on the test.
（蔓蒂花一個小時做這項測驗。）

Sandy also spent one hour on the test.
（珊蒂也花一個小時做這項測驗。）

↳ Sandy spent <u>as much time on the test</u> as Mandy does.
（珊蒂花了和蔓蒂一樣多的時間在做這項測驗。）

Q5. She is tall.
（她個子高。）

Her sister is even taller.
（她姐姐個子更高。）

↳ She is <u>not as/so tall</u> as her sister.
（她沒有她姐姐高。）

Q6. Paul runs fast.
（保羅跑得快。）

Ted runs even faster.
（泰德跑更得快。）

↳ Paul runs <u>not as/so fast as</u> Ted.
（保羅跑得沒有泰德快。）

Q7. Dolphins are smart animals.
（海豚是聰明的動物。）

Whales are smarter than dolphins.
（鯨魚比海豚聰明。）

↳ Dolphins are <u>not as smart</u> as whales.
（海豚沒有鯨魚聰明。）

Q8. My father works for 8 hours a day.
（我父親一天工作八個小時。）

He worked for 14 hours a day before.
（他以前一天工作四小時。）

↳ My father does not work for <u>as many hours</u> as he did before.
（我父親現在工作的時數沒有以前那麼多。）

Q9. This baby drinks little milk.
（這嬰兒奶喝得很少。）

Other babies drink more than she (does).
（其他嬰兒喝得比她多。）

↳ This baby doesn't drink <u>as much milk</u> as others do.
（這嬰兒不像其他嬰兒一樣喝那麼多奶。）

☞ milk 是不可數名詞，要用much 或 little 來修飾。

Q10. He weighs 90kg.
（他體重 90 公斤。）

Everyone in his family weighs less than 90kg.
（他家裡每個人體重都不到 90 公斤。）

↳ No one in his family <u>weighs as much</u> as he.
（他家裡沒有人體重和他一樣那麼重。）

☞ 從題目第二句的 weighs less 可推知，要表達「（某人）體重很重」是「weigh much」，所以「（體重）沒有像某人一樣重」是 not weigh as much as sb.。

Q11. All the boys on the team plays soccer well.

（隊上的男生足球都踢得不錯。）

Donald plays the best.

（杜南德踢得最好。）

↳ No other boy on the team **plays soccer as well** as Donald.

（隊上的男生沒有人足球踢得像杜南德一樣好。）

Q12. This river is 300 km long.

（這條河 300 公里長。）

That river is 150 km long.

（那條河 150 公里長。）

↳ This river is **twice as long** as that one.

（這條河是那條河的兩倍長。）

☞ 空格後面是 as that one，而 one 就是指 river，顯然本題要考的是倍數詞搭配原級比較的用法：「A 是 B 的兩倍…（長／寬／高／厚…等）」可以用「A + be動詞 + twice/double + as + long/wide/high/thick... + as」的句型來表達。另外，「兩倍」通常不用 two times 來表達。

Q13. She bought 6 dresses.

（她買了六件洋裝。）

I bought 3 dresses.

（我買了三件洋裝。）

↳ I bought **half as many dresses** as she (did).

（我買的洋裝件數是她的一半。）

Q14. They own 10 cars.

（他們有 10 部車。）

We own 50 cars.

（我們有 50 部車。）

↳ We own **5 times as many cars as** they do.

（我們擁有的車子數量是他們的五倍。）

Q15. You earn 120 thousand.

（你賺十二萬。）

I only earn 30 thousand.

（我只賺三萬。）

↳ You earn <u>four times as much money</u> as I do.

（你賺的錢是我的四倍。）

☞ 空格後面是 as I do，顯然本題要考的是倍數詞搭配原級比較的用法：「A 賺的錢是 B 的幾倍」可以用「A + earn + 倍數詞 + as much money as + B (do/does)」的句型來表達。

解題焦點：

比較級的合併句型可分為四種：
一、具體的數量比較／二、抽象程度的比較
三、以比較級表達最高級／四、兩者之間的比較

一、具體的數量比較級

可具體比較數量的包括身高、體重、年齡…等，具體比較數量時，可以寫出用來做比較的數量和名詞，而在不需寫明差異程度時可予以省略。

例 Jean is twenty-four years old.

Darcy is twenty-six years old.

☞ Jean is (two years old) younger than Darcy.

二、抽象程度的比較

難易的程度、有趣或枯燥的、英俊的或美貌的…等形容詞，無法以具體數字來修飾比較，因此比較級前面常加上 much、even…等副詞來表達程度上的差異。

例 Novels are interesting.

Comic books are even more interesting.

☞ Novels are less interesting than comic books.

三、以比較級表達最高級

利用比較級來表達最高級的句型用法，請參見句型改寫主題 6。

例 They all have pretty faces.

Elizabeth has the prettiest face.

☞ None of them has a prettier face than Elizabeth (does).

四、兩者之間的比較

要表達「兩者當中較⋯的」時，雖然看似比較級的形式，因為有「在兩者當中」（of the two），比較級前面仍須加上冠詞 the。

例 Jeff is handsome.

William is more handsome than Jeff.

☞ William is the more handsome of the two.

重點文法 快速查!!

形容詞比較級的變化法則

形容詞音節	比較級如何變化	字尾	例子
單音節或雙音節	字尾-er	一般情況	small → smaller
		字尾有 e，直接加 r	pale → paler
		字尾子音+y，去 y 加 ier	pretty → prettier
		單音節短母音，重複子音字尾+er	thin → thinner
三個音節以上	more + 形容詞原級		beautiful → more beautiful

常用的不規則變化形容詞

原級	比較級	最高級
good	better	the best
bad	worse	the worst
much	more	the most
many	more	the most
little	less	the least

259

Q1. Serena is 20 years old.

Catherine is 23 years old.

↳ Catherine is _____ than Serena.

Q2. The television is 7,000 dollars.

The stereo is 17,000 dollars.

↳ The stereo is _____ than the television.

Q3. My weight is 55 kg.

John's weight is 65 kg.

↳ John is _____ than I am.

Q4. Speaking English is easy.

Speaking Spanish is not so easy.

↳ Speaking English is easier _____.

Q5. Swimming is hard to learn.

Surfing is even hard to learn.

↳ Surfing is harder _____.

Q6. Ian teaches six classes.

Yvonne teaches four classes.

↳ Yvonne teaches _____ than Ian does.

Q7. The boys behaved well yesterday.

The girls behaved not so well.

↳ _____ than the boys did yesterday.

Q8. John is very bright.

None of us is as bright as he.

↳ _____ than all of us.

Q9. Everyone has a good idea.

Kevin has the best idea.

↳ No one _____ than Kevin.

Q10. Storybooks are interesting.

Comic books are even more interesting.

↳ Storybooks are _____ than comic books.

Q11. All the men here are rich.

Mr. Katz is the richest.

↳ All the men _____ than Mr. Katz here.

Q12. Each lake in Canada is large.

Great Bear is the largest one.

↳ In Canada, each lake _____ than Great Bear.

Q13. Hank is handsome.

Leo is more handsome than Hank.

↳ Leo is _____ of the two.

Q14. Kenting is a nice place.

Taroko is nicer than Kenting.

↳ Taroko is _____ of the two.

Q15. Rice is delicious.

Pasta is not as delicious as rice.

↳ Pasta is _____ of the two.

示範 解答   中英文對照大解析

Q1. Serena is 20 years old.
（西莉娜 20 歲。）

Catherine is 23 years old.
（凱薩琳 23 歲。）

↳ Catherine is (three years) older than Serena.
（凱薩琳年紀比西莉娜大 (三歲)。）

Q2. The television is 7,000 dollars.
（這部電視要價七千元。）

The stereo is 17,000 dollars.
（這音響要一萬七千元。）

↳ The stereo is (10,000 dollars) more expensive than the television.
（音響比電視貴 (一萬元)。）

Q3. My weight is 55kg.

（我的體重是 55 公斤。）

John's weight is 65 kg.

（約翰的體重是 65 公斤。）

↳ John is **(10 kg) heavier** than I am.

（約翰比我重 (10 公斤)。）

☞ 空格後面是 than I am，顯然本題要考的是比較級的用法：「A（體重）比 B 重（幾公斤）」可以用「A + be動詞 + 幾公斤 + heavier than + B (be動詞)」的句型來表達。

Q4. Speaking English is easy.

（講英文很簡單。）

Speaking Spanish is not so easy.

（講西班牙文不是那麼簡單。）

↳ Speaking English is easier <u>than speaking Spanish</u>.

（講英文比講西班牙文簡單。）

Q5. Swimming is hard to learn.

（游泳很難學。）

Surfing is even hard to learn.

（潛水更難學。）

↳ Surfing is harder <u>to learn than swimming</u>.

（潛水比游泳更難學。）

Q6. Ian teaches six classes.

（伊安教六個班。）

Yvonne teaches four classes.

（伊娃教四個班。）

↳ Yvonne teaches <u>fewer classes</u> than Ian does.

（伊娃教的班比伊安少。）

Q7. The boys behaved well yesterday.
（昨天男孩子們很守規矩。）

The girls behaved not so well.
（女孩子們不是那麼守規矩。）

↳ <u>The girls behaved worse</u> than the boys did yesterday.
（昨天女孩子們的規矩比男孩子們差。）

☞ 本題考的是副詞比較級用法。雖然 well 的比較級是 better，但空格後面的被比較對象是 the boys，所以依題意，合併句要表達的是「女孩表現比男孩差。」可以先思考 behave badly，再改成 behave worse。

Q8. John is very bright.
（約翰很聰明。）

None of us is as bright as he.
（我們沒有人像他一樣聰明。）

↳ <u>John is brighter</u> than all of us.
（約翰比我們所有人都聰明。）

Q9. Everyone has a good idea.
（每個人都有好主意。）

Kevin has the best idea.
（凱文想出的主意最棒。）

↳ No one <u>has better idea</u> than Kevin.
（沒有人想出比凱文更好的主意。）

Q10. Storybooks are interesting.
（故事書很有趣。）

Comic books are even more interesting.
（漫畫書更有趣。）

↳ Storybooks are <u>less interesting</u> than comic books.
（故事書沒有比漫畫有趣。）

Q11. All the men here are rich.

（這裡所有的男人都很富有。）

Mr. Katz is the richest.

（卡茲先生最富有。）

↳ All the men <u>are less rich</u> than Mr. Katz here.

（這裡所有的男人都沒卡茲先生富有。）

☞ 因為「被比較的對象」（than 後面的名詞）是最富有的 Mr. Katz，因此合併句要表達的是「沒有比…更富有」。「沒有比較富有」可以用 less rich 或 not richer 來表示。

Q12. Each lake in Canada is large.

（加拿大境內所有的湖泊都很大。）

Great Bear is the largest one.

（大熊湖是最大的一座湖。）

↳ In Canada, each lake <u>is less large</u> than Great Bear.

（在加拿大，每一座湖都沒有大熊湖大。）

Q13. Hank is handsome.

（漢克很帥。）

Leo is more handsome than Hank.

（里歐比漢克帥。）

↳ Leo is <u>the more handsome</u> of the two.

（里歐是兩個人當中比較帥的那個。）

Q14. Kenting is a nice place.

（墾丁是個好地方。）

Taroko is nicer than Kenting.

（太魯閣比墾丁好。）

↳ Taroko is <u>the nicer place</u> of the two.

（太魯閣是兩個地方當中比較好的。）

Q15. Rice is delicious.

（米很好吃。）

Pasta is not as delicious as rice.

（義大利麵不像米那麼好吃。）

↳ Pasta is <u>the less delicious</u> of the two.

（義大利麵是兩者當中比較不好吃的。）

句 子 重 組

❶ 重組的題目中，考生必須根據提示，將所有不連貫的英文字串，排列成一個結構完整且有意義的英文句子。特別要注意的是句首字母的大寫，以及句尾的標點符號。

❷ 本書針對重組的命題趨勢，將考題歸納為 18 種文法主題，百分之百的嚴選內容，提供考生有系統的學習。

本書嚴選 句子重組的 18 個文法主題

解題焦點：

> 不及物動詞後面不必接受詞，就可以完整地表達語意，有時可以接副詞來修飾動詞，若是否定語氣則在動詞前面加否定的助動詞或其他否定副詞（never, seldom...）。本單元可分為四種常見句型：
> 一、肯定句型／二、祈使句型
> 三、Yes/No 問句型／四、5W1H 疑問句型。

一、肯定句型

　　S + 助動詞（ + not）+ V（ + 副詞）.
　　S +（副詞 1）+ V +（副詞 2）.

　　例 sing / happily / birds

　　☞ Birds sing happily.

二、祈使句型

　　助動詞 + not + V + 副詞.
　　V + 副詞, please.

　　例 here / smoke / don't

　　☞ Don't smoke here.

三、Yes/No 問句型

　　助動詞（ + not）+ S + V（ + 副詞）?

　　例 you / try / won't / again

　　☞ Won't you try again.

四、5W1H 疑問句型

　　疑問詞 + 助動詞（ + not）+ S + V（ + 副詞）?

　　例 did / weekend / go / where / you / last

　　☞ Where did you go last weekend.

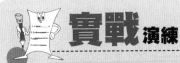

Q1. go / upstairs / don't

↳ _____.

Q2. come / , / please / in

↳ _____.

Q3. didn't / anywhere / we / go

↳ _____.

Q4. now / we / leave / can't

↳ _____?

Q5. cat / silently / the / walks

↳ _____.

Q6. going / rain / it's / to

↳ _____.

Q7. won't / the / start / car

↳ _____.

Q8. flag / the / in / the / is / flapping

↳ _____ wind.

Q9. the / moon / the / west / rises / in / does

↳ _____?

Q10. flashed / a / just / shooting / star

↳ _____ by.

Q11. the / accidentally / boy / inside / locked / was

↳ _____.

Q12. the / be / fixed / will / problem

↳ _____.

Q13. run / how / fast / you / can

↳ _____?

Q14. will / they / arrive / when/

↳ _____?

Q15. eat / where / going / are / we / to

↳ _____?

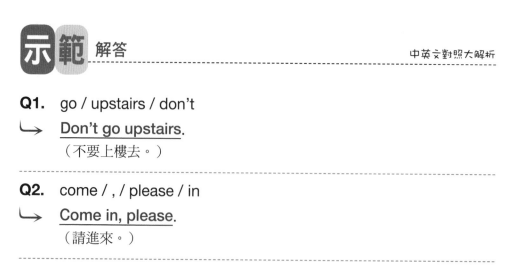

示範 解答 　　　　　　　　　　　　　　中英文對照大解析

Q1. go / upstairs / don't

↳ <u>Don't go upstairs</u>.
（不要上樓去。）

Q2. come / , / please / in

↳ <u>Come in, please</u>.
（請進來。）

Q3. didn't / anywhere / we / go

↳ <u>We didn't go anywhere</u>.
（我們沒去任何地方。）

Q4. now / we / leave / can't

↳ <u>Can't we leave now</u>?
（我們現在不能離開嗎？）

Q5. cat / silently / the / walks

↳ <u>The cat walks silently</u>.
（貓走路無聲無息。）

Q6. going / rain / it's / to

↳ <u>It's going to rain</u>.
（要下雨了。）

Q7. won't / the / start / car

↳ <u>The car won't start</u>.
（車子沒辦法啟動。）

Q8. flag / the / in / the / is / flapping

↳ <u>The flag is flapping in the</u> wind.
（旗幟在風中飛舞。）

Q9. the / moon / the / west / rise / in / does

↳ <u>Does the moon rise in the west</u>?
（月亮在西方升起嗎？）

☞ 句尾已提示問號（?），所以要用助動詞 does 開頭來引導問句，主詞是 the moon，後接原形動詞 rise，最後再放地方副詞 in the west 即可。

Q10. flashed / a / just / shooting / star

↳ <u>A shooting star just flashed</u> by.

（有一顆流星剛閃過。）

☞ 本句最後一個字提示為 by，顯然前面要有個動詞，跟它形成不及物動詞片語。只有 flashed 可以放在 by 前面，flash by 是「閃過」的意思。

Q11. the / accidentally / boy / inside / locked / was

↳ <u>The boy was accidentally locked inside</u>.

（男孩不小心被鎖在裡面了。）

Q12. the / be / fixed / will / problem

↳ <u>The problem will be fixed</u>.

（問題會解決的。）

Q13. run / how / fast / you / can

↳ <u>How fast can you run</u>?

（你可以跑多快？）

Q14. will / they / arrive / when

↳ <u>When will they arrive</u>?

（他們什麼時候抵達？）

Q15. eat / where / going / are / we / to

↳ <u>Where are we going to eat</u>?

（我們要去哪裡吃飯？）

主題 36 主詞 + be 動詞 + 名詞

Focus 解題焦點：

> be 動詞後面接名詞作為主詞補語，主詞與主詞補語可能是名詞、動名詞、不定詞等。此類句型的考題可分為三種句型：
> 一、肯定句型／二、5W1H 問句型／三、Yes/No 問句型

一、肯定句型

S + be 動詞 +（not）+ N

例 believe / to / is / to / see

☞ To see is to believe.

二、5W1H 問句型

疑問詞 + S + be 動詞 +（not）+ N?

例 ball / is / shape / what / the

☞ What shape is the ball?

三、Yes/No 問句型

be 動詞（+ not）+ S + N?

例 scientist / are / a / you

☞ Are you a scientist?

重點文法 快速查!!

be 動詞時態變化一覽表

時態	人稱	單數	複數
現在式	第一人稱	am	are
	第二人稱	are	
	第三人稱	is	
過去式	第一人稱	was	were
	第二人稱	were	
	第三人稱	was	
未來式		will be	

GRAMMAR

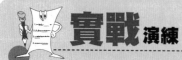

Q1. is / this / CD / player / a

↳ _____.

Q2. mother / her / a / housewife / is

↳ _____.

Q3. is / learning / teaching

↳ _____.

Q4. to / believe / see / is / to

↳ _____.

Q5. size / these / not / shoes / are / my

↳ _____.

Q6. the / age / are / the / kids / same / of

↳ _____.

Q7. the / is / three / hundred / total

↳ _____ dollars.

Q8. is / mine / that / not

↳ _____.

Q9. mine / the / is / not / problem

↳ _____.

Q10. my / music / isn't / of / type

↳ This _____ .

Q11. is / everything / money / not

↳ _____ .

Q12. your / eyes / are / what / color

↳ _____ ?

Q13. what / is / your / age / daughter's

↳ _____ ?

Q14. is / what / earth's / the / shape

↳ _____ ?

Q15. that / is / who / boy

↳ _____ ?

示範 解答　　　　　　　　　　　　　中英文對照大解析

Q1. is / this / CD / player / a

↳ This is a CD player.
（這是一台 CD 播放機。）

Q2. mother / her / a / housewife / is

↳ Her mother is a housewife.
（他媽媽是一名家庭主婦。）

Q3. is / learning / teaching

↳ <u>Teaching is learning</u>.

（教學相長。）

☞ 答案當然也可以寫成 Learning is teaching.。

Q4. to / believe / see / is / to

↳ <u>To see is to believe</u>.

（眼見為憑。）

☞ 答案當然也可以寫成 To believe is to see.。

Q5. size / these / not / shoes / are / my

↳ <u>These shoes are not my size</u>.

（這些鞋子不是我的尺寸。）

Q6. the / age / are / the / kids / same / of

↳ <u>The kids are of the same age</u>.

（這些小孩子同年齡。）

☞ 「of + 名詞」= 形容詞。主詞是 kids，be 動詞 are 後面要接主詞補語，如果主詞補語是名詞的話，必須跟主詞有「對等」關係，所以本句不能寫成 The kids are the same age.。

Q7. the / is / three / hundred / total

↳ <u>The total is three hundred</u> dollars.

（一共是三百元。）

Q8. is / mine / that / not

↳ <u>That is not mine</u>.

（那不是我的。）

Q9. mine / the / is / not / problem

↳ <u>The problem is not mine</u>.

（這不是我的問題。）

Q10. my / music / isn't / of / type

↳ This <u>isn't my type of music</u>.
（這不是我喜歡的那種音樂類型。）

Q11. is / everything / money / not

↳ <u>Money is not everything</u>.
（金錢不是一切。）

Q12. your / eyes / are / what / color

↳ <u>What color are your eyes</u>?
（你的眼睛是什麼顏色？）

Q13. what / is / your / age / daughter's

↳ <u>What is your daughter's age</u>?
（你女兒的年齡多大？）

☞ 句尾有問號的提示，所以這是個問句，疑問詞 what 要放在句首變成大寫的 What。daughter's 是所有格，後面一定要有名詞，所以只能放 age（年齡）

Q14. is / what / earth's / the / shape

↳ <u>What is the earth's shape</u>?
（地球是什麼形狀？）

Q15. that / is / who / boy

↳ <u>Who is that boy</u>?
（那男孩是誰？）

主題 37 | 主詞 + 及物動詞 + 名詞

 Focus 解題焦點：

> 及物動詞顧名思義就是此類動詞必須「及物」，也就是後面一定要有「人、事、物」作為其受詞，如此才能表達完整的意思。此類句型的考題可分為三種：
>
> 一、肯定句型／二、5W1H 問句型／三、Yes/No 問句型。

一、肯定句型

　　S（+ 助動詞 + not）+ V + N

　　例 not / do / I / coffee / drink

　　☞ I do not drink coffee.

二、5W1H 問句型

　　疑問詞 +（助動詞 + not）S + V + N?

　　例 buy / you / where / your / skirt / did

　　☞ Where did you buy your skirt?

三、Yes/No 問句型

　　（助動詞 + not）+ S + V + N?

　　例 you / money / have / do

　　☞ Do you have money?

重點文法 快速查!!

常用的及物動詞

buy（買）	say（說）	bring（帶）
lose（失去）	drink（喝）	have（有）
answer（回答）	own（擁有）	love（愛）
eat（吃）	know（知道）	choose（選擇）
steal（偷）	break（打破）	get（得到）
hear（聽見）	need（需要）	catch（捉住）

實戰演練

考驗你的重組能力！

Q1. don't / meat / cows / eat

↳ _____.

Q2. I / anything / say / didn't

↳ _____.

Q3. his / nobody / name / knows

↳ _____.

Q4. I / bring / can / my / pet / the / bus / onto

↳ _____.

Q5. may / one / you / choose / either

↳ _____.

Q6. of / you / buy / did / wine / a / bottle

↳ _____ .

Q7. who / questions / answer / my / can

↳ _____ .

Q8. owned / you / pet / have / ever / a

↳ _____ .

Q9. have / you / lost / what

↳ _____ ?

Q10. stolen / my / was / watch

↳ _____ .

Q11. someone / my / broken / vase / has

↳ _____ .

Q12. computer / do / have / a / you

↳ _____ ?

Q13. can / I / a / by / taxi / get / phone

↳ _____ ?

Q14. you / do / dinner / make / every / day

↳ _____ ?

Q15. will / me / love / you / always

↳ _____ ?

解答 中英文對照大解析

Q1. don't / meat / cows / eat

↳ <u>Cows don't eat meat</u>.

（母牛不吃肉。）

☞ eat 是及物動詞，後面一定要有受詞，可以當受詞的名詞有 cows 與 meat，顯然 eat meat（是「牛吃肉」而不是「肉吃牛」）才是比較合理的搭配。

Q2. I / anything / say / didn't

↳ <u>I didn't say anything</u>.

（我沒說任何話。）

Q3. his / nobody / name / knows

↳ <u>Nobody knows his name</u>.

（沒有人知道他的名字。）

Q4. I / bring / can / my / pet / the / bus / onto

↳ <u>Can I bring my pet onto the bus</u>?

（我可帶我的寵物上巴士嗎？）

Q5. may / one / you / choose / either

↳ <u>You may choose either one</u>.

（你可選其中一個。）

Q6. of / you / buy / did / wine / a / bottle

↳ <u>Did you buy a bottle of wine</u>?

（你買了一瓶酒嗎？）

Q7. who / questions / answer / my / can

↳ <u>Who can answer my questions</u>?

（誰可以回答我的問題？）

Q8. owned / you / pet / have / ever / a

↳ Have you ever owned a pet?
（你曾養過寵物嗎？）

Q9. have / you / lost / what

↳ What have you lost?
（你掉了什麼東西？）

Q10. stolen / my / was / watch

↳ My watch was stolen.
（我的錶被偷了。）

Q11. someone / my / broken / vase / has

↳ Someone has broken my vase.
（有人打破了我的花瓶。）

Q12. computer / do / have / a / you

↳ Do you have a computer?
（你有電腦嗎？）

Q13. can / I / a / by / taxi / get / phone

↳ Can I get a taxi by phone?
（我可以打電話叫計程車嗎？）

Q14. you / do / dinner / make / every / day

↳ Do you make dinner every day?
（你每天做晚餐嗎？）

Q15. will / me / love / you / always

↳ Will you always love me?
（你會永遠愛我嗎？）

主題 38 | 主詞 + 及物動詞片語 + 名詞

Focus 解題焦點：

及物動詞片語至少會有兩個字，大多是「及物動詞 + 介系詞」的形式，後面接名詞作受詞時，有時可拆開，有時不可拆開。通常接代名詞時要拆開來，把代名詞擺在兩字中間。但必須注意，有些及物動詞片語不管在什麼情況下都不能拆開。此類句型的考題分為兩類：
一、可拆開使用／二、不可拆開使用。

一、可拆開使用

例 the / mother / my / up / picked / pencil

☞ My mother <u>picked</u> the pencil <u>up</u>.

My mother <u>picked up</u> the pencil.

例 picked / my / it / up / mother.

☞ My mother <u>picked it up</u>.

二、不可拆開使用

例 over / all / boss / the / my / stands / time / me

☞ My boss <u>stands over me</u> all the time.

重點文法 快速查!!

不可拆開使用之及物動詞片語

arrive at（抵達）	run into（遇見，撞到）
look into（調查）	go through（用盡）
call on（拜訪）	stand over（監視）
result in（導致）	lead to（導致）
get over（克服，恢復）	take after（與…相像）
run across（遇上，越過）	look after（照顧）
go over（複習）	wait on（伺候）

GRAMMAR

實戰演練

考驗你的重組能力！

Q1. they / on / the / turned / conditioner / air

↳ _____.

Q2. her / put / helmet / she / on

↳ _____.

Q3. I / my / take / should / off / shoes

↳ _____?

Q4. give / clothes / away / let's / the / old

↳ _____.

Q5. lock / did / safe / you / up

↳ _____?

Q6. all / the / up / food / on / plate / your

↳ Eat _____.

Q7. please / the / away / rubbish / clear

↳ _____.

Q8. are / away / going / you / to / throw / TV / this

↳ _____?

Q9. bring / chairs / can / you / those / in

↳ _____?

284

Q10. switch / lights / remember / the / to / off

↳ _____ .

Q11. you / heat / need / up / pizza / frozen / to / the

↳ _____ .

Q12. will / the / pick / me / up / airport / you / at / the

↳ _____ ?

Q13. put / all / toys / the / away

↳ _____ .

Q14. bring / I them / may / in / now

↳ _____ ?

Q15. I / my / can't / mind / make / up

↳ _____ .

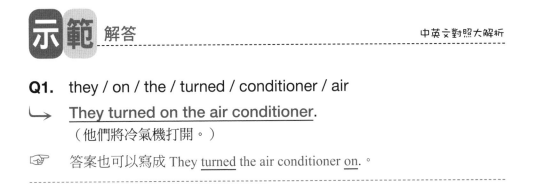

示範 解答 ------------------------------- 中英文對照大解析

Q1. they / on / the / turned / conditioner / air

↳ **They turned on the air conditioner.**
（他們將冷氣機打開。）

☞ 答案也可以寫成 They <u>turned</u> the air conditioner <u>on</u>.。

02. her / put / helmet / she / on

↳ <u>She put on her helmet</u>.
（她帶上她的安全帽。）

☞ 答案也可以寫成 She <u>put</u> her helmet <u>on</u>. 。

Q3. I / my / take / should / off / shoes

↳ <u>Should I take off my shoes</u>?
（我應該脫鞋嗎？）

Q4. give / clothes / away / let's / the / old

↳ <u>Let's give away the old clothes</u>.
（我們把舊衣服給人吧！）

Q5. lock / did / safe / you / up

↳ <u>Did you lock up the safe</u>?
（你有鎖保險箱嗎？）

Q6. all / the / up / food / on / plate / your

↳ Eat <u>up all the food on your plate</u>.
（把你盤子裡的食物全吃光。）

Q7. please / the / away / rubbish / clear

↳ <u>Please clear the rubbish away</u>.
（請把垃圾清掉。）

Q8. are / away / going / you / to / throw / TV / this

↳ <u>Are you going to throw away this TV</u>?
（你要把這台電視丟掉嗎？）

☞ 這裡的 throw away this TV 也可以寫成 throw this TV away。

Q9. bring / chairs / can / you / those / in

↳ <u>Can you bring in those chairs</u>?
（你可以把那些椅子拿進來嗎？）

Q10. switch / lights / remember / the / to / off

↳ Remember to switch off the lights.

（記得把燈開掉。）

Q11. you / heat / need / up / pizza / frozen / to / the

↳ You need to heat up the frozen pizza.

（你必須把冷凍披薩加熱。）

Q12. will / the / pick / me / up / airport / you / at / the

↳ Will you pick me up at the airport?

（你會到機場來接我嗎？）

☞ 提示句尾有問號，所以用助動詞 will 開頭，後面接主詞 you。其中受格 的 me 必須擺在 pick 和 up 中間，形成 pick me up「及物動詞片語 + 受 詞」的組合，最後剩下的字就是形成地方副詞片語（at the airport）的部 分了。

Q13. put / all / toys / the / away

↳ Put away all the toys.

（把所有的玩具收好。）

Q14. bring / I them / may / in / now

↳ May I bring them in now?

（我現在可以帶他們進來嗎?）

☞ 這裡的 bring them in 不可寫成 bring in them。

Q15. I / my / can't / mind / make / up

↳ I can't make up my mind.

（我無法下決定。）

☞ make up one's mind 是個固定的片語，表示「（某人）做決定」，因此不 可寫成 make one' s mind up。

句子重組

39 | 主詞 +be 動詞 + 形容詞 + 介系詞 + 名詞

Focus 解題焦點：

這類型的題目，是要在形容詞後面接固定與該形容詞搭配的介系詞，然後再接名詞。此類考題可分為四種：
一、肯定句型／二、Yes / No 問句型
三、祈使句型／四、5W1H 問句型

一、肯定句型

S + be 動詞（+ not）+ adj + 介系詞 + 名詞

例 at / I / speech / am / good

☞ I <u>am good at</u> speech.

二、Yes / No 問句型

be 動詞 + S（+ not）+ adj + 介系詞 + 名詞

例 with / are / work / busy / you

☞ <u>Are</u> you <u>busy with</u> work?

三、祈使句型

Be + adj + 介系詞 + 名詞
Don't be + adj + 介系詞 + 名詞

例 be / trivial / about / don't / things / angry

☞ Don't <u>be angry about</u> trivial things.

四、5W1H 問句型

Who + be 動詞 + adj + 介系詞 + 名詞？
Which + N + be 動詞 + S + adj + 介系詞？
What + be 動詞 + S + adj + 介系詞？

例 are / in / you / subject / which / interested

☞ Which subject <u>are</u> you <u>interested in</u>?

重點文法 快速查!!

常見 be 動詞 + 形容詞 + 介系詞的片語

be afraid of（害怕，恐懼）	be happy with/about（對…滿意）
be angry about/at/with（對…生氣）	be inferior to（劣於…）
be annoyed at/with（對…惱怒）	be superior to（優於…）
be aware of（知道，意識到…）	be interested in（對…有興趣）
be busy with（忙著…）	be kind to（對…親切）
be crazy about（對…瘋狂／著迷）	be quick at（對…手腳很快／很敏捷）
be cruel to（對…是殘忍的）	be sure of/about（對…確信）
be dear to（對…來說很珍貴）	be satisfied with（對…滿意）
be enthusiastic about（熱衷於…）	be sorry for（對…感到遺憾或抱歉）
be excited about（對…感到興奮）	be surprised at（對…感到驚訝）
be fond of（喜歡…）	be tired of（對…感到厭倦）
be generous with（對…慷慨／大方）	be worried about（憂慮著…）
be good at（擅長…）	be gentle with（對…(人)溫柔，輕輕擺弄…(某物)）
be poor at（不擅長…）	be sick with（生了…病）
be short of（缺乏…）	be famous for（以…聞名）

GRAMMAR

Part 1・單句寫作 ▶▶ 03 句子重組

Q1. was / meeting / Walt / from / absent / the

↳ _____ .

Q2. fond / he / is / sports / of

↳ _____ .

Q3. were / we / danger / not / the / aware / of

↳ _____ .

Q4. about / everybody / trip / is / the / excited

↳ _____ .

Q5. of / you / are / figures / sure / the

↳ _____ ?

Q6. so / scenery / there/ the / beautiful / about / excited

↳ I was _____ .

Q7. careful / plate / be / hot / with / the

↳ _____ .

Q8. be / him / don't / of / afraid

↳ _____ .

Q9. generous / money / he / is / with / his

↳ _____ .

Q10. the / isn't / for / people / food / ten / enough

↳ _____ .

Q11. for / he / wasn't / happy / you

↳ _____ ?

Q12. they / weren't / satisfied / that / with

↳ _____ ?

Q13. neighborhood / familiar / who / this / is / with

↳ _____ ?

Q14. you / good / which / at / subject / are

↳ _____ ?

Q15. have / with / what / busy / been / you

↳ _____ ?

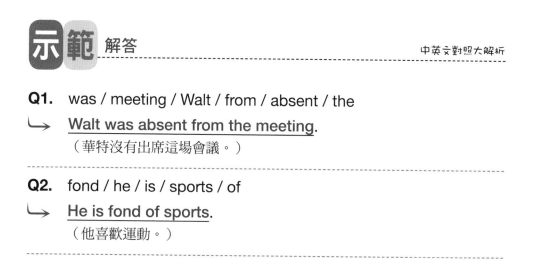

示範 解答 　　　　　　　　　　　　　中英文對照大解析

Q1. was / meeting / Walt / from / absent / the

↳ <u>Walt was absent from the meeting</u>.
（華特沒有出席這場會議。）

Q2. fond / he / is / sports / of

↳ <u>He is fond of sports</u>.
（他喜歡運動。）

Q3. were / we / danger / not / the / aware / of

↳ We were not aware of the danger.
（我們沒有意識到有危險。）

Q4. about / everybody / trip / is / the / excited

↳ Everybody is excited about the trip.
（每個人對這趟旅行都感到興奮。）

Q5. of / you / are / figures / sure / the

↳ Are you sure of the figures?
（你確定是這些數字嗎？）

Q6. so / scenery / there/ the / beautiful / about / excited

↳ I was so excited about the beautiful scenery there.
（我對於那裡的美景感到相當興奮。）

Q7. careful / plate / be / hot / with / the

↳ Be careful with the hot plate.
（小心盤子很熱。）

Q8. be / him / don't / of / afraid

↳ Don't be afraid of him.
（不用怕他。）

Q9. generous / money / he / is / with / his

↳ He is generous with his money.
（他在錢這方面很大方。）

Q10. the / isn't / for / people / food / ten / enough

↳ The food isn't enough for ten people.
（這些食物不夠十個人吃。）

Q11. for / he / wasn't / happy / you

↳ Wasn't he happy for you?

（他不為你感到高興嗎？）

Q12. they / weren't / satisfied / that / with

↳ Weren't they satisfied with that?

（他們對那結果不滿意嗎？）

Q13. neighborhood / familiar / who / this / is / with

↳ Who is familiar with this neighborhood?

（誰熟悉這個社區？）

Q14. you / good / which / at / subject / are

↳ Which subject are you good at?

（你擅長哪一門科目?）

Q15. have / with / what / busy / been / you

↳ What have you been busy with?

（你一直在忙什麼？）

☞ 句尾提示為問號（?），因此應以疑問詞 what 開頭。後面接完成式 be 動詞 have been。busy 及介系詞 with 形成詞組 "busy with"，表示「忙於⋯」。

主詞 + 連綴動詞 + 形容詞

Focus 解題焦點：

「連綴動詞」屬於不及物動詞的一種，後面必須有「主詞補
語」（通常是形容詞或名詞）語意才會完整，在文法中也被
稱為「不完全不及物動詞」。考題可分為三種：
一、肯定句型／二、5W1H 問句型／三、Yes / No 句型。

一、 肯定句型
S + V + adj
例 sad / looked / she
☞ She looked sad.

二、5W1H 問句型
疑問詞 + 助動詞 + S + V + adj
例 look / she / why / sad / did
☞ Why did she look sad?

三、Yes / No 問句型
助動詞 + S + V + adj
例 look / she / sad / did
☞ Did she look sad?

重點文法 快速查!!

常見後面必須接補語的連綴動詞	
感官型連綴動詞（感官動詞）	一般連綴動詞
smell（聞起來…）	be 動詞（am, is, are...）
feel（感覺起來…）	become/turn/go/come（變得，變成…）
look（看起來…）	keep/stay（保持著…）
sound（聽起來…）	go/come（變得，變成…）
taste（嚐起來…）	seem（似乎…）

GRAMMAR

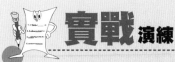

Q1. smells / the / sweet / perfume

↳ _____.

Q2. soft / and / smooth / feels / this

↳ _____.

Q3. the / horrible / soup / tastes

↳ _____.

Q4. the / pleasant / sounds / music

↳ _____.

Q5. the / good / pictures / very / look

↳ _____.

Q6. the / are / turning / brown / leaves

↳ _____.

Q7. are / we / older / growing

↳ _____.

Q8. has / the / sour / milk / turned

↳ _____.

Q9. feel / tired / I / so

↳ _____.

Q10. your / has / true / dream / come

↳ _____.

Q11. has / the / dirty / river / become

↳ _____.

Q12. did / they / become / how / popular

↳ _____?

Q13. look / why / so / she / unhappy / does

↳ _____?

Q14. you / feel / do / nervous

↳ _____?

Q15. gone / the / has / meat / bad

↳ _____?

示範 解答 ⋯⋯⋯⋯⋯⋯⋯⋯⋯⋯⋯⋯⋯⋯⋯⋯⋯⋯⋯⋯ 中英文對照大解析 ⋯⋯⋯⋯⋯⋯⋯⋯⋯⋯⋯

Q1. smells / the / sweet / perfume

↳ The perfume smells sweet.
（這香水聞起來有甜味。）

Q2. soft / and / smooth / feels / this

↳ This feels soft and smooth.
（這東西感覺起來很柔順。）

Q3. the / horrible / soup / tastes

↳ The soup tastes horrible.
（這湯嚐起來很糟糕。）

Q4. the / pleasant / sounds / music

↳ The music sounds pleasant.
（這音樂聽起來很悅耳。）

Q5. the / good / pictures / very / look

↳ The pictures look very good.
（這些照片看起來很棒。）

Q6. the / are / turning / brown / leaves

↳ The leaves are turning brown.
（樹葉正在變黃。）

Q7. are / we / older / growing

↳ We are growing older.
（我們一直在長大／變老中。）

Q8. has / the / sour / milk / turned

↳ The milk has turned sour.
（牛奶酸掉了。）

Q9. feel / tired / I / so

↳ I feel so tired.
（我感覺好累。）

Q10. your / has / true / dream / come

↳ Your dream has come true.
（你的夢想已經成真。）

Q11. has / the / dirty / river / become

↳ The river has become dirty.
（這條河已經變髒了。）

Q12. did / they / become / how / popular

↳ How did they become popular?
（他們是如何變得受歡迎的？）

Q13. look / why / so / she / unhappy / does

↳ Why does she look so unhappy?
（為什麼她看起來這麼不快樂？）

Q14. you / feel / do / nervous

↳ Do you feel nervous?
（你覺得緊張嗎？）

Q15. gone / the / has / meat / bad

↳ Has the meat gone bad?
（這肉有變壞嗎？）

主題 41 | 主詞 + 及物動詞 + 名詞 + 形容詞／名詞

Focus 解題焦點：

這類及物動詞後面加受詞／名詞之後，必須再接形容詞或名詞，意思才會完整。此類及物動詞又稱為「不完全及物動詞」，受詞後面的形容詞或名詞稱為「受詞補語」。可分為四種句型：

一、肯定句型／二、Yes / No 問句型
三、5W1H 問句型／四、祈使句型

一、肯定句型
S + V + O + adj./n.

例 her / kept / mother / child / the / quiet

☞ In the concert, **the mother kept her child quiet**.

二、Yes / No 問句型
助動詞 + S + V + O + adj./n.?

例 like / would / hair / you / curly / your

☞ **Would you like your hair curly** ?

三、5W1H 問句型
疑問詞 + 助動詞 + S + V + O + adj./n.?

例 consider / did / liar / him / a / why / you

☞ **Why did you consider him a liar**?

四、祈使句型
V + O + adj
Don't + V + O + adj

例 leave / alone / me

☞ **Leave me alone**, please.

重點文法 快速查!!

常見接受詞後必須再接補語的不完全及物動詞

舉例說明	中文意義
cut + it + open	把它剪／切開來
find + 事情 + easy	發現某事很簡單
get + 事情 + done	把某事完成了
leave + 人 + alone	不去理會某人
make + it + a rule	將某事定為例行事項
consider + herself + an adult	視她自己為成年人
elect + 人 + 身分／職位	將某人選為某職位者
drive + 人 + crazy	令某人瘋狂
let + 人 + down	令某人失望
paint + 物件 + 顏色	把某物漆成某種顏色
name + 人 + 名字	把某人取名為什麼名字
keep + 地方 + clean	將某地方保持整潔
ask + 人 + to-V	要求某人去做某事
have + 物件 + P.P.	把某物進行某種處理

實戰演練

考驗你的重組能力！

Q1. she / her / skirts / likes

↳ _____ short.

Q2. white / wall / painted / hey / the

↳ _____ .

Q3. young / green / dyed / the / hair / man / his

↳ _____ .

Q4. is / a / in / hero / village / he / considered / the

↳ _____ .

Q5. happy / to / we / you / see / want

↳ _____ .

Q6. birds / to / set / free / going / the

↳ They are _____ .

Q7. a / he / makes / rule / jogging / go / it / to

↳ _____ in the morning.

Q8. make / my / I'll / short / speech

↳ _____ .

Q9. the / you / door / could / open / leave

↳ _____ ?

Q10. asked / me / the / later/ garbage / away / to / throw

↳ My mother _____ .

Q11. to / I / need / bicycle / my / have / fixed

↳ _____ .

Q12. parents / your / let / worry / don't / much / too

↳ _____ .

Q13. the / flat / with / a / can / smash / hammer

↳ _____ .

Q14. tips / find / she / the / useful / did

↳ _____ ?

Q15. David / named / they / newborn / the / baby

↳ _____ .

 解答 　　　　　　　　　　　　　　中英文對照大解析

- -

Q1. she / her / skirts / likes

↳ <u>She likes her skirts</u> short.
　（她喜歡穿短裙。）

☞ 句尾提示為short，是個形容詞，所以應往「動詞 + 受詞 + 形容詞」的方向思考，本句只有 "like her skirt short" 的組合。

- -

Q2. white / wall / painted / hey / the

↳ <u>They painted the wall white</u>.
　（他們把牆漆成白色。）

- -

Q3. young / green / dyed / the / hair / man / his

↳ <u>The young man dyed his hair green</u>.
　（那個年輕人把他的頭髮染成綠色。）

☞ 單字選項中的形容詞有 young 及 green，一般會想到「形容詞 + 名詞」的搭配，但這裡有動詞 dyed，是個不完全及物動詞，接受詞之後必須再接補語（形容詞或名詞），所以這裡有一個形容詞會擺在名詞後面。"dyed his hair green" 是最合理的組合，表示「將他的頭髮染成綠色」。

- -

Q4. is / a / in / hero / village / he / considered / the

⮑ He is considered a hero in the village.

（他在這村落被視為是個英雄。）

☞ 單字選項中有 is 和 considered 兩個字可以當動詞，但沒有連接詞，所以這兩個字應組成被動式動詞 is considered。consider（視⋯為⋯）是個不完全及物動詞，接受詞之後必須再接補語（形容詞或名詞），所以 is considered 後面應該擺一個名詞，作為主詞補語。這裡 “ He is considered a hero” 是最合理的組合，表示「他被視為一位英雄」。

Q5. happy / to / we / you / see / want

⮑ We want to see you happy.

（我們想看到你快樂。）

Q6. birds / to / set / free / going / the

⮑ They are going to set the birds free.

（他們要把鳥兒放走。）

Q7. a / he / makes / rule / jogging / go / it / to

⮑ He makes it a rule to go jogging in the morning.

（他早上都固定去慢跑。）

Q8. make / my / I'll / short / speech

⮑ I'll make my speech short.

（我會簡短做演說。）

Q9. the / you / door / could / open / leave

⮑ Could you leave the door open?

（你可以讓門開著嗎？）

Q10. asked / me / the / later/ garbage / away / to / throw

⮑ My mother asked me to throw away the garbage later.

（我媽媽要求我等一下去倒垃圾。）

Q11. to / I / need / bicycle / my / have / fixed

↳ <u>I need to have my bicycle fixed</u>.
（我必須將我的腳踏車送修。）

Q12. parents / your / let / worry / don't / much / too

↳ <u>Don't let your parents worry too much</u>.
（別讓你的父母過於擔心。）

Q13. the / flat / with / a / can / smash / hammer

↳ <u>Smash the can flat with a hammer</u>.
（用榔頭把這罐頭打扁。）

Q14. tips / find / she / the / useful / did

↳ <u>Did she find the tips useful</u>?
（她認為那些提示有用嗎？）

Q15. David / named / they / newborn / the / baby

↳ <u>They named the newborn baby David</u>.
（他們將這新生兒取名為大衛。）

主題 42 | There + be 動詞 + 主詞

Focus 解題焦點：

「there + be 動詞」後面的名詞是句子的主詞，所以嚴格來說，它是個「倒裝句」，但初學者不必去研究它的句構，只要記住這個句型就是「有…」的意思。在考題中可分為兩種句型：

一、直述句型／二、Yes / No 問句型。

一、直述句型

There（＋助動詞）＋ be 動詞 ＋ 主詞

例 bird / there / a / in / is / tree / the

☞ <u>There is a bird in the tree.</u>

二、Yes / No 問句型

be 動詞 ＋ there ＋主詞？

助動詞 ＋ there ＋ be ＋ 主詞？

例 something / is / new / there

☞ <u>Is there something new</u>?

重點文法 快速查!!

「There be」句型總整理

句型	中文意義
There is ＋ 單數主詞	有…
There are ＋ 複數主詞	有…
There will be ＋ 單／複數主詞	（未來）將會有…
There must be ＋ 單／複數主詞	一定有…
There may / might / would / can be ＋ 單／複數主詞	可能有…
There should be ＋ 單／複數主詞	應該有…

GRAMMAR

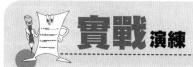

Q1. and / is / rat / there / a / big

↳ _____ some rabbits.

Q2. one / there's / entrance / only

↳ _____.

Q3. there's / doubt / no / answer / about / the

↳ _____.

Q4. problems / are / some / there / here

↳ _____.

Q5. are / for / there / enough / guests / the / chairs

↳ _____?

Q6. too / there's / the / much / air / pollution / in

↳ _____.

Q7. many / there're / of / activities / types / on / campus

↳ _____.

Q8. only / this / there's / a / city / park / in

↳ _____.

Q9. much / noise / coming / too / from / next-door / the

└→ There's _____ neighbor.

Q10. there / traffic / is / so / much / late

└→ _____?

Q11. difference / there / any / be / won't

└→ _____.

Q12. won't / supplies / a / problem / there / be / with / the

└→ _____.

Q13. must / better / be / there / a / way

└→ _____.

Q14. must / somewhere / there / mistake / be / a

└→ _____.

Q15. there / wasn't / another / one

└→ _____ by that name?

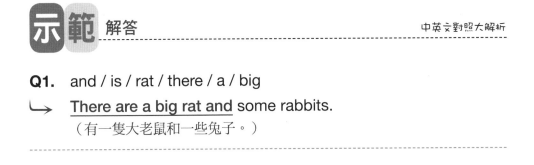

示範 解答

中英文對照大解析

Q1. and / is / rat / there / a / big

└→ **There are a big rat and** some rabbits.
（有一隻大老鼠和一些兔子。）

Q2. one / there's / entrance / only

↳ <u>There's only one entrance</u>.
（只有一個入口。）

Q3. there's / doubt / no / answer / about / the

↳ <u>There's no doubt about the answer</u>.
（這個答案是沒有疑問的。）

Q4. problems / are / some / there / here

↳ <u>There are some problems here</u>.
（這裡有一些問題。）

☞ 這是「There be...」的句型，雖然單字選項中有 there 也有 here，但 There are some problems here. 會比 Here are some problems there. 更加合理。

Q5. are / for / there / enough / guests / the / chairs

↳ <u>Are there enough chairs for the guests</u>?
（有足夠的椅子給賓客們嗎？）

Q6. too / there's / the / much / air / pollution / in

↳ <u>There's too much pollution in the air</u>.
（空氣污染太嚴重了。）

Q7. many / there're / of / activities / types / on / campus

↳ <u>There're many types of activities on campus</u>.
（大學校園裡的活動有非常多的類型。）

Q8. only / this / there's / a / city / park / in

↳ <u>There's only a park in this city</u>.
（這個城市裡只有一座公園。）

Q9. much / noise / coming / too / from / next-door / the

↳ There's <u>too much noise coming from the next-door</u> neighbor.
（隔壁鄰居那兒傳來太多噪音。）

Q10. there / traffic / is / so / much / late

↳ <u>Is there much traffic so late</u>?
（這麼晚了路上車流還很多嗎？）

Q11. difference / there / any / be / won't

↳ <u>There won't be any difference</u>.
（不會有任何不同。）

Q12. won't / supplies / a / problem / there / be / with / the

↳ <u>There won't be a problem with the supplies</u>.
（供給不會有問題的。）

Q13. must / better / be / there / a / way

↳ <u>There must be a better way</u>.
（一定會有個更好的方法。）

Q14. must / somewhere / there / mistake / be / a

↳ <u>There must be a mistake somewhere</u>.
（一定是哪裡出錯了。）

Q15. there / wasn't / another / one

↳ <u>Wasn't there another one</u> by that name?
（那時沒有一個人是叫這名字的嗎？）

☞ 句尾的 by that name 是個形容詞片語，作後位修飾，所以前面必須放個名詞或代名詞，只有 another one 是合理的選擇。因為是個問句，所以 be 動詞 wasn't 擺在句首。

解題焦點：

> 授予動詞當然是及物動詞的一種，只是它後面必須有兩個受詞，才能表達完整的語意。主要句型為：S（＋助動詞）＋授予 V + O1+ O2。其中 O1 稱為「間接受詞（I.O.）」，O2 為「直接受詞（D.O.）」。另外，它還有另一種句型可以表示：S（＋助動詞）＋授予 V + O2 + 介系詞 + O1。

主要句型

S（＋助動詞）＋授予 V + D.O. + I.O.

例 hug / I / a / him / gave

☞ I gave him a hug.

= I gave a hug to him.

重點文法 快速查!!

考題中常見的授予動詞	
句型	中文意義
S + do/ask + 人 + a favor	給予／請求某人幫忙
S + buy/sell + 人 + 物	買／賣給某人某物
S + pass + 人 + 物	傳遞某物給某人
S + give + 人 + 物	給某人某物
S + show + 人 + 物	把某物給某人看
S + tell + 人 + 事情	告訴某人某事
S + write + 人 + a letter	寫給某人一封信
物 + cost + 人 + 金額	某物花了某人多少錢
S + spare + 人 + some time	為某人挪出一些時間
S + save + 人 + some money	為某人省下一些錢
S + envy + 人 + 事物	羨慕某人（擁有）某物

GRAMMAR

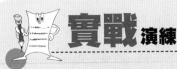

Q1. the / he / me / scooter / sold

↳ _____.

Q2. her / money / I / some / lent

↳ _____.

Q3. pass / salt / me / the / please / to

↳ _____.

Q4. feed / food / the / let's / dog / some

↳ _____.

Q5. dollars / pay / should / me / you / 500

↳ _____.

Q6. we / should / her / present / send / a

↳ _____?

Q7. can / 15 / spare / me / you / minutes

↳ _____?

Q8. do / me / a / you / favor / would

↳ _____?

Q9. much / did / you / dictionary / cost / how / this

↳ _____?

Q10. you / this / trouble / save / a / will / lot / of

↳ _____ .

Q11. envy / how / happy / I / you / your / family

↳ _____ !

Q12. you / I / ask / a / may / question

↳ _____ ?

Q13. the / did / he / press / what / tell

↳ _____ ?

Q14. you / bought / snacks / who / these

↳ _____ ?

Q15. me / bring / Swiss / some / chocolate / you

↳ Would you please _____ ?

示範 解答

中英文對照大解析

Q1. the / he / me / scooter / sold

↳ He sold me the scooter.
（他賣給我這輛摩托車。）

Q2. her / money / I / some / lent

↳ I lent her some money.
（我借給她一些錢。）

Q3. pass / salt / me / the / please / to

↳ Please pass the salt to me.

☞ 沒有主詞，有 please，顯然是個祈使句，應以 Please 開頭，動詞是 pass，
且有個 to，可構成「pass 物 to 人」（傳遞某物給某人）的句型。
（請把鹽遞給我。）

Q4. feed / food / the / let's / dog / some

↳ Let's feed the dog some food.
（我們給這隻狗餵些食物吧。）

Q5. dollars / pay / should / me / you / 500

↳ You should pay me 500 dollars.
（你應該要付我五百元。）

Q6. we / should / her / present / send / a

↳ Should we send her a present?
（我們應該送她一份禮物嗎？）

Q7. can / 15 / spare / me / you / minutes

↳ Can you spare me 15 minutes?
（你可以空出 15 分鐘給我嗎／可以打擾你 15 分鐘嗎？）

Q8. do / me / a / you / favor / would

↳ Would you do me a favor?
（你可以幫我個忙嗎？）

Q9. much / did / you / dictionary / cost / how / this

↳ How much did this dictionary cost you?
（這本字典花你多少錢？）

Q10. you / this / trouble / save / a / will / lot / of

↳ This will save you a lot of trouble.
（這會省掉你很多麻煩。）

Q11. envy / how / happy / I / you / your / family

↳ How I envy you your happy family!

（我有多羨慕你有個幸福的家庭呢！）

☞ 句尾是驚嘆號（！），這是個以疑問詞為首的感嘆句，所以第一個字要寫下 How。本題重點是 envy 在此當授予動詞，後面必須有兩個受詞，要先寫間接受詞（人），再寫直接受詞（事物）：envy you your happy family。

Q12. you / I / ask / a / may / question

↳ May I ask you a question?

（我可以問你個問題嗎？）

Q13. the / did / he / press / what / tell

↳ What did he tell the press?

（他對記者們說了什麼？）

Q14. you / bought / snacks / who / these

↳ Who bought you these snacks?

（誰買給你這些點心呢？）

Q15. me / bring / Swiss / some / chocolate

↳ Would you please bring me some Swiss chocolate?

（可以麻煩你幫我帶些瑞士巧克力嗎？）

句子重組

主題 44 │ 主詞 + 及物動詞 + 受詞 + 原形動詞

Focus 解題焦點：

> 這裡的及物動詞也是「不完全及物動詞」的一種，主要以「使役動詞」及「知覺／感官動詞」為主。所以接受詞之後必須再接「受詞補語」，如此語意才算完整，而這裡的受詞補語以「原形動詞」為代表。

一、使役動詞

S + 使役 V + O + 原形 V...

例 to / the / better/ taste / he / tried / dish / make

☞ He tried to make the dish taste better.

二、知覺動詞

S + 知覺 V + O + 原形 V...

例 him / I / saw / cry

☞ I saw him cry.

NOTE：這些動詞也被稱為「感官動詞」，在此以「知覺動詞」稱之，是為了區別兩者於不同句型中運用。感官動詞用於「S + V + C」中，而知覺動詞用於「S + V + O + C」的句型中。

三、動詞 help

S + help + O + 原形 V...

例 his / I / finish / helped / homework / him

☞ I helped him finish his homework.

重點文法 快速查!!

此類句型中常見的不完全及物動詞

知覺動詞	使役動詞與 help
S + feel + 受詞 + 原形 V	S + make + 受詞 + 原形 V
S + see + 受詞 + 原形 V	S + have + 受詞 + 原形 V
S + watch + 受詞 + 原形 V	S + let + 受詞 + 原形 V
S + hear + 受詞 + 原形 V	S + help + 受詞 + 原形 V

實戰演練

考驗你的重組能力!

Q1. did / shake / feel / the / you / house

↳ _____?

Q2. me / mom / jump / , / watch

↳ _____.

Q3. we / didn't / him / out / go / notice

↳ Sorry, _____.

Q4. steal / saw / the / me / who / bike

↳ _____?

Q5. way / think / what / you / makes / this

↳ _____?

Q6. we / help / shall / finish / him / his / job

↳ _____ ?

Q7. can't / wants / let / he / him / we / do / whatever

↳ _____ .

Q8. have / fix / I'll / car / the / the / mechanic

↳ _____ .

Q9. have / this / Room 123 / to / baggage / taken / please

↳ _____ .

Q10. you / complain / ever / heard / about / a / buyer / have

↳ _____ the product?

Q11. made / they / my / me / give / away / collection

↳ _____ for free.

Q12. play / in / their / the / let / own / ways / kid

↳ _____ .

Q13. can / make / newer / the / how / house / we / look

↳ _____ ?

Q14. could / you / how / her / have / her / change / mind

↳ _____ ?

Q1. did / shake / feel / the / you / house

↳ Did you feel the house shake?
（你感覺到房子在搖嗎？）

Q2. me / mom / jump / , / watch

↳ Watch me jump, Mom.
（看我跳喔，媽媽。）

Q3. we / didn't / him / out / go / notice

↳ Sorry, we didn't notice him go out.
（到不起，我們沒注意到他走出去。）

Q4. steal / saw / the / me / who / bike

↳ Who saw me steal the bike?
（誰看見我偷了腳踏車嗎？）

Q5. way / think / what / you / makes / this

↳ What makes you think this way?
（什麼原因讓你這麼想？）

Q6. we / help / shall / finish / him / his / job

↳ Shall we help him finish his job?
（我們應該幫他完他的工作嗎？）

Q7. can't / wants / let / he / him / we / do / whatever

↳ We can't let him do whatever he wants.
（我們不能讓他為所欲為。）

Q8. have / fix / I'll / car / the / the / mechanic

↳ <u>I'll have the mechanic fix the car</u>.
（我會叫修車師傅修好這車子。）

Q9. have / this / Room 123 / to / baggage / taken / please

↳ <u>Please have this baggage taken to Room 123</u>.
（請把這行李拿到 123 號房。）

Q10. you / complain / ever / heard / about / a / buyer / have

↳ <u>Have you ever heard a buyer complain about</u> the product?
（你曾聽過買家抱怨這項商品嗎？）

Q11. made / they / my / me / give / away / collection

↳ <u>They made me give away my collection</u> for free.
（他們迫使我免費送出我的收藏品。）

☞ 有兩個動詞 made 與 give 但沒有連接詞，可以用「使役動詞 + 受詞 + 原形動詞」的句型，形成 They made me give away... 的句子。

Q12. play / in / their / the / let / own / ways / kid

↳ <u>Let the kid play in their own ways</u>.
（讓孩子們用自己的方法玩。）

Q13. can / make / newer / the / how / house / we / look

↳ <u>How can we make the house look newer</u>?
（我們要怎麼讓房子看起來新一點？）

Q14. could / you / how / her / have / her / change / mind

↳ <u>How could you have her change her mind</u>?
（你怎麼有辦法讓她改變心意？）

解題焦點：

此句型中的介系詞分為兩種情況：
一、視語意使用的介系詞
二、和特定動詞搭配使用的介系詞

一、視語意使用的介系詞

例 for / my / a doll / mother / me / made

☞ My mother <u>made</u> a doll <u>for</u> me.

二、和特定動詞搭配使用的介系詞

例 spent / Tony / on / lot / a / car / his

☞ Tony <u>spent</u> a lot <u>on</u> his car.

重點文法 快速查!!

動詞搭配特定介系詞的例子

動詞搭配介系詞	中文意義
remind sb. of sth.	提醒某人某事
spend/waste... (time, money) on...	花／浪費…（金錢、時間）在…（某事上）
award sth. to sb.	獎賞某人某物
congratulate sb. on sth.	為某事恭喜某人
blame sb. for sth.	因某事責備某人

GRAMMAR

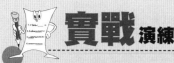 **實戰** 演練

考驗你的重組能力!

Q1. made / her / a / dress / for / she / daughter

↳ _____.

Q2. on / car / spent / much / money / how / have / you / this

↳ _____?

Q3. your / save / some / for / please / food / father

↳ _____.

Q4. will / choose / the / they / best / school

↳ _____ for Tom.

Q5. offered / the / was / to / Jeff / job

↳ _____.

Q6. boys / write / to / many / letters / Molly

↳ _____.

Q7. we / owe / bank / of / lots / money / to / still / the

↳ _____.

Q8. car / won't / anyone / he / lend / his / to

↳ _____.

Q9. wife / his / his / always / reminds / daughter / him / of

↳ _____.

Q10. stop / didn't / you / from / him / that / doing / why

↳ _____ ?

Q11. late / blamed / was / Kent / for / arriving

↳ _____ .

Q12. the / Tina / awarded / prize / is / to / first

↳ _____ .

Q13. one / guests / success / congratulated / the / her / her

↳ _____ .

Q14. on / waste / too / games / much / don't / time / computer

↳ _____ .

Q15. the / I / explain / boss / this / must / to

↳ _____ ?

示範 解答 　　　　　　　　　　　　中英文對照大解析

Q1. made / her / a / dress / for / she / daughter

↳ <u>She made a dress for her daughter.</u>
　　（她做了件洋裝給她女兒。）

Q2. on / car / spent / much / money / how / have / you / this

↳ <u>How much money have you spent on this car</u>?
　　（你已經花了多少錢在這部車上？）

Q3. your / save / some / for / please / food / father

↳ <u>Please save some food for your father</u>.

（請留一些食物給你爸爸。）

Q4. will / choose / the / they / best / school

↳ <u>They will choose the best school</u> for Tom.

（他們將為湯姆選擇最好的學校。）

Q5. offered / the / was / to / Jeff / job

↳ <u>The job was offered to Jeff</u>.

（這份工作給了傑夫。）

Q6. boys / write / to / many / letters / Molly

↳ <u>Many boys write letters to Molly</u>.

（很多男孩子寫信給茉莉。）

Q7. we / owe / bank / of / lots / money / to / still / the

↳ <u>We still owe lots of money to the bank</u>.

（我們還欠銀行很多錢。）

Q8. car / won't / anyone / he / lend / his / to

↳ <u>He won't lend his car to anyone</u>.

（他不會把他的車借給任何人。）

Q9. wife / his / his / always / reminds / daughter / him / of

↳ <u>His daughter always reminds him of his wife</u>.

（他的女兒總是讓他想起他的妻子。）

Q10. stop / didn't / you / from / him / that / doing / why

↳ <u>Why didn't you stop him from doing that</u>?
（你怎麼不阻止他去做那件事？）

☞ 句尾提示問號（？），因此應以疑問詞 why 開頭，然後接助動詞 didn't 與主詞 you。注意有動詞 stop 與介系詞 from 可形成 stop... from...（阻止…去做…）的片語。

Q11. late / blamed / was / Kent / for / arriving

↳ <u>Kent was blamed for arriving late</u>.
（肯特因為遲到受到責備。）

Q12. the / Tina / awarded / prize / is / to / first

↳ <u>The first prize is awarded to Tina</u>.
（頭獎頒給了提娜。）

☞ 從 awarded 與 is 兩個單字來看，這是個被動語態的句子，動詞是 is awarded，後面好搭配介系詞 to，形成「獎 + is awarded to + 人」的句型。

Q13. one / guests / success / congratulated / the / her / her

↳ <u>The guests congratulated her on her success</u>.
（賓客們為她的成功向她道賀。）

Q14. on / waste / too / games / much / don't / time / computer

↳ <u>Don't waste too much time on computer games</u>.
（不要浪費太多時間在電玩上。）

Q15. the / I / explain / boss / this / must / to

↳ <u>Must I explain this to the boss</u>?
（我必須向老闆解釋這件事嗎？）

----

46 It + be 動詞 + 形容詞／名詞 + 動名詞

Focus 解題焦點：

這個主題是在句子開頭利用虛主詞 it 帶出所要強調的形容詞或名詞，而真正的主詞置於最後，以動名詞呈現。也就是將原句「S + be 動詞 + Adj./N」改為「It + be 動詞 + Adj./N + S」。可依其強調的重點分為兩類：
一、強調名詞／二、強調形容詞

一、強調名詞

It + be 動詞+ N + S

例 no / it / over / use / is / milk / spilt / crying

☞ It is no use crying over spilt milk.

二、強調形容詞

It + be 動詞 + Adj + S

例 mother / it / being / difficult / a / is

☞ It is difficult being a mother.

重點文法 快速查!!

強調句型的對照與解析		
	強調名詞	強調形容詞
強調句型	It + be 動詞 + N + S	It + be 動詞 + Adj + S
	It is no use crying over spilt milk.	It is difficult being a mother.
原句型	S + be 動詞 + N	S + be 動詞 + Adj
	Crying over spilt milk is no use.	Being a mother is difficult.

GRAMMAR

Q1. to / it / talking / you / was / nice

↳ _____.

Q2. a / parent / is / hard / it / being

↳ _____.

Q3. the / internet / helpful / it's / having

↳ _____.

Q4. it / was / fun / to / Brazil / traveling

↳ _____?

Q5. writer / isn't / as / easy / a / living / making / it / a

↳ _____.

Q6. is / milk / no / it / use / spilt / crying / over

↳ _____.

Q7. no / good / front / it's / spending / in / of / hours / TV

↳ _____.

Q8. it / a / dangerous / tiger / isn't / feeding

↳ _____?

Q9. his / death / was / a / shock / of / hearing

↳ It _____.

Q10. was / a / it / letting / risk / drive / him

↳ _____.

Q11. would / Ted / no / be / with / it / use / arguing

↳ _____.

Q12. it / money / be / giving / a / would / waste / him

↳ _____.

Q13. won't / complaining / be / it / good / to / your / any / boss

↳ _____.

Q14. for / five / worth / dollars / it / paying / thousand

↳ It wasn't _____.

Q15. would / out / it / be / a / her / pleasure / taking

↳ _____.

示範 解答 　　　　　　　　　　　　中英文對照大解析

Q1. to / it / talking / you / was / nice

↳ <u>It was nice talking to you</u>.
　（和你交談是愉快的。）

Q2. a / parent / is / hard / it / being

↳ <u>It is hard being a parent</u>.
　（為人父母不是容易的事。）

Q3. the / internet / helpful / it's / having

→ It's helpful having the internet.
（有網路是很大的幫助。）

Q4. it / was / fun / to / Brazil / traveling

→ Was it fun traveling to Brazil?
（巴西之旅好玩嗎？）

Q5. writer / isn't / as / easy / a / living / making / it / a

→ It isn't easy making a living as a writer.
（以作家為生計不是件容易的事。）

Q6. is / milk / no / it / use / spilt / crying / over

→ It is no use crying over spilt milk.
（覆水難收。）

Q7. no / good / front / it's / spending / in / of / hours / TV

→ It's no good spending hours in front of TV.
（花幾小時在看電視並不好。）

Q8. it / a / dangerous / tiger / isn't / feeding

→ Isn't it dangerous feeding a tiger?
（餵老虎吃東西不是很危險嗎？）

Q9. his / death / was / a / shock / of / hearing

→ It was a shock hearing of his death.
（聽到他的死訊令人震驚。）

☞ 提示以 It 開頭，動詞只有 was 可選，因此這是個虛主詞 it 為首的強調句型，真主詞是動名詞 hearing，但要加上介系詞 of，hear of 是「聽到…」的意思。最後要注意的是，名詞 shock 為可數，前面要放不定冠詞 a。

328

Q10. was / a / it / letting / risk / drive / him

↳ It was a risk letting him drive.

（讓他開車有風險。）

Q11. would / Ted / no / be / with / it / use / arguing

↳ It would be no use arguing with Ted.

（跟泰得爭辯沒有用。）

Q12. it / money / be / giving / a / would / waste / him

↳ It would be a waste giving him money.

（給他錢根本就是一種浪費。）

Q13. won't / complaining / be / it / good / to / your / any / boss

↳ It won't be any good complaining to your boss.

（跟老闆抱怨事情不會有什麼好處。）

Q14. for / five / worth / dollars / it / paying / thousand

↳ It wasn't worth paying five thousand dollars for it.

（花五千元在這東西上根本不值得。）

☞ 提示以 It wasn't 開頭，後面必須接補語，單字選項中也只有 worth 是正確的選擇。「worth + Ving」是個固定用語，表示「值得...（做某事）」，而 Ving 當然是非 paying 莫屬了，接著只要會「pay + 金額 + for + 物」的用語，答案就出來了。

Q15. would / out / it / be / a / her / pleasure / taking

↳ It would be a pleasure taking her out.

（能和她出去約會一種榮幸。）

解題焦點：

及物動詞後面的受詞，除了一般名詞之外，也可能是動名詞或不定詞，可分為四類：一、只能接動名詞；二、只能接不定詞；三、能接動名詞和不定詞，且意義相近；四、能接動名詞和不定詞，但意義不同。

一、只能接動名詞

例 I / singing / enjoy

☞ I enjoy singing.

二、只能接不定詞

例 I / to / want / sing

☞ I want to sing.

三、能接動名詞和不定詞，而且意義相近

例 hate / I / coffee / drinking

☞ I hate drinking coffee.

= I hate to drink coffee.

四、能接動名詞和不定詞，但意義不同

例 I / singing / stop

☞ I stop singing.（原本在唱歌，現在先停了下來。）

例 I / to / sing / stop

☞ I stop to sing.（原本在做別的事，現在先停下來去唱歌。）

重點文法 快速查!!

本單元常用動詞比較表

動詞類型	單字舉例
只能接動名詞	enjoy, mind, keep, continue, practice, avoid, give up, finish…
只能接不定詞	want, intend, plan, decide, seek, promise
能接動名詞和不定詞，且意義相近	hate, like, begin, start, stand, prefer
能接動名詞和不定詞，但意義不同	try, forget, remember, stop

實戰演練

考驗你的重組能力！

Q1. hates / the / she / dishes / doing

↳ _____ .

Q2. enjoys / he / with / talking / her

↳ _____ .

Q3. you / for / here / mind / a / do / waiting / moment

↳ _____ ?

Q4. we / searching / continue / shall

↳ _____ ?

Q5. practice / times / the / story / telling / several

↳ You'd better _____ .

Q6. want / don't / I / work / with / anymore / him / to

↳ _____.

Q7. you / rocking / the / can / chair / stop

↳ _____?

Q8. you / decided / smoking / have / to / quit

↳ _____?

Q9. book / she / begun / has / writing / a

↳ _____?

Q10. they / that / keep / why / saying / do

↳ _____?

Q11. own / your / site / try / creating / web

↳ Why don't you _____?

Q12. Queen / I'll / forget / the / in / seeing / London / never

↳ _____.

Q13. before / you / me / remember / can't / seeing

↳ _____?

Q14. to / earlier / happened / explain / had / what

↳ He attempted _____.

Q15. did / you / give / pilot / being / why / a / up

↳ _____?

示範 解答

Q1. hates / the / she / dishes / doing

↳ **She hates doing the dishes**.
（她討厭洗碗。）

Q2. enjoys / he / with / talking / her

↳ **He enjoys talking with her**.
（他喜歡和她說話。）

Q3. you / for / here / mind / a / do / waiting / moment

↳ **Do you mind waiting here for a moment**?
（你介意在此等候一下嗎？）

Q4. we / searching / continue / shall

↳ **Shall we continue searching**?
（我們要繼續搜尋嗎？）

Q5. practice / times / the / story / telling / several

↳ You'd better **practice telling the story several times**.
（你最好練習幾次說故事。）

Q6. want / don't / I / work / with / anymore / him / to

↳ **I don't want to work with him anymore**.
（我再也不想和他一起工作。）

Q7. you / rocking / the / can / chair / stop

↳ **Can you stop rocking the chair**?
（你可以不要再搖那椅子了嗎？）

Q8. you / decided / smoking / have / to / quit

↳ <u>Have you decided to quit smoking</u>?

（你決定要戒菸了嗎？）

Q9. book / she / begun / has / writing / a

↳ <u>Has she begun writing a book</u>?

（她已經開始要寫書了嗎？）

Q10. they / that / keep / why / saying / do

↳ <u>Why do they keep saying that</u>?

（為什麼他們一直那麼說？）

Q11. own / your / site / try / creating / web

↳ Why don't you <u>try creating your own web site</u>?

（你為什麼不試著架設一個自己的網站呢？）

Q12. Queen / I'll / forget / the / in / seeing / London / never

↳ <u>I'll never forget seeing the Queen in London</u>.

（我永遠不會忘記在倫敦見到了女皇。）

Q13. before / you / me / remember / can't / seeing

↳ <u>Can't you remember seeing me before</u>?

（你不記得以前見過我嗎？）

Q14. to / earlier / happened / explain / had / what

↳ He attempted <u>to explain what had happened earlier</u>.

（他試圖解釋稍早前發生了什麼事。）

Q15. did / you / give / pilot / being / why / a / up

↳ <u>Why did you give up being a pilot</u>?

（你為什麼放棄成為一名飛行員？）

句子重組

48 主詞 + 及物動詞 + 受詞 + 現在分詞

Focus 解題焦點：

這類及物動詞，與如先前在「主題 44」中提及的一樣，屬於「不完全及物動詞」，主要有兩種類型：一、知覺動詞／二、其他動詞

一、知覺動詞

・ V + O + V-ing → 強調動作正在發生或進行

NOTE：這裡的 V-ing 不是「動名詞」，而是「現在分詞」。

・ V + O + 原形 V → 強調整個過程

例 the / you / distance / sobbing / did / in / someone / hear

☞ Did you hear someone sobbing in the distance?

二、其他動詞

例 you / fast / anyone / can / running / so / image

☞ Can you image anyone running so fast?

重點文法 快速查!!

此類句型中常見的不完全及物動詞

知覺動詞	feel（覺得） watch（看見） hear（聽到）	see（看見） notice（注意） smell（聞到）
其他動詞	catch（捉住） mind（介意） bear（忍受） keep（保持）	leave（放任、任由） imagine（想像） get（使） find（發現）

GRAMMAR

Q1. you / smell / don't / burning / something

↳ _____?

Q2. stomach / wildly / felt / growling / her / Janice

↳ _____.

Q3. crying / help / you / hear / did / for / someone

↳ _____?

Q4. grabbing / your / see / the / robber / handbag

↳ Did anyone _____?

Q5. being / you / have / seen / a / hit / kid

↳ _____ ever _____?

Q6. let / catch / me / again / you / doing / don't / that

↳ _____!

Q7. can / working / them / we / get / how / hard

↳ _____?

Q8. not / the / leave / do / running / water

↳ _____!

Q9. he / himself / found / girl / attracted / being / to / the

↳ _____.

Q10. nose / can't / bear / her / people / fun / making / she / of

↳ _____.

Q11. you / image / cruelly / can / treating / anyone / dogs / so

↳ _____?

Q12. the / felt / and / shaking / out / ran / I / house

↳ _____ at once.

Q13. kept / an / hour / him / waiting / you've / for

↳ _____.

Q14. caught / the / cell / phone / him / we / stealing

↳ _____.

Q15. your / you / age / mind / do / me / asking

↳ _____?

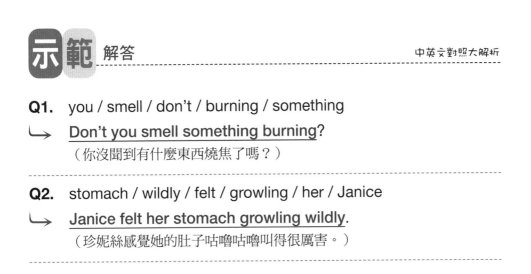

示範 解答 　　　　　　　　　　　　　　中英文對照大解析

Q1. you / smell / don't / burning / something

↳ **Don't you smell something burning**?

（你沒聞到有什麼東西燒焦了嗎？）

Q2. stomach / wildly / felt / growling / her / Janice

↳ **Janice felt her stomach growling wildly.**

（珍妮絲感覺她的肚子咕嚕咕嚕叫得很厲害。）

Q3. crying / help / you / hear / did / for / someone

↳ Did you hear someone crying for help?

（你們有沒有聽到有人在喊救命？）

Q4. grabbing / your / see / the / robber / handbag

↳ Did anyone see the robber grabbing your handbag?

（有人看見搶匪搶你的手提包嗎？）

Q5. being / you / have / seen / a / hit / kid

↳ Have you ever seen a kid being hit?

（你曾看過一個孩子被打嗎？）

Q6. let / catch / me / again / you / doing / don't / that

↳ Don't let me catch you doing that again!

（別讓我抓到你在做那件事！）

Q7. can / working / them / we / get / how / hard

↳ How can we get them working hard?

（我們要如何讓他們認真工作呢？）

☞ 句尾問號提示應以疑問詞 How 開頭，然後接助動詞 can 與主詞 we。接著看到 get 與 working 應想到「get + O + Ving」的用法。雖然 get 在意義上與使役動詞 make、have 意思一樣，但其運用的句型並不相同，應特別注意。

Q8. not / the / leave / do / running / water

↳ Do not leave the water running!

（不要放任水一直流！）

Q9. he / himself / found / girl / attracted / being / to / the

⮡ He found himself being attracted to the girl.

（他發現自已被那女孩吸引住了。）

☞ found 在此為 find 的過去式，運用於「find + O + Ving」的句型。"be attracted to" 表示「被…（某人）吸引」，to 後面要接「人」（the girl）。

Q10. nose / can't / bear / her / people / fun / making / she / of

⮡ She can't bear people making fun of her nose.

（她無法忍受別人取笑她的鼻子。）

Q11. you / image / cruelly / can / treating / anyone / dogs / so

⮡ Can you image anyone treating dogs so cruelly?

（你能想像有人對狗如此殘忍嗎？）

Q12. the / felt / and / shaking / out / ran / I / house

⮡ I felt the house shaking and ran out at once.

（我感覺房子正在搖動且立刻跑了出去。）

Q13. kept / an / hour / him / waiting / you've / for

⮡ You've kept him waiting for an hour.

（你已經讓他等了一個小時了。）

Q14. caught / the / cell / phone / him / we / stealing

⮡ We caught him stealing the cell phone.

（我們抓到他在偷手機。）

Q15. your / you / age / mind / do / me / asking

⮡ Do you mind me asking your age?

（你介意我問一下你的年齡嗎？）

☞ 很多人都知道「mind + Ving」的用法，所以可能很直接地就寫下 mind asking 了，但會發現最後 me 這個受格不知道要擺哪，於是乾脆擺在 asking 後面，變成 asking me your age，整句也變成「你介意問我你的年齡嗎？」這樣奇怪的語意。記住，mind 也可以用在「mind + O + Ving」的句型中喔！

句子重組

主題 49 | It + be 動詞 + 形容詞／名詞 + 不定詞

Focus 解題焦點：

這個主題是在句子開頭利用虛主詞 it 帶出所要強調的形容詞或名詞，而真正的主詞置於最後，以不定詞呈現。可依其強調的重點分為兩類：
一、強調名詞／二、強調形容詞

一、強調名詞

It + be 動詞 + N + 不定詞

例 is / up / pity / to / such / a / it / a / opportunity / good / give

☞ It is a pity to give up such a good opportunity.

二、強調形容詞

It + be 動詞 + Adj + 不定詞

例 with / it / to / is / talk / you / nice

☞ It is nice to talk with you.

重點文法 快速查!!

強調句型的對照與解析

	強調名詞	強調形容詞
強調句型	It + be 動詞 + N + to-V	It + be 動詞 + Adj + to-V
	It is a pity to give up such a good opportunity.	It is nice to talk with you.
原句型	S (to-V) + be 動詞 + N	S (to-V) + be 動詞 + Adj
	To give up such a good opportunity is a pity.	To talk with you is nice.

GRAMMAR

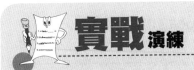

Q1. is / them / to / impossible / it / convince

↳ _____.

Q2. him / is / useless / rely / it / to / on

↳ _____.

Q3. lose / it / careless / tickets / of / was / you / to / the

↳ _____.

Q4. was / their / kind / help / of / it / to / them / offer

↳ _____.

Q5. to / your / would / be / company / it / great / have

↳ _____.

Q6. be / again / won't / it / all / easy / to / over / start

↳ _____.

Q7. is / business / it / difficult / begin

↳ _____.

Q8. is / for / loved / children / it / important / to / feel

↳ _____.

Q9. is / make / time / change / to / it / a

↳ _____.

Q10. a / day / pity / such / to / nice / spoil / it's / a

↳ _____.

Q11. him / was / a / it / go / mistake / to / let

↳ _____.

Q12. leader / it's / to / be / fun / a / class / no

↳ _____.

Q13. day / it / a / outdoors / pleasant / to / go / such / was

↳ _____.

Q14. you / into / it / so / nice / to / was / run

↳ _____.

Q15. a / it / ride / that / bike / hard / isn't / to

↳ _____.

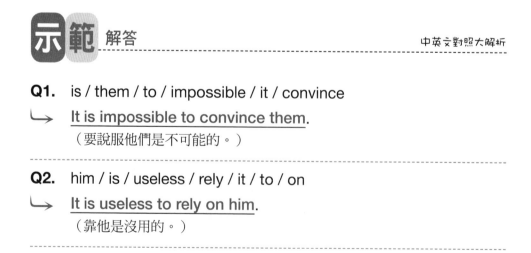

示範 解答　　　　　　　　　　　　　　　　中英文對照大解析

Q1. is / them / to / impossible / it / convince

↳ It is impossible to convince them.
（要說服他們是不可能的。）

Q2. him / is / useless / rely / it / to / on

↳ It is useless to rely on him.
（靠他是沒用的。）

Q3. lose / it / careless / tickets / of / was / you / to / the

↳ <u>It was careless of you to lose the tickets</u>.
（你把票遺失真是太不小心了。）

☞ 在「It + be動詞 + adj. + to-V」句型中，形容詞與不定詞中間也可能加入「對某人而言」或「某人令人感覺如何」的用語，前者為「for + 人」，後者則為「of + 人」。

Q4. was / their / kind / help / of / it / to / them / offer

↳ <u>It was kind of them to offer their help</u>.
（他們能提供協助真是好心。）

Q5. to / your / would / be / company / it / great / have

↳ <u>It would be great to have your company</u>.
（有你陪伴就太好了。）

☞ 如果把這裡的 company 當成「公司」的意思，會不知道這個字要擺哪！company 還有另個意思是「陪伴」，前面常跟著人稱所有格，表示「某人的陪伴」。

Q6. be / again / won't / it / all / easy / to / over / start

↳ <u>It won't be easy to start all over again</u>.
（要整個重新來過並不容易。）

Q7. is / business / it / difficult / begin

↳ <u>It is difficult to begin a business</u>.
（創業維艱。）

Q8. is / for / loved / children / it / important / to / feel

↳ <u>It is important for children to feel loved.</u>
（讓孩子感受到被愛是很重要的。）

Q9. is / make / time / change / to / it / a

↳ <u>It is time to make a change</u>.
（是該改變的時候了。）

Q10. a / day / pity / such / to / nice / spoil / it's / a

↳ It's a pity to spoil such a nice day.
（浪費這麼美好的一天真是可惜。）

Q11. him / was / a / it / go / mistake / to / let

↳ It was a mistake to let him go.
（讓他走是一個錯誤。）

Q12. leader / it's / to / be / fun / a / class / no

↳ It's no fun to be a class leader.
（當班長並不好玩。）

Q13. day / it / a / outdoors / pleasant / to / go / such / was

↳ It was such a pleasant day to go outdoors.
（這真是個走向戶外的美好日子。）

☞ 單字選項中有 such，後面要接名詞，可能是單數也可能複數名詞，但可別把這裡的 outdoors 當作複數名詞了，它是個副詞，表示「往戶外」；go outdoors 就是「走出戶外」的意思。

Q14. you / into / it / so / nice / to / was / run

↳ It was so nice to run into you.
（遇到你真好。）

Q15. a / it / ride / that / bike / hard / isn't / to

↳ It isn't that hard to ride a bike.
（騎腳踏車沒那麼難。）

Focus 解題焦點：

> 本句型中 be 動詞後面的名詞子句是主詞補語。應注意的是，這個名詞子句就是個有主詞、動詞…等基本元素的完整句子，且通常由一個「從屬連接詞」來引導，但有時是可以省略的。此類從屬連接詞主要有三類：
> 一、連接詞／二、關係代名詞／三、關係副詞

一、連接詞

　例 doesn't / problem / change / he / to / at / want / the / is / that / all
　☞ The problem is that he doesn't want to change at all.

二、關係代名詞

　例 love / whom / is / I / this
　☞ This is whom I love.

三、關係副詞

　例 leave / that / she / why / chose / to / is
　☞ That is why she chose to leave.

 快速查!!

引導名詞子句的從屬連接詞可分為三類	
連接詞	that, whether, if（不充當子句中的任何元素）
關係代名詞	what, whatever, who, whoever, whom, whose, which
關係副詞	when, where, how, why

GRAMMAR

Q1. is / he / thinks / how

↳ This _____.

Q2. this / for / what / you're / is / looking

↳ _____?

Q3. expected / is / I / like / everything / what

↳ _____.

Q4. where / lived / this / childhood / is / I / in / my

↳ _____.

Q5. wants / forgiveness / what / your / is / she

↳ _____.

Q6. is / called / why / it's / that

↳ _____ "Lucky"?

Q7. why / that / is / you / her / like

↳ _____?

Q8. is / I / love / whom / he

↳ _____.

Q9. are / they / who / saved / my / life

↳ _____?

Q10. who / singer / kidnapped / he / famous / the

   ↳ Is _____ ?

Q11. forget / is / password / that / the / I

   ↳ The trouble _____ .

Q12. do / my / is / this / that / you / don't / suggestion

   ↳ _____ .

Q13. would / down / decision / shop / their / they / close / the

   ↳ _____ was that _____ .

Q14. tomorrow / the / whether / worry / is / it / will / only / rain

   ↳ _____ .

Q15. we / choice / the / is /another / question / have

   ↳ _____ if _____ .

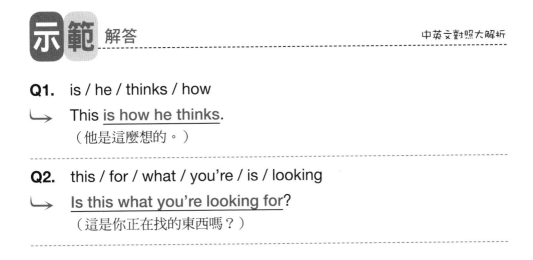

示範 解答　　　　　　　　　　　中英文對照大解析

Q1. is / he / thinks / how

   ↳ This **is how he thinks**.
     （他是這麼想的。）

Q2. this / for / what / you're / is / looking

   ↳ **Is this what you're looking for**?
     （這是你正在找的東西嗎？）

Q3. expected / is / I / like / everything / what

↳ <u>Everything is like what I expected</u>.

（一切正如我所預料。）

☞ 單字選項中有 like，但它不是動詞，而是個介系詞，表示「像⋯一樣」，後面要接名詞，但整句如果寫成 What I expected is like everything.（我所期待的是好像每一件事情。），雖然結構是正確的，但語意是不自然的。

Q4. where / lived / this / childhood / is / I / in / my

↳ <u>This is where I lived in my childhood</u>.

（這是我小時候住的地方。）

Q5. wants / forgiveness / what / your / is / she

↳ <u>Your forgiveness is what she wants</u>.

（你的原諒就是她想要的。）

Q6. is / called / why / it's / that

↳ <u>Is that why it's called</u> "Lucky"?

（那就是為什麼它被稱作「幸運」的原因嗎？）

☞ 句尾是問號，但可別直接就把疑問詞 why 放到句首了，因為從單字選項的 is 及 it's 可知，有兩個 be 動詞，所以疑問詞 why 在此的功能應是引導一個子句：why it's called "Lucky"。所以句首應放 be 動詞 is，那麼主詞當然就是 that 了。

Q7. why / that / is / you / her / like

↳ <u>Is that why you like her</u>?

（那就是為什麼你喜歡她的原因嗎？）

Q8. is / is / love / whom / he

↳ <u>He is whom I love</u>.

（他是我所愛的人。）

Q9. are / they / who / saved / my / life

↳ Are they who saved my life?

（他們是救了我一命的人嗎？）

Q10. who / singer / kidnapped / he / famous / the

↳ Is he who kidnapped the famous singer?

（他是綁架那位知名歌手的人嗎？）

Q11. forget / is / password / that / the / I

↳ The trouble is that I forget the password.

（麻煩的是我忘了密碼。）

Q12. do / my / is / this / that / you / don't / suggestion

↳ My suggestion is that you don't do this.

（我的建議是你不要做這件事。）

Q13. would / down / decision / shop / their / they / close / the

↳ Their decision was that they would close down the shop.

（他們的決定是他會把這家店收起來。）

Q14. tomorrow / the / whether / worry / is / it / will / only / rain

↳ The only worry is whether it will rain tomorrow.

（唯一要擔心的是明天會不會下雨。）

Q15. we / choice / the / is / another / question / have

↳ The question is if we have another choice.

（問題是我們不知道還有沒有機會。）

主題 51 | 數字與倍數詞的相關句型

> **Focus** 解題焦點：
>
> 此類句型主要是透過「數字」來表達人事物的外型或狀態，
> 也許是靜態，也許是動態的。主要有兩種句型：
> 一、be 動詞＋數字＋單位（-s）＋形容詞
> 二、倍數詞＋原級／比較級

一、be 動詞＋數字＋單位（-s）＋形容詞

例 meters / 1.5 / is / Anne / tall

☞ Anne is 1.5 meters tall.

二、倍數詞＋原級／比較級

例 cars / fast / twice / HSR trains / as / run / as / can

☞ HSR trains can run twice as fast as cars.

例 is / Nancy / years / Alice / older / two / than

☞ Alice is two years older than Nancy.

重點文法 快速查!!

常用的度量單位	
centimeter（=cm）（公分／釐米）	kilogram（=kg）（公斤）
meter（=m）（公尺／米）	inch（=in）（英吋）
kilometer（=km）（公里）	foot（=ft）（英呎）
milligram（=mg）（毫克）	yard（=yd）（碼）
gram（=g）（克）	mile（英哩）

GRAMMAR

Q1. is / tall / 1.7 / Sam / meters

↳ _____ .

Q2. the / is / thick / centimeters / glass / two

↳ _____ .

Q3. meters / ceiling / is / high / four / the

↳ _____ .

Q4. is / wide / the / 385 / river / kilometers

↳ _____ .

Q5. two / street / is / this / about / miles / hundred

↳ _____ long.

Q6. is / old / only / five / he / years

↳ _____ ?

Q7. swimming / and / feet / is / three / half / pool / a / the

↳ _____ deep.

Q8. Great Wall / is / the / around / 6, 700 / long / kilometers

↳ _____ .

Q9. wide / is / 20 / meters / meters / long / and / 16

↳ The house _____ .

Q10. wall / is / 12 / thick / the / inches / and

↳ _____ 80 inches high.

Q11. here / is / 38 / far / from / kilometers

↳ The temple _____.

Q12. big / is / as / as / the / moon / twice

↳ The Mars _____.

Q13. gas / air / is / 2.5 / the / heavy / times / as / as

↳ _____.

Q14. car / goes / 5 / scooter / the / times / the

↳ _____ faster than _____.

Q15. farther / Jeremy / 2 / feet / jumped

↳ _____ than Walter.

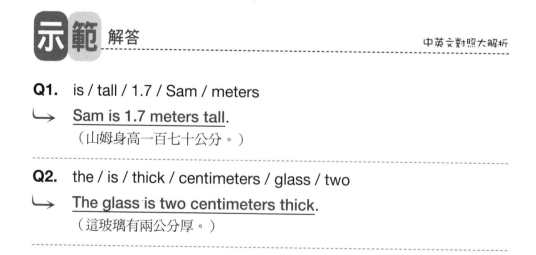

示範 解答

中英文對照大解析

Q1. is / tall / 1.7 / Sam / meters

↳ Sam is 1.7 meters tall.
（山姆身高一百七十公分。）

Q2. the / is / thick / centimeters / glass / two

↳ The glass is two centimeters thick.
（這玻璃有兩公分厚。）

352

Q3. meters / ceiling / is / high / four / the

↳ <u>The ceiling is four meters high</u>.

（天花板有四公尺高。）

Q4. is / wide / the / 385 / river / kilometers

↳ <u>The river is 385 kilometers wide</u>.

（這條何有 385 公里寬。）

Q5. two / street / is / this / about / miles / hundred

↳ <u>This street is about two hundred miles</u> long.

（過條街大約有兩百英哩長。）

Q6. is / old / only / five / he / years

↳ <u>Is he only five years old</u>?

（他只有五歲大嗎？）

Q7. swimming / and / feet / is / three / half / pool / a / the

↳ <u>The swimming pool is three and a half feet</u> deep.

（這游泳池有 3.5 英呎深。）

Q8. Great Wall / is / the / around / 6, 700 / long / kilometers

↳ <u>The Great Wall is around 6, 700 kilometers long</u>.

（中國長城大約有六千七百公里長。）

☞ Great Wall 是個專有名詞，但其前要加上 The，置於句首當主詞。around 在這裡是個副詞，表示「大約」，放在數字（6700）前面修飾，所以這裡要表達是「大約6700公里長」，要寫成 around 6700 kilometers long。

Q9. wide / is / 20 / meters / meters / long / and / 16

↳ The house <u>is 20 meters long and 16 meters wide</u>.

（這房子有 20 公尺長、16 公尺寬。）

Q10. wall / is / 12 / thick / the / inches / and

↳ <u>The wall is 12 inches thick and</u> 80 inches high.
（這道牆有 12 吋厚、80 吋高。）

Q11. here / is / 38 / far / from / kilometers

↳ The temple <u>is 38 kilometers far from here</u>.
（那座廟距離這裡 38 公里遠。）

Q12. big / is / as / as / the / moon / twice

↳ The Mars <u>is twice as big as the moon</u>.
（火星是月球的兩倍大。）

Q13. gas / air / is / 2.5 / the / heavy / times / as / as

↳ <u>The gas is 2.5 times as heavy as air</u>.
（天然氣是空氣的 2.5 倍重。）

Q14. car / goes / 5 / scooter / the / times / the

↳ <u>The car goes 5 times</u> faster than <u>the scooter</u>.
（汽車跑得比輕型機車快五倍。）

Q15. farther / Jeremy / 2 / feet / jumped

↳ <u>Jeremy jumped 2 feet farther</u> than Walter.
（傑瑞米跳得比華特遠兩英呎。）

☞ 從句尾提示字詞 than Walter 以及唯一的動詞是 jumped 來看，這是個帶有副詞比較級的句子，而這裡的副詞比較級就是 farther，它的原級是 far。數量詞 2 feet 置於比較級 farther 前面，表示「更遠兩公尺」。

句子重組

主題 **52** | 形容詞的後位修飾用法

Focus 解題焦點：

「形容詞的後位修飾」就是形容詞擺在名詞（片語）的後面作為修飾語就如同前一個主題中，「數字 + 單位 + 形容詞」的用法，也是形容詞擺在單位名詞後面修飾。但在這裡，之所以要擺在後面是因為字數過長，無法以單一形容詞擺在名詞前面來修飾。主要有三種用法：一、形容詞子句／二、分詞片語／三、介系詞片語

一、形容詞子句

例 was / book / by / Mark Twin / the / is / written / interesting / which

☞ The book which was written by Mark Twin is interesting.

二、分詞片語

例 book / by / Mark Twin / the / is / written / interesting

☞ The book written by Mark Twin is interesting.

三、介系詞片語

例 walking / the / hat / clown's / a / man / a / I / house / the / I / in

☞ I noticed a man in a clown's hat walking into the house.

 快速查!!

分詞片語分為主動與被動兩種型態	
主動型態	被動型態
The man standing by the door is my husband. =（還原為形容詞子句）The man who stands/ is standing by the door is my husband.	The car (being) stolen two days ago is mine. =（還原為形容詞子句）The car which/that was stolen two days ago is mine.

Part 1 · 單句寫作 ▶▶ 03 句子重組

GRAMMAR

355

Q1. is / cradle / sleeping / in / the / is / who

↳ The baby _____ my nephew.

Q2. talking / whom / the / man / Jane / is / to

↳ Do you know _____?

Q3. is / written / by / book / which / is / this / him / the

↳ _____.

Q4. which / a / snow / high / was / covered / with / mountain

↳ We saw _____.

Q5. walked / lady / the / has / just / past / is / that

↳ _____ my manager.

Q6. like / is / the / tourists / many / this / stay / hotel / to

↳ _____ where _____.

Q7. helps / people / doctor / a / is / a / sick / person / who

↳ _____.

Q8. people / cinema / is / a / where / place / see / a / movies

↳ _____.

Q9. which / book / yesterday / the / you / bought

↳ Please show me _____.

356

Q10. where / the / we're / going / place / is

↳ _____ an island.

Q11. is / a / this / reading / worth / book

↳ _____ .

Q12. long / is / the / hair / man / with / where

↳ _____ ?

Q13. is / the / violin / boy / playing / who / the

↳ _____ ?

Q14. book / by / Mark Twin / the / is / written / interesting

↳ _____ .

Q15. was / painted / the / wall / picture / the / on

↳ _____ by Mr. Lin.

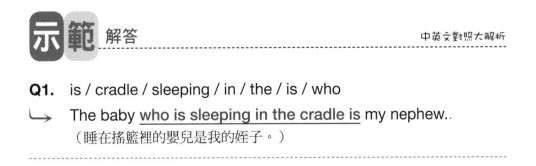

示範 解答 　　　　　　　　　　　　　　　　中英文對照大解析

Q1. is / cradle / sleeping / in / the / is / who

↳ The baby <u>who is sleeping in the cradle is</u> my nephew..
（睡在搖籃裡的嬰兒是我的姪子。）

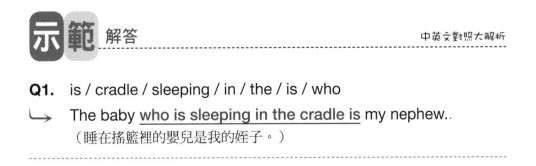

357

Q2. talking / whom / the / man / Jane / is / to

↳ Do you know <u>the man whom Jane is talking to</u>?
（你認識在和珍交談的那名男子嗎？）

☞ know 後面一定要有受詞，而所提供的單字中還有動詞 is，顯然可以接名詞子句，也就是 whom Jane is talking to（Jane 正在交談的人），但最後剩下 the 和 man 呢？剛好也可以擺在 know 後面作為其受詞，再接前面提到的 whom Jane is talking to，但這時候的它就變成形容詞子句，修飾 the man。

Q3. is / written / by / book / which / is / this / him / the

↳ <u>This is the book which is written by him</u>.
（這就是他寫的那本書。）

Q4. which / a / snow / high / was / covered / with / mountain

↳ We saw <u>a high mountain which was covered with snow</u>.
（我們見到了一座被雪覆蓋的高山。）

Q5. walked / lady / the / has / just / past / is / that

↳ <u>The lady that has just walked past is</u> my manager.
（剛才走過去的女士是我的經理。）

Q6. like / is / the / tourists / many / this / stay / hotel / to

↳ <u>This is the hotel</u> where <u>many tourists like to stay</u>.
（這是很多觀光客喜歡投宿的飯店。）

☞ 句子中間有 where，表示可能引導名詞子句或形容詞子句。首先，應確認它後面的句子要怎麼寫。"where many tourists like to stay" 是最佳的組合，前面再放 This is，形成 This is where many tourists like to stay.，但最後剩下 the 和 hotel 呢？剛好也可以擺在 This is 後面作為其主詞補語，再接前面提到的 "where many tourists like to stay"。

Q7. helps / people / doctor / a / is / a / sick / person / who

↳ <u>A doctor is a person who helps sick people</u>.
（醫生是幫助病患的人。）

Q8. people / cinema / is / a / where / place / see / a / movies

↳ A cinema is a place where people see movies.

（電影院是人們看電影的地方。）

Q9. which / book / yesterday / the / you / bought

↳ Please show me the book which you bought yesterday.

（請讓我看一下你昨天買的那本書。）

Q10. where / the / we're / going / place / is

↳ The place where we're going is an island.

（我們要去的那個地方是一座島嶼。）

Q11. is / a / this / reading / worth / book

↳ This is a book worth reading.

（這是一本值得閱讀的書。）

Q12. long / is / the / hair / man / with / where

↳ Where is the man with long hair?

（那個長髮的男子在哪？）

Q13. is / the / violin / boy / playing / who / the

↳ Who is the boy playing the violin?

（那個在拉小提琴的男孩子是誰？）

Q14. book / by / Mark Twin / the / is / written / interesting

↳ The book written by Mark Twin is interesting.

（馬克吐溫寫的那本書很有趣。）

Q15. was / painted / the / wall / picture / the / on

↳ The picture on the wall was painted by Mr. Lin.

（牆上那幅畫是林先生畫的。）

Part **2** 段落寫作

100% 得分要領

☑ 文法正確 ☑ 語句流利

☑ 內容切題 ☑ 主題連貫

Writing 6

段落寫作 完全達陣守則

　　段落寫作有別於單句寫作，並不單單把一堆句子擺在一起就算完工了，首行縮排、文法和拼字的正確性是最基本的，除此之外，還要注意語意的表達是否前後連貫，還有文章的脈絡是否合乎邏輯。

　　看圖寫作的重點在於，將圖形的意象轉換為文字，而不是天馬行空地胡扯一堆，這是看圖寫作最簡單、也最難的地方：圖畫的提示似乎便利了考生的寫作，但也因為考題給了這點方便，使考生無法隨心所欲地發揮自己所擅長的寫作題材，或避開自己沒有把握的字彙或文法。舉例來說，圖中有一隻狗在游泳（A dog is swimming.），如果不知道狗的英文是 dog，或不知道 swim 的現在分詞要重複字尾 m，恐怕就很難在這個題目上拿到分數了，千萬別小看段落寫作，它嚴屬地考驗考生的寫作功力。建議考生平時就要多做文法演練，增加自己使用文法的靈活度和熟練度，而且還要勤於擴充字彙，才不會因為字彙不足而飲恨。

　　另外還要注意，許多考生在段落寫作中最常犯的毛病就是文不對題。常見的情況是，考生沒有仔細思考圖畫所要表達的主題，看到什麼就寫什麼，結果句子和句子之間沒有意義上的連結，整篇文章呈現失焦狀態，許多閱卷老師對於這樣的情況頗為扼腕，因為考生並不見得是英文程度不好，而就算整篇文章的文法沒有錯誤，閱卷老師頂多也只能掬一把同情淚，給一點點同情分數，要拿到高分是不可能的。另一種常見的情形是，文句敘述和圖完全沒有關聯，完全無視於圖畫的存在，有這種現象的考生，在答題時千千萬萬要提醒自己：「再多看圖畫一眼吧」！

TIPS 段落寫作搶分一族

- ✿ **Step 1.** 平日多做文法練習，增加靈活度及熟練度。
- ✿ **Step 2.** 擴充字彙，無往不利。
- ✿ **Step 3.** 仔細觀察圖片，找出圖片所要表達的主要內容。
- ✿ **Step 4.** 根據圖片內容，構思一段主題前後連貫且劇情符合邏輯的短文。
- ✿ **Step 5.** 發揮你在 Part 1 所學到的文法基礎，寫出流利且正確的句子。
- ✿ **Step 6.** 交卷之前務必依據 Step3 至 Step5，再次檢視答題過程。

段落寫作

寵物篇

請依照題目的要求,寫出一篇約 50 字的短文。這個 PART 的評分要點包括:重點表達的完整性、文法、用字、拼字、字母大小寫及標點符號。

相關字彙 快速查!!

a cat (cats) 貓

a dog (dogs) 狗

a bunny (bunnies) 兔子

a bird (birds) 鳥

a parrot (parrots) 鸚鵡

keep a pet 養寵物

a pet (pets) 寵物

a kitten (kittens) 小貓

a puppy (puppies) 小狗

a mouse (mice) 鼠

a fish (fish) 魚

a turtle (turtles) 烏龜

a pet carrier 寵物提籃

GRAMMAR

363

**實戰**演練

寫作測驗 1. Alice 有一隻狗，幾乎形影不離。請根據以下三張圖，寫出一篇約 50 字的短文。

A　　　　　B　　　　　C

_____

_____

_____

_____

_____

_____

_____

_____

_____

_____

▶▶ 參考解答請見 p.367

寫作測驗 2. Ken 的媽媽送了一隻小狗給他當十歲的生日禮物,有一天小狗不見了。請根據以下三張圖,寫一篇約 50 字的短文。

A　　　　　　　B　　　　　　　C

1.

Alice 有一隻狗，幾乎形影不離。請根據以下三張圖，寫出一篇約 50 字的短文。

A

B

C

▶▶ 參考解答

Alice **keeps a dog**. When Alice **watches TV**, it lies by her feet. When Alice **goes jogging**, it runs **by her side**. If Alice has to take a bus, she would put it in a **pet carrier**. However, there are still some places where her dog can't go with her, including the movie theaters and some restaurants.

▶▶ 中文翻譯

Alice 養了一隻狗。當 Alice 看電視的時候，牠就趴在她的腳邊。當 Alice 去慢跑時，牠就跑在她的旁邊。如果 Alice 必須去搭公車時，她會把牠放在一個寵物提籃裡。然而，還是有些地方是她的狗不能和她一起去的，包括電影院和一些餐廳。

2.

Ken 的媽媽送了一隻小狗給他當十歲的生日禮物。有一天小狗不見了。請根據以下三張圖,寫一篇約 50 字的短文。

A   **B**   **C**

▶▶ 參考解答

    It was Ken's 10-year-old birthday. He was happier than ever when he received **a puppy as a gift** from his mother. Ken and his new friend **spent so much great time together**. One day, Ken couldn't find his **pet** and **nearly burst into tears**. Suddenly, he broke tears into laughter when the little animal **showed up and ran to him**.

▶▶ 中文翻譯

那是 Ken 十歲的生日,當他從母親那兒接獲一隻小狗作為禮物時,他開心得不得了。Ken 和他的新朋友一起渡過了許多快樂時光。有一天,Ken 找不到他的寵物,且他幾乎要嚎啕大哭了。突然,當那小動物出現且跑向他時,他馬上破涕為笑了。

生活篇

請依照題目的要求，寫出一篇約 50 字的短文。這個 PART 的評分要點包括：重點表達的完整性、文法、用字、拼字、字母大小寫及標點符號。

相關字彙 快速查!!

winter vacation 寒假	summer vacation 暑假
see a doctor 看醫生	spring vacation 春假
go to bed 上床睡覺	go to school 上學
have a headache 頭痛	catch a cold 感冒
get hurt 受傷	cough 咳嗽
classroom 教室	bathroom 浴室
get up 起床	rest room 廁所
have a stomachache 胃痛	have/catch a flu 得了流行性感冒
do the cleaning 做清潔工作	sneeze 打噴嚏
living room 客廳	bedroom 寢室
	dorm 宿舍

GRAMMAR

實戰演練

考驗你的寫作能力！

▶▶參考解答請見 p.375

寫作測驗 **1.** 請根據以下三張圖，寫一篇約 50 字的短文，描述 Tammy 暑假期間中某一天的生活。

_____

_____

_____

_____

_____

_____

_____

_____

_____

_____

Part 2 · 段落寫作 ▶▶ 02 生活篇

▶▶參考解答請見 p.376

寫作
測驗 **2.** 今早你身體不舒服,媽媽帶你去看醫生,醫生檢查後告訴你得了
流感。請根據以下三張圖,寫一篇約 50 字的短文。

A　　　B　　　C

_____

_____

_____

_____

_____

_____

_____

_____

_____

_____

▶▶參考解答請見 p.377

寫作測驗 3. 學生有責任保持教室整潔,請根據以下三張圖,寫一篇約 50 字的短文,描述學生的清潔工作情形。

A　　　B　　　C

▶▶參考解答請見 p.378

寫作
測驗 **4.** 在 Emma 前往美國念大學之前從未離家過，所以她相當不適應在外孤單過夜的日子。請根據以下三張圖，寫一篇約 50 字的短文。

▶▶ 參考解答請見 p.379

寫作測驗 5. Kate 每天過著規律的生活,她放學回家後就很快地把功課先做完了。請根據以下三張圖,寫一篇約 50 字的短文。

A   B   C

_____

_____

_____

_____

_____

_____

_____

_____

_____

_____

_____

▶▶ 參考解答請見 p.380

寫作測驗 6. 湯姆的太太出門去了，留下他和兒子獨處，湯姆和太太道別之後聽到玻璃摔破的聲音。請根據以下圖片，描述他們兩人相處的情形。

A　B　C

範 解答

1.
　　請根據以下三張圖，寫一篇約 50 字的短文，描述 Tammy 暑假期間中某一天的生活。

A

B

C

▶▶ 參考解答

　　It is **summer vacation**. Tammy **doesn't get up early** in order to go to school. He usually **misses his breakfast**. After lunch, he **sticks in front of the computer playing games**. His mother **isn't happy with** his unhealthy life, so she takes him to the **swimming pool** to learn how to swim.

▶▶ 中文翻譯

現在是暑假，湯米不必為了去上學而早起。他通常都會錯過早餐。在吃完午餐後，他就一直待在電腦前打電玩。他媽媽很不高興他過這種不健康的生活，於是帶他到游泳池去學游泳。

2.

今早你身體不舒服，媽媽帶你去看醫生，醫生檢查後告訴你得了流感。請根據以下三張圖，寫一篇約 50 字的短文。

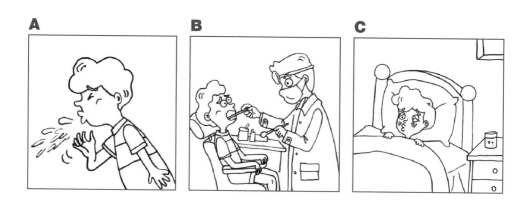

▶▶ **參考解答**

This morning, I woke up and **didn't feel well. My mother took me to see a doctor.** First, the doctor **took my temperature.** Then he **checked my throat,** and found it red and swollen. The doctor said that I had caught a flu. He suggested that I should **rest and drink** as much **water** as possible.

▶▶ **中文翻譯**

今天早上我起床之後感覺不舒服。我母親帶我去看醫生。首先，醫生幫我量了體溫，然後檢查我的喉嚨，並發現我的喉嚨又紅又腫。醫生說我感冒了。他建議我盡可能多休息及多喝水。

3.

學生有責任保持教室整潔,請根據以下三張圖,寫一篇約 50 字的短文,描述學生的清潔工作情形。

A　　　　　　　**B**　　　　　　　**C**

▶▶ **參考解答**

　　Students are responsible for keeping the classroom **tidy and clean. They** usually **do the cleaning** at the end of a day. They **have their different duties:** some have to sweep or mop the floors; some tidy up the desks and chairs; and others **collect the garbage** and **throw it away.** After all, they are the ones who mess up the classroom.

▶▶ **中文翻譯**

學生有責任保持教室整潔,他們通常在一天結束的時候做清潔工作。他們各有不同的職責:有人得掃地或拖地,有人得把桌椅排整齊;其他人則把垃圾整理起來並拿出去丟掉。畢竟,他們就是把教室弄亂的人。

4.

在 Emma 前往美國念大學之前從未離家過，所以她相當不適應在外孤單過夜的日子。請根據以下三張圖，寫一篇約 50 字的短文。

A    **B**    **C**

▶▶ 參考解答

    Emma had never spent a night away from home until she entered the college in America. She was reluctant to part from her parents at the airport. How she missed her family back in Taiwan! Feeling lonely in the dorm, she always sobbed herself to sleep for the first whole month.

▶▶ 中文翻譯

艾瑪未曾離開家在外過夜，直到她在美國念大學時。她在機場時很不情願地和她的父母道別。她有多麼思念在台灣的家人啊！第一個月在校舍裡，她感覺自己很孤單，她總是一直哭到睡著。

5.

Kate 每天過著規律的生活，她放學回家後就很快地把功課先做完了。請根據以下三張圖，寫一篇約 50 字的短文。

A

B

C

▶▶ 參考解答

　　Kate leads a regular life. She finishes her homework right back from school. She has only fruits and vegetables for dinner. She goes to bed at 9 o'clock, and gets up early at 6 o'clock sharp. Kate believes that by this way, she may remain in good health and live to the age of a hundred.

▶▶ 中文翻譯

凱特過著規律的生活。她放學回來後會馬上完成她的作業，晚餐她只吃蔬果。她九點就上床睡覺，且一大早六點整起床。凱特相信，藉由這樣的生活方式，她可以保持身體健康，活到一百歲。

6.

湯姆的太太出門去了，留下他和兒子獨處，湯姆和太太道別之後聽到玻璃摔破的聲音。請根據以下圖片，描述他們兩人相處的情形。

A

B

C

▶▶ 參考解答

Tom waved at his wife as she walked away, just before he heard glass breaking and his son crying. He saw him standing by a vase in pieces on the floor. The boy held up his hand, and it was covered in blood. Tom rushed him into the bathroom and cleaned off his hand. After it was well bandaged up, Tom started sweeping up the glass pieces.

▶▶ 中文翻譯

湯姆的太太離去時，他向她揮揮手。然後，就他聽到打破玻璃以及他兒子在哭泣的聲音。他看到他站在散落一地的花瓶碎片旁。孩子伸出手，手上一片血淋淋。湯姆火速將他帶到浴室去把手清洗乾淨。孩子的手包紮好之後，湯姆開始清掃碎玻璃。

0③ ▶▶

職 業 篇

請依照題目的要求,寫出一篇約 50 字的短文。這個 PART 的評分要點包括:重點表達的完整性、文法、用字、拼字、字母大小寫及標點符號。

 相關字彙 快速查!!

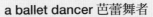

	an artist 藝術家
a dancer 舞者	a ballet dancer 芭蕾舞者
a musician 音樂家	a guitarist 吉他手
a pianist 鋼琴手	a singer 歌手
a violinist 小提琴手	an actor 男演員
a painter 畫家	a novelist 小說家
a writer 作家	a secretary 秘書
a cook 廚師	a dentist 牙醫
a doctor 醫生	a nurse 護士
a scientist 科學家	an engineer 工程師
a gardener 花匠,園丁	a farmer 農夫
a mailman 郵差	a worker 工人
a bus driver 公車司機	a pilot 飛行員
a policeman 員警	a student 學生
a teacher 教師	a professor 教授

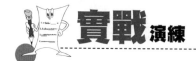
實戰演練

▶▶ 參考解答請見 p.383

寫作測驗 **1.** Gina 是一名學生，她的夢想是成為一名舞者，請根據以下三張圖，寫一篇約 50 字的短文。

B   C

_____

_____

_____

_____

_____

_____

_____

_____

_____

_____

_____

▶▶ 參考解答請見 p.384

| 寫作
測驗 | 2. | Jason 從小就愛玩飛機，長大後還當上了飛行員。請根據以下三張
圖，寫一篇約 50 字的短文。 |

A

B

C

_____

_____

_____

_____

_____

_____

_____

_____

_____

_____

_____

 解答

1.

> Gina 是一名學生,她的夢想是成為一名舞者,請根據以下三張圖,寫一篇約 50 字的短文。

▶▶ 參考解答

Gina is a student. She is at school from 7:30 a.m. to 5:00 p.m. After school she can't go home directly because she has to take a ballet class. Becoming a famous dancer has been Gina's dream since she was very young. Therefore, even though she has to work so hard, she still enjoys her life very much.

▶▶ 中文翻譯

吉娜是一名學生。她早上七點半到下午五點在學校上學。放學後她不能直接回家,因為她還要去上芭蕾舞課。從她很小的時候,成為一位著名的舞者就一直是吉娜的夢想。因此,即使她必須這麼辛苦,她還是相當樂在其中。

2.

　　Jason 從小就愛玩飛機，長大後還當上了飛行員。請根據以下三張圖，寫一篇約 50 字的短文。

A 　**B** 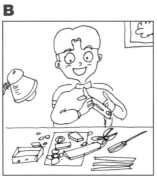　**C**

▶▶ 參考解答

　　Jason is really fond of **airplanes**. When he was a kid, his favorite game was to fly **paper planes** folded by his father. Then he started to build **model planes**. His dream of **flying a real plane** has come true --- he's a pilot now. He thinks it's wonderful that he can work for what he is interested in.

▶▶ 中文翻譯

Jason 真的很喜歡飛機。當他還是個小孩的時候，他最喜歡的遊戲就是玩父親摺的紙飛機。然後他開始組裝模型飛機。他駕駛真正飛機的夢想已經實現了——現在他是一名飛行員。他認為可以和興趣結合的工作真是太棒了。

Part 2 ● 段落寫作 ▼ 03 職業篇

04 ▶▶

交 通 篇

請依照題目的要求,寫出一篇約 50 字的短文。這個 PART 的評分要點包括:重點表達的完整性、文法、用字、拼字、字母大小寫及標點符號。

相關字彙 快速查!!

crosswalk 行人穿越道	pavement 人行道
bus stop 公車站	train station 火車站
street 街道	road 路
taxi 計程車	freeway 高速公路
take a bus 搭公車	ambulance 救護車
bicycle/bike 腳踏車	MRT=Mass Rapid Transit 捷運
traffic jam 塞車	scooter 機車
traffic accident 交通事故	flat tire 爆胎
traffic lights 紅綠燈,交通號誌燈	run through a red light 闖紅燈
street sign 街道標誌	traffic rule(s) 交通規則
by... 以…為交通工具	ask direction(s) 問路
	on foot 步行

GRAMMAR

實戰 演練

考驗你的寫作能力！

▶▶ 參考解答請見 p.391

| 寫作測驗 | 1. | Patty 和朋友約了下午六點見面，但是她被會議絆住，且又遇上了塞車。請根據以下三張圖，寫一篇約 50 字的短文。 |

A

B

C

_____

_____

_____

_____

_____

_____

_____

_____

_____

_____

_____

▶▶ 參考解答請見 p.392

寫作
測驗
2. 上星期一你在上學途中目睹了一場車禍，請根據以下三張圖，寫一篇約 50 字的短文。

▶▶ 參考解答請見 p.393

寫作測驗 3. Tony 為了準備考試而熬夜讀書,隔天在公車上睡著而忘了下車,並錯過了考試時間。請根據以下三張圖,寫一篇約 50 字的短文。

A

B

終點站

C

_____

_____

_____

_____

_____

_____

_____

_____

_____

_____

▶▶ 參考解答請見 p.394

寫作測驗 **4.** Adam 跟媽媽說今天在放學回家途中，有個說英語的外國人向他問路。請根據以下三張圖，寫一篇約 50 字的短文。

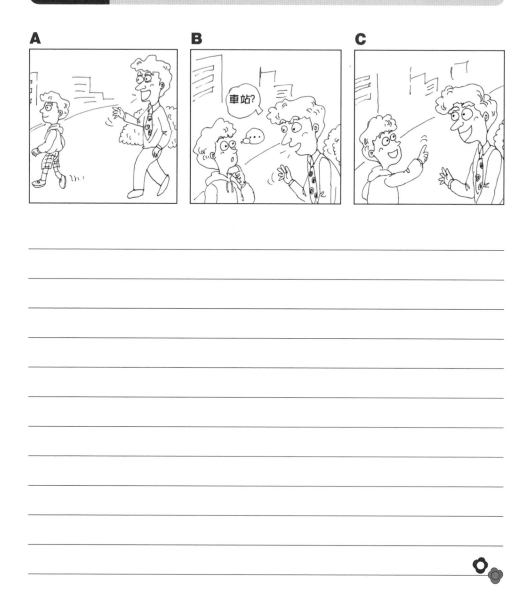

解答

中英文對照大解析

1.

Patty 和朋友約了下午六點見面,但是她被會議絆住,且又遇上了塞車。請根據以下三張圖,寫一篇約 50 字的短文。

A	B	C

▶▶ 參考解答

　　Patty was going to meet a friend at 6 p.m. but she was still attending a meeting at 5:30 p.m. Right after the meeting, she called her friends to apologize and wanted them to wait for her. She jumped into her car, but it was already 5:55. The worst is that it seemed there was a traffic jam, so all the vehicles are moving extremely slowly.

▶▶ 中文翻譯

佩蒂和朋友約晚上六點要見面,不過她下午五點半時還在開會。就在會議後她馬上就打電話給她的朋友道歉,並請她們等她一下。她跳上她的車,但已經五點五十五分了。最糟的是,似乎塞車了,因此所有車輛都只能極度緩慢地前進著。

Part 2 · 段落寫作 ▶▶ 04 交通篇

391

2.

上星期一你在上學途中目睹了一場車禍，請根據以下三張圖，寫一篇約 50 字的短文。

A

B

C

▶▶ 參考解答

　　Last Monday, on my way to school, I saw a **traffic accident**. A **woman riding a scooter** was **hit by a truck**. She was thrown away from her **motorcycle** which was **badly damaged**. The truck driver quickly came to the woman to check if she was injured. Finally, **the police** arrived at the **accident scene**.

▶▶ 中文翻譯

上星期一，我在上學途中看到了一場車禍。一名騎著摩托車的婦人被一輛卡車撞到，她從她的摩托車摔了出去，而摩托車也嚴重受損。卡車司機趕緊來到婦人身旁查看她有沒有受傷，最後，員警抵達了事故現場。

3.

Tony 為了準備考試而熬夜讀書，隔天在公車上睡著而忘了下車，並錯過了考試時間。請根據以下三張圖，寫一篇約 50 字的短文。

A　　　　　　　**B**　　　　　　　**C**

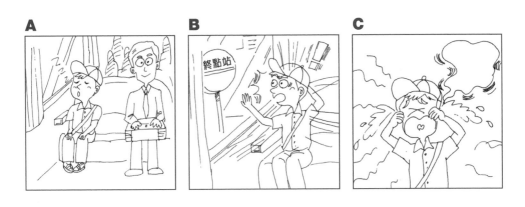

▶▶ 參考解答

Last night Tony **stayed up late** preparing for an important exam. He was so tired that he **fell asleep on the bus** to school this morning. When the bus came to the **terminal**, the bus driver woke him up. Tony couldn't help but cry loudly because it was **too late** for him **to take the exam**.

▶▶ 中文翻譯

昨天晚上 Tony 熬夜準備一場重要的考試。由於太累了，他今天早上在前往學校的公車上睡著了。當公車來到終點站時，公車司機叫醒了他。Tony 忍不住大聲哭了起來，因為他已經來不及參加考試了。

4.

Adam 跟媽媽說今天在放學回家途中,有個說英語的外國人向他問路。請根據以下三張圖,寫一篇約 50 字的短文。

▶▶ 參考解答

　　Adam is very excited about today's special experience. He told his mother about it: he helped a man who speaks English. This afternoon, **on his way home from school,** a foreigner asked him about **the direction to the train station.** Adam did his best to help the foreigner get to the place successfully.

▶▶ 中文翻譯

亞當對今天的特殊經驗感到相當興奮。他告訴他媽媽這件事:他幫助一位講英文的男子。今天下午,在放學回家路上,有一位外國人問他到火車站怎麼走。亞當盡他最大努力成功地幫助那位外國人去到了他要去的地方。

05 ▶▶

飲 食 篇

請依照題目的要求，寫出一篇約 50 字的短文。這個 PART 的評分要點包括：重點表達的完整性、文法、用字、拼字、字母大小寫及標點符號。

相關字彙 快速查!!

dining room 飯廳	restaurant 餐廳
convenience store 便利商店	McDonald 麥當勞
fast-food restaurant 速食店	buffet 自助餐
food 食物	a meal 一餐
noodles 麵食	rice 米飯
vegetable 蔬菜	steak 排餐
fruit 水果	meat 肉
tea 茶	coffee 咖啡
chocolate 巧克力	milk 牛奶
bread 麵包	cake 蛋糕
drinks 飲料	ice cream 冰淇淋
juice 果汁	coke 可樂
hamburgers 漢堡	sandwich 三明治
pizza 披薩	French fries 薯條
fish 魚肉	beef 牛肉
pork 豬肉	chicken 雞肉
Chinese food 中餐	Western-style food 西餐
	seafood 海鮮

▶▶ 參考解答請見 p.398

寫作測驗 1. 有一天你到餐廳吃飯，卻忘了帶錢，根據以下三張圖，寫一篇約 50 字的短文。

A　　　B　　　C

_____

_____

_____

_____

_____

_____

_____

_____

_____

_____

_____

_____

▶▶ 參考解答請見 p.399

寫作測驗 2. 人人愛吃的食物不同，要決定一起吃什麼可能不是件容易的事。請根據以下三張圖，寫一篇約 50 字的短文。

A　　　　　　B　　　　　　C

 1.

有一天你到餐廳吃飯，卻忘了帶錢，根據以下三張圖，寫一篇約 50 字的短文。

▶▶ 參考解答

　　One day I went to a **cafeteria** for lunch. After **ordering my meal**, I found I **had left my money in the office**. I was so **embarrassed** that I didn't know what to do next. Fortunately, one of **my co-workers** appeared and **helped me pay for** my food. She really is my lifesaver!

▶▶ 中文翻譯

有一天我去自助餐廳吃午飯，點完餐後，我發現我把錢忘在辦公室裡了。我糗得不知道接下來該怎麼辦。幸好，我一位同事出現了，並幫我付了食物的錢。她真是我的救星！

2.

人人愛吃的食物不同，要決定一起吃什麼可能不是件容易的事。請根據以下三張圖，寫一篇約 50 字的短文。

A

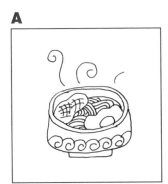

B

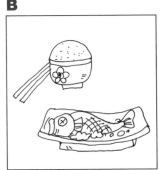

C

▶▶ 參考解答

It can be difficult to decide what to **eat** for every **meal**, not to mention sometimes you want to **enjoy a meal together** with your friends or your family. One may like **rice**, another like **noodles**, and the other like **steak**. To make the decision on where to go can be a headache and can result in unhappiness.

▶▶ 中文翻譯

決定每一餐要吃什麼可能會有困難，更別 有時候你要和朋友或家人聚在一起享用一餐了。有人喜歡吃飯，有人喜歡吃麵，還有人喜歡吃牛排。要做出去哪吃飯的決定，可能是件令人頭痛的事，且可能帶來不愉快。

06 ▶▶

休 閒 篇

請依照題目的要求，寫出一篇約 50 字的短文。這個 PART 的評分要點包括：重點表達的完整性、文法、用字、拼字、字母大小寫及標點符號。

相關字彙　快速查!!

holiday 假期
Kenting 墾丁
beach 沙灘
department store 百貨公司
shopping mall 購物商場
go to see a movie 去看電影
go hiking 遠足，徒步旅行
enjoy the nature 享受大自然
hobby 嗜好
watch TV 看電視
do exercise 做運動
comic books 漫畫書

on the weekend 在週末
Sun-Moon Lake 日月潭
Yang Ming Mountain 陽明山
zoo 動物園
movie theater 電影院
go shopping 逛街
go climbing 攀爬
go on a picnic 野餐
have fun/have a god time 玩得開心
listen to music 聽音樂
pastime 消遣
drawing 畫畫

GRAMMAR

實戰演練

寫作測驗 **1.** 請根據以下三張圖，寫一篇約 50 字的短文，描述 Ben 和家人到日月潭旅遊的經過。

A

B

C

_____

_____

_____

_____

_____

_____

_____

_____

_____

_____

_____

Part 2 · 段落寫作 ▼▼ 06 休閒篇

▶▶ 參考解答請見 p.406

寫作 測驗 2. 請根據以下三張圖，寫一篇約 50 字的短文，描寫這一家人在沙灘上的活動情形。

_____

_____

_____

_____

_____

_____

_____

_____

_____

_____

▶▶ 參考解答請見 p.407

寫作
測驗　**3.**　　請根據以下三張圖，寫一篇約 50 字的短文，描寫坐雲霄飛車
　　　　　　　（roller coaster）緊張刺激的過程。

A

B

C

▶▶ 參考解答請見 p.408

寫作測驗 **4.** 到百貨公司購物，你通常可以逛上好幾個小時。請根據以下圖片，描述你逛百貨公司的情形。

A　　　　　　　　B　　　　　　　　C

_____

_____

_____

_____

_____

_____

_____

_____

_____

_____

_____

解答

請根據以下三張圖，寫一篇約 50 字的短文，描述 Ben 和家人到日月潭旅遊的經過。

▶▶ 參考解答

Ben made a trip to Sun-Moon Lake with his family. They went there by bus. The scenery there was very beautiful. The lake was big and calm. They first went boating on the lake, and then they went on a hike around the lake. When feeling tired, they lay down on the lawn side by side watching the starry sky.

▶▶ 中文翻譯

Ben 和家人到日月潭旅遊，他們搭乘巴士前往。那兒的風景非常美麗。湖面大又平靜。她們先在湖上划船，然後沿著湖散步。當他們覺得累了，就肩並肩躺在草地上欣賞著星空。

2.

請根據以下三張圖，寫一篇約 50 字的短文，描寫這一家人在沙灘上的活動情形。

A   B   C

▶▶ 參考解答

At the beach, two children are digging the sand with shovels and pails. They build a sand castle while their parents lie resting under a beach umbrella. The boy was in such a hurry that he knocked over the sand castle. His sister looks at his funny gesture and laughs hard, and so do his parents.

▶▶ 中文翻譯

在沙灘上，兩個小孩用鏟子和提桶正在挖沙子。當他們在蓋沙堡時，他們的父母則在海灘傘下躺著休息。小男孩太過急忙了，所以把沙堡給弄倒了。他的姊姊看見他滑稽的動作大笑不已，他的父母也在笑著。

3.

請根據以下三張圖，寫一篇約 50 字的短文，描寫坐雲霄飛車（roller coaster）緊張刺激的過程。

A   **B**   **C**

▶▶ 參考解答

    My palms were sweating. Today was the day I overcome my fear of roller coasters. I bravely marched to the waiting line; I boarded the car; I was ready to take off! Super fast speeds and sharp turns made the ride very exciting. I had an awesome day and decided I will come again next week.

▶▶ 中文翻譯

我的手掌在流汗。今天我就要克服坐雲霄飛車的恐懼了。我勇敢地走向等候的隊伍；我上了車廂；我要出發囉！超快的速度和急轉彎讓我有了一趟非常刺激的體驗。我的這一天真是精采，且我決定下星期還要再來。

4.

到百貨公司購物，你通常可以逛上好幾個小時。請根據以下圖片，描述你逛百貨公司的情形。

A

B

C

▶▶ **參考解答**

Every time I go to the department store, I can spend several hours shopping. It is for me like a day trip. I always think I'm just going to get a dress, but I usually end up coming out with shoes, earrings and other stuff that goes with the dress. Anyway, the department store is the best place to go to, rain or shine!

▶▶ **中文翻譯**

每次我去百貨公司時，我總能花上好幾個小時購物。對我來說，它就像是一日遊。我總是以為我會只買一件洋裝，但通常最後會買了鞋子、耳環和其他搭配洋裝的配件。不管怎樣，百貨公司是最棒的去處，無論下雨或晴天！

PART 2.
段落寫作

氣象篇

請依照題目的要求，寫出一篇約 50 字的短文。這個 PART 的評分要點包括：重點表達的完整性、文法、用字、拼字、字母大小寫及標點符號。

快速查!!

spring 春天	weather 天氣
fall 秋天	summer 夏天
hot 炎熱的	winter 冬天
cold 冷的	cool 涼涼的
humid 潮濕的	warm 溫暖的
cloud 雲	freezing 酷寒的
shower 陣雨	snow 雪
storm 暴風雨	typhoon 颱風
breeze 微風	wind 風
cold front 冷空氣、冷鋒	heat 熱氣
	sweat 流汗

Part 2 · 段落寫作 ▶▶ 07 氣象篇

GRAMMAR

409

實戰演練

考驗你的寫作能力！

▶▶ 參考解答請見 p.413

寫作測驗 **1.** 你和父母到動物園去玩，在遊園時卻下起了大雨。請根據以下三張圖，寫一篇約 50 字的短文。

A

B

C

_____

_____

_____

_____

_____

_____

_____

_____

_____

_____

▶▶ 參考解答請見 p.414

**寫作
測驗** **2.** 仲夏的天氣像烤箱一樣熱，所以到山上去享受清涼的空氣、美麗的景色並享用特別的餐點，應該是很享受的事。請根據以下三張圖，寫一篇約 50 字的短文。

A

B

C

▶▶ 參考解答請見 p.415

寫作
測驗　**3.**　請根據以下三張圖，寫一篇約50字的短文，描寫颱風過後停電造成生活上的困擾。

A　　　　　　　　B　　　　　　　　C

_____

_____

_____

_____

_____

_____

_____

_____

_____

_____

解答

1.

你和父母到動物園去玩，在遊園時卻下起了大雨。請根據以下三張圖，寫一篇約 50 字的短文。

A

B

C

▶▶ 參考解答

　　Last Saturday, my parents and I **went to the zoo**. We wanted to see the newborn koalas; but before we could see them, it started to **pour**. We ran quickly into a **pavilion**. While waiting for the **rain** to stop, we took out the food from the backpack and happily ate it up.

▶▶ 中文翻譯

上星期六，我和爸媽去動物園。我們想去看剛出生的無尾熊；但在我們能看到無尾熊之前，天空開始下起了大雨。我們快速地跑進一座涼亭。我們在等待雨停的同時，從背包裡拿出食物，並開心地把食物吃光光。

2.

仲夏的天氣像烤箱一樣熱,所以到山上去享受清涼的空氣、美麗的景色並享用特別的餐點,應該是很享受的事。請根據以下三張圖,寫一篇約 50 字的短文。

A   **B**   **C**

▶▶ 參考解答

    It feels like an oven out there. We're almost dying in this summer heat! Is going hiking in the mountains a great idea? Fresh, cool air and beautiful scenery seem two good reasons to get out of the city. What's more? Maybe we could sample some special food! OK! Let's take a trip to the mountain.

▶▶ 中文翻譯

外面熱得像烤箱,我們快被這種嚴夏暑氣給熱死了!去山上健行是個好主意嗎?清涼的空氣和美麗的風景似乎是逃離城市的兩個好理由。還有什麼?也許我們可以品嚐些特產。好吧!我們要去山上玩吧!

3.

請根據以下三張圖，寫一篇約50字的短文，描寫颱風過後停電造成生活上的困擾。

A   **B**   **C**

▶▶ 參考解答

A strong **typhoon** caused a massive **blackout** last night. We could barely see things by the dim light of **candles** and **flashlights**. We couldn't watch TV and turn on the **air-conditioning** or the electric fan! We felt so bored and so hot. I turned and tossed all night, and woke up tired due to the poor sleep quality.

▶▶ 中文翻譯

昨夜一個強烈颱風造成大規模停電。我們幾乎無法藉由蠟燭和手電筒的微弱光線看清楚東西。我們沒辦法看電視，也無法使用冷氣或電扇。我們覺得好無聊且很熱。我一整晚翻來覆去，且醒來時感覺很疲倦，因為睡眠品質太差了。

MEMO

英檢初級寫作
實戰完整模擬試題

本測驗共有兩部分。第一部份為單句寫作，第二部份為段落寫作。測驗時間為 40 分鐘。

第一部分：單句寫作（50%）

請將答案寫在答案紙上對應的題號旁，如有文法、用字、拼字、標點符號、大小寫等之錯誤，將予扣分。

第 1～5 題句子改寫

請依題目之提示，將原句依指定型式改寫，並將改寫的句子**完整**地寫在答案紙上。**注意：須寫出提示之文字及標點符號。**

例：題目：I receive a letter from her.

    She sent _____ .

在答案紙上寫：***She sent a letter to me. / She sent me a letter.***

---

1. Leave early because you don't want to miss the bus.（用 so that）
   Leave _____ .

2. People don't use this bridge very often.（用被動式）
   This bridge _____ .

3. I'd rather have tea than coffee.（用 would prefer）
   _____ .

4. Peter invited Alice to the concert.（改寫成被動式）
   Alice _____ Peter.

5. Alex went to Korea yesterday and he is there now.（用 has）
   _____ .

第 6～10 題：句子合併

請依照題目指示，將兩句合併成一句，並將合併的句子完整地寫在答案紙上。注意：須寫出提示之文字及標點符號。

例：He goes swimming.

    He does it once a week.

題目：He _____ once a week.

在答案紙上寫：***He goes swimming once a week.***

---

6. Helen's job is boring.
    Helen is bored.（用 because）
    _____.

7. There are not many chairs.
    Not everybody can get a chair to sit down.（用 enough... to）
    _____.

8. I have a brother.
    My brother is studying Chinese in college.（用 who）
    _____.

9. Tom asked Grace something.
    Jane went home early.（用 why）
    _____.

10. Terry can't see anything.
    She has to wear glasses.
    _____ without _____.

第 11～15 題：重組
請將題目中所有提示的字詞整合成一個有意義的句子，並將重組的句子完整地寫在答案紙上。注意：須寫出提示之文字及標點符號。（答案中必須使用所有提示的字詞，且不能隨意增減字詞，否則不予計分。）

> 例：題目：They _____?
>   Jack / me / call
>   在答案紙上寫：***They call me Jack.***

11. The new _____.
    good / is / restaurant / Baseline / Road / on / very

12. It _____.
    raining / hour / ago / an / started

13. They _____.
    plenty / to / money / seem / of / have

14. Mark _____.
    eat / that / nervous / he / so / was / couldn't

15. They _____.

    paint / house / themselves / didn't / the

第二部分：段落寫作（50%）

題目：約翰（John）是個學生，而且他的生活很有規律，下面幾張圖為 John 平常一天的生活。請依照下面的圖片，用大約 50 個字來描述他每一天的生活作息。

全民英語能力分級檢定測驗

初級寫作能力測驗答案紙（不夠請自行影印）

座位號碼： 　　　　　　　　　　　　試卷別： _____

第一部分：單句寫作（50%），請依題目序號並於<u>框線內</u>作答，寫出完整的
句子。

1. _____

_____

2. _____

_____

3. _____

_____

4. _____

_____

5. _____

_____

6. _____

_____

7. _____

_____

8. _____

_____

9. _____

_____

10. _____

_____

11. _____

_____

12. _____

_____

13. _____

_____

14. _____

_____

15. _____

_____

座位號碼：

第二部分：段落寫作（50%），請於框線內作答，勿隔行書寫。

1 _____

_____

_____

_____

5 _____

_____

_____

_____

_____

10 _____

_____

_____

_____

_____

評分用識別碼：_____

第一部分 單句寫作

第 1～5 題：句子改寫

1. **Leave early because you don't want to miss the bus.（用 so that）**

   （早點離開，因為你不會想錯過公車。）

   Leave ＿＿＿＿＿＿＿＿＿＿＿＿＿＿.（早點離開才不會錯過公車。）

   答題解說

   答案：Leave early so that you won't miss the bus. 這是一句「祈使句」，有命令的口吻，雖然沒有主詞，但祈使句的主詞是 you。用 so that（以便…，那麼…）來引導表目的的副詞子句，也就是說，leave early 和 you don't want to miss the bus 有因果關係，這一點可以從題目中的 because 看出。但 because 改成 so that 之後，就要用 won't 來取代原本的 "don't want to"，語意上會比較合理。

   破題關鍵

   so that（所以、因此）用以引導表示「目的，結果」的副詞子句。另一個寫法是 in order that。

2. **People don't use this bridge very often.（用被動式）**

   （人們並不常使用這座橋。）

   This bridge ＿＿＿＿＿＿＿＿＿＿＿＿＿.（這座橋不常被使用。）

   答題解說

   答案：This bridge isn't used very often. 把主動句中的受詞放到句首，要採用被動式「be 動詞 + 過去分詞」，而原本的主動式句子是以 people、everyone... 等「非特定對象」當主詞，在轉為被動式之後，可予以省略。

   破題關鍵

   被動式 = be 動詞+過去分詞。若原本主動式以 people、everyone... 等非特定對象當主詞，則可省略。

3. **I'd rather have tea than coffee.**（用 would prefer）

   （我能可喝茶也不要喝咖啡。）

   _____.（我會比較想喝茶。）

   答案：I'd prefer to have tea.「would rather A than B」是「跟 B 比起來，比較想要 A」的意思，而「would prefer to-V」是「比較想要做 A」(would prefer to 比 would like to 的感覺更為強烈)。所以直接寫 would prefer to have tea 即可。本題有個陷阱，首先 prefer 單獨使用時可以接 V-ing 或 to-V，但改為 would prefer 時，後面就只能接不定詞 to-V；第二，prefer 單獨使用時，有 prefer A to B（較喜歡 A 更甚於 B）的用法。但是 would prefer 沒有這種用法。而且，如果我們說 "I prefer tea to coffee."，這句話指的是平常所表現出來的態度，表示「我對茶的喜愛更勝於咖啡。」但是，I would rather have tea than coffee. 這句話真正的意思是，在當下，我想要喝茶更勝於咖啡，並不一定跟我們平常的態度有絕對的關係。兩者間語意的差別需多加留意。

   破題關鍵

   would rather A = would prefer to A。前者 A 前面有助動詞 would，所以要接原形動詞，後者 to 是不定詞的 to，後面需接原形動詞。

4. **Peter invited Alice to the concert.**（改成被動式）

   （彼得邀請愛麗絲去聽一場音樂會。）

   Alice _____ Peter.
   （愛麗絲受彼得的邀請去聽一場音樂會。）

   答題解說

   答案：Alice was invited to the concert by Peter. 主動、被動的句型如下：
   主動：主詞＋動詞＋受詞
   被動：受詞＋be 動詞＋過去分詞＋by＋主詞
   在這裡，Peter 是很明確的一個人，所以 by Peter 是不能省略的。

   破題關鍵

   被動式＝be 動詞＋過去分詞＋by＋人（動作執行者）。另外，「invite sb. to＋地方」改成被動式之後變成「be invited to＋地方」。

5. **Alex went to Korea yesterday and he is there now.（用 has）**

（艾利克斯昨天去韓國，且他現在在那裡了。）

_____. （艾利克斯已經去了韓國。）

答題解說

答案：Alex has gone to Korea. 題目提示用 has，表示要用 has gone to 來改寫這個句子。「have/has gone to 地方」的意思是「已經去了某地」，所以目前人就在那個地方。如果要說「曾經去過某地」，則要改成「have/has been to 地方」，這表示人現在並不在那裡。

破題關鍵

從過去式的 "went to" 以及現在式的 "is there now" 可推知，改寫句要考你 "have/has gone to" 的用法，表示「已經去了某地（目前人在那裡）」。

第 6～10 題：句子合併

6. **Helen's job is boring.**
   Helen is bored.（用 because）

（Helen 的工作很無聊。）
（Helen 感到厭煩。）

_____.

（Helen 感到厭煩，因為她的工作很無聊。）

答題解說

答案：Helen is bored because her job is boring. 首先，要了解形容詞 boring 和 bored 意義上的不同。一個觀念要記住：-ed 用來形容「人」，-ing 用來形容「事物」。boring 是「（事物）令人感到無趣的」，當然，「人」本身，也可能是「令人感到無趣的」，不過 bored 就一定是用來表達「人的感受」，表示「（某人）感到無聊的」。類似的字彙還有：interesting / interested、surprising / surprised、exciting / excited、confusing / confused、disappointing / disappointed…等。

破題關鍵

用連接詞 because 來連接兩個句子。第一句顯然是「因」，第二句是「果」。也可以寫成 "Because Helen's job is boring, she is bored."。另外應注意的是，because 置於句首時後面要加逗號（,）但置於句中時，通常不加逗號。

425

7. **There are not many chairs.**
   Not everybody can get a chair to sit down.（用 enough... to）
   （沒有很多張椅子。）
   （並不是每個人都有椅子可以坐。）

   _____.
   （沒有足夠的椅子可以讓每個人坐下來。）

   答題解說

   答案：There are not enough chairs for everybody to sit down. 首先，我們要讀懂題目中的否定是全部的否定還是部分的否定。當 not 與 all、both、every、always 等連用時，表示「部分否定」（並非全部都是..)，而題目限定用 enough... to，所以必須用否定才能符合句意。enough 後面顯然要接名詞，而題目中只有 chairs 可用，所以可以把第一句的 not many chairs 改成 not enough chairs，後面接「for + 人 + to-V」即可，也就是「人」= everyone，to-V = to sit down。

   破題關鍵

   enough... to-V 表示「足夠的…可以做某事」。兩句應合併成「There are not enough... for… to...」（沒有足夠的…可以讓…做…）的句型。

8. **I have a brother.**
   My brother is studying Chinese in college.（用 who）
   （我有一個哥哥。）
   （我哥哥在大學念中文。）

   _____.
   （我有個哥哥，在大學念中文。）

   答題解說

   答案：I have a brother, who is studying Chinese in college. 這兩個句子共同之處就是 brother 這個字，以 who 為關係代名詞引導關係子句，而 brother 就是關係代名詞 who 的先行詞，亦即 who 在句中取代 brother 而將兩個句子合併。另外注意，由於題目第一句已經清楚表示說話者只有「一個哥哥／弟弟」，所以 who 的前面應該要加逗點，屬於「非限定用法」的關係子句。如果 who 前面不加逗號而寫成 I have a brother who is studying Chinese in college.，那意思會變成「我有一個在大學念中文的哥哥。」（表示說話者不是只有一個哥哥），所以這跟原本題目要表達的意思不同。

   破題關鍵

   題目提示用 who，表示要用關係代名詞 who 來連接兩句，但要注意關係代名詞的限定與非限定用法。

9. **Tom asked Grace something.**
   Jane went home early.（用 why）

   （Tom 問 Grace 某件事。）
   （Jane 很早就回家了。）

   _____.
   （Tom 問 Grace 為什麼 Jane 很早就回家了。）

   答題解說

   答案：Tom asked Grace why Jane went home early. 看題目時要聯想到 Tom 問 Grace 的 something 是指什麼，如此才能知道合併後的句子怎麼寫。why 除了可以放在句首當引導疑問句的疑問詞之外，也可以用來引導「間接問句」，此時就可以用來連接兩個句子，並符合本題的句意與提示。疑問詞 why 所引導的間接問句是個「名詞子句」，應用「肯定句」的結構。

   破題關鍵

   題目提示用 why，表示要用疑問詞 why 來連接兩句，也就是 why 引導間接問句的用法。這時候要注意 why 後面要用肯定句的語態。

10. **Terry can't see anything.**
    She has to wear glasses.

    （Terry 什麼也看不到。）
    （她必須戴眼鏡。）

    _____ without _____.
    （Terry 沒有眼鏡的話什麼也看不到。）

    答題解說

    答案：Terry can't see anything without (wearing) glasses. 首先要了解題目的兩個句子所要傳達的意思：Terry 看不見，她必須戴眼鏡 → Terry 不戴眼鏡的話什麼都看不見，因為題目已限定要用 without，就必須把這個字帶進合併的句子裡：without glasses 或是 without wearing glasses。另外注意，glasses 當「眼鏡」的意思時，一定要用複數形，如果是單數 glass 則表示「玻璃」或「玻璃杯」。

    破題關鍵

    without + 名詞／動名詞（Ving），表示「若無…」、「沒有…的話」。"not... without..." 是雙重否定用法，表示「沒有…就不能…」。

第 11～15 題：句子重組

11. The new <u>restaurant on Baseline Road is very good.</u>

（在 Baseline 路上的那家新餐廳非常棒。）

答題解說

從提供的「The new ＿＿＿＿＿＿＿＿＿＿＿.」以及「good / is / restaurant / Baseline / Road / on / very」內容來看，new 後面要放名詞，而介系詞 on 後面也要放名詞，所以組成 "The new restaurant on Baseline Road"，作為句子的主詞是最適當的，剩下的「good / is / very」三個字，就組成「be 動詞＋主詞補語」即可。

破題關鍵

本題關鍵只要把句子的主詞組合起來，剩下的就很容易擺放了。雖然 "on Baseline Road" 看似地方副詞片語，通常置於句尾，但如果寫成 "The new restaurant is very good on Baseline Road."（那家新餐廳在 Baseline 路上非常棒。）是比較不自然的句子。

12. It <u>started raining an hour ago.</u>

（一個小時前開始下雨。）

答題解說

從提供的「It ＿＿＿＿＿＿＿＿＿＿.」以及「raining / hour / ago / an / started」內容來看，提示的句首 It 是主詞，只有 started 可以當動詞，而「hour / ago / an」正好形成 an hour ago（一小時前），那麼剩下的 raining 就只有放在 started 後面當受詞了。

破題關鍵

句子已經給你主詞了，就要把動詞找出來，本句單字選項中也只有 started 可以當動詞。

13. They <u>seem to have plenty of money.</u>

（他們似乎很有錢。）

答題解說

從提供的「They ＿＿＿＿＿＿＿＿＿＿.」以及「plenty / to / money / seem / of / have」內容來看，提示的句首 They 是主詞，其中有 seem 和 have 可以當動詞。雖然沒有任何連接詞可以連接這兩個動詞，但有個 to，所以可以構成 "seem to have"（似乎有…），那麼剩下的 plenty、money、of 就可以組成 have 的受詞

"plenty of money"。

看到 seem 以及 to 直接聯想的 seem to-V 的用法，另外 plenty of... 表示「滿滿的，很多的」。

14. Mark was so nervous that he couldn't eat.

（馬克緊張到吃不下東西。）

答題解說

從提供的「Mark _____.」以及「eat / that / nervous / he / so / was / couldn't」內容來看，提示的句首 Mark 是主詞，其中有 eat 和 was 可以當動詞，也有連接詞 so 或 so that 可以連接這兩個動詞，顯然還有第二個主詞，那當然是 he 來擔綱了。接著 was 後面要有形容詞 nervous 當主詞補語，以及助動詞 couldn't 可以擺在 eat 前面，自然可構成 Mark was nervous 以及 he couldn't eat 兩個句子。剩下 so 與 that 可以用兩種情況：Mark was nervous so that he couldn't eat. 以及 Mark was so nervous that he couldn't eat.，前者較不符合語意與邏輯，故正確答案應為 Mark was so nervous that he couldn't eat.。

破題關鍵

so... that... 表示「如此…以致於…」，而 so that... 表示「以便…」、「那麼…」，兩者語意上的差別應分辨清楚。

15. They didn't paint the house themselves.

（他們不是自己粉刷這房子。）

答題解說

從提供的「They _____.」以及「paint / house / themselves / didn't / the」內容來看，提示的句首 They 是主詞，其中只 paint 可以當動詞，且是個及物動詞，它的受詞就是 the house，而不會是 themselves，paint themselves 是不合邏輯的說法。所以剩下的 didn't 就擺在動詞 paint 前面，而 themselves 在此可以當副詞，表示「靠他們自己」。

破題關鍵

本題關鍵在於分辨 themselves 是當受詞還是副詞，既然 paint themselves 是不合邏輯的，那麼 themselves 當然是副詞的用法。

第二部分 段落寫作

寫作範例

John gets up at seven o'clock every morning. He has breakfast at home and has to arrive at school before eight thirty. At school, John likes PE class best because he doesn't have to sit still in the classroom. The school ends at a quarter to five. John usually goes home with his sister. On their way home, sometimes they stop at a comic book shop. John's family normally have dinner at seven o'clock. After dinner his family watch TV together and have a chitchat. Then John goes to bed at ten o'clock.

中文翻譯

約翰每天早上七點起床。他在家裡吃飯且必須在七點半前到達學校。在學校，約翰最喜歡體育課，因為他不必挺直地坐在教室裡。學校四點四十五分放學。約翰通常跟他妹妹一起回家。在回家的路上，有時候他們會到漫畫店待一下子。約翰的家人平常都七點時吃晚餐。晚餐後他們一家人會一起看電視，並且閒聊一下。然後約翰會在十點的時候上床睡覺。

答題解說

英檢初級的這道題，幾乎都是看圖描述的題目，所以有必要先把與圖案裡面出現的人事物相關英文表達用語準備好。例如第一張圖有小男孩去上學（go to school / arrive at school）以及指著八點半（at eight thirty）的時鐘。第二張圖有小男孩與小女孩／兄妹／姊弟一起放學（go home with... after school），以及點出四點四十五分（a quarter to five / at 4:45 p.m.）的時間；第三張圖顯示一家人在晚上七點一起吃晚餐（have dinner together）。而單憑上述圖片中的敘述尚無法將平常一天的生活做一個完整的描述，所以為了寫一篇較完整而豐富的短文，可以穿插一些日常生活的事件。例如幾點起床（get up）、吃早餐（breakfast）、喜歡學校的什麼課（ex. PE、math、English...）、放學後會去那裡溜搭一下（stop by...）以及完成回家作業（homework）…等等。

語言學習NO.1

國際學村　LA PRESS 語研學院 Language Academy Press

學英語

自然懂的 英文文法 一步步跟著學！

59堂 English Grammar Course 簡單明晰，遞組連貫的文法精華課程 學新的同時建立完整的網絡圖像的！ 只要會中文就能學會的漸進式英文文法重建

學韓語

實境式 照單全收 圖解韓語單字 不用背

超過1500張實境圖解 誕生於中的人事物成為你的韓文字素！

視覺記憶韓語單字，深入了解韓國文化

朴炫英

學日語

第二外語

我的第一本 泰語發音

最有趣、好學的泰語發音入門書

一次弄懂泰語裡難的母音、子音、尾音、聲調等所有規則無負擔

THAI Starter!

考多益

HACKERS × 國際學村

新制多益 NEW TOEIC 單字大全 Vocabulary

2018起多益更新單字資訊完全掌握！

30天激增300分的多益字彙！ 最能反映多益現況的權威單字書！

David Cho

8種版本音檔・配合不同學習需求

考日檢

新日檢 JLPT N5

合格模試 3回模擬試題

解析本

全新仿真模考題！ 含詳盡完整解析，滿分不是夢！

考韓檢

NEW TOPIK II 新韓檢 中高級

試題全面解析

全方位拆解中高級考古題試卷

考英檢

各級機關、學校、企業、補習班指定購買

全新！NEW GEPT 全民英檢 初級 聽力&閱讀 題庫解析

新制修訂版

6回試題完全掌握最新內容與趨勢！

110年起最新版做英檢初級體型

想獲得最新最快的 語言學習情報嗎？

歡迎加入 國際學村&語研學院粉絲團

台灣廣廈 國際出版集團
Taiwan Mansion International Group

國家圖書館出版品預行編目（CIP）資料

NEW GEPT 新制全民英檢初級寫作必考題型 / 國際語言中
心委員會著. -- 初版. -- 新北市：國際學村, 2022.01
　　面；　公分
　　ISBN 978-986-454-196-6（平裝）
　　1.英語　2.讀本

805.1892　　　　　　　　　　　　110019731

● 國際學村

NEW GEPT 新制全民英檢初級寫作必考題型

一本囊括「句子改寫、合併、重組」的解題重點及常見作文題目，徹底破解英檢
最常考題型，一看到題目就能寫出正確答案！

作　　　者／國際語言中心委員會	編輯中心編輯長／伍峻宏・編輯／許加慶 封面設計／何偉凱・內頁排版／菩薩蠻數位文化有限公司 製版・印刷・裝訂／皇甫・秉成

行企研發中心總監／陳冠蒨　　　　　　線上學習中心總監／陳冠蒨
媒體公關組／陳柔彣　　　　　　　　　產品企製組／黃雅鈴
綜合業務組／何欣穎

發　行　人／江媛珍
法 律 顧 問／第一國際法律事務所 余淑杏律師・北辰著作權事務所 蕭雄淋律師
出　　　版／國際學村
發　　　行／台灣廣廈有聲圖書有限公司
　　　　　　地址：新北市235中和區中山路二段359巷7號2樓
　　　　　　電話：（886）2-2225-5777・傳真：（886）2-2225-8052

代理印務・全球總經銷／知遠文化事業有限公司
　　　　　　地址：新北市222深坑區北深路三段155巷25號5樓
　　　　　　電話：（886）2-2664-8800・傳真：（886）2-2664-8801
郵 政 劃 撥／劃撥帳號：18836722
　　　　　　劃撥戶名：知遠文化事業有限公司（※單次購書金額未達1000元，請另付70元郵資。）

■出版日期：2022年1月　　　　　ISBN：978-986-454-196-6
　　　　　　2024年4月4刷　　　　版權所有，未經同意不得重製、轉載、翻印。